<u>HEADCASE</u>

Charles D. Thomas

Author's Note: This is a work of fiction. While real clinics, hospitals and churches are mentioned by name, everything about them, all of the characters and all of their actions, are 100% fictional. This note, however, is non-fiction.

For Laura:

"How she, so pure and sweet and beautiful, can think of marrying me, I cannot understand, but I praise and thank God it is so."

Headcase

I have become a reproach to all my enemies and even to my neighbors, a dismay to those of my acquaintance; when they see me in the street they avoid me. I am forgotten like a dead man, out of mind. I am as useless as a broken pot.

- Psalm 31:11-1

1

"Sick, Mr. Plowman. You're sick, sick, sick. You have a bad chemical imbalance and you are in deep denial about it."

Dr. Patel stared at me but I said nothing. A dense fog of awkwardness descended on the consulting room. I felt like I was at a junior high school dance. But really, what did Patel expect me to say? We'd played this game before. Patel gave his "chemical imbalance" lecture followed immediately with a "these-pills-correct-the-imbalance" spiel. I'd heard it many times before. Patel seemed to think the words "chemical imbalance" would make me feel better about being crazy.

Just so you know, chemical imbalance is shrink talk for what everyone else calls crazy. It's psychiatric sleight of hand designed to motivate patients to take pills. To get the "buy in," as they say. I knew the game well.

By the time of that interview with Dr. Patel, I'd been a mental patient long enough to know how psychiatrists ticked. I'd observed the movement of their wheels and springs close up during my time in the state mental hospital in Kalamazoo and could predict their movements just like I could predict a watch's.

My ability to understand psychiatrists worked as well here at the Community Mental

Health Center as it did in the state hospital. Not to be immodest, but I could have taught a class for the newly crazy if I'd wanted to: Jack Plowman's Guide to Succeeding as a Mental Patient.

But the system being like it was, no one was going to let me teach a class like that. I was crazy, messed up, the part that gets removed from the assembly line by Quality Control.

They brought the bin full of us defectives here so they could shine a bright spotlight onto our defective psyches. The cracks were so pretty to them. Patel, like most mental health people, seemed to see everything that was wrong with me but nothing that was right.

So I had my reasons for sitting there wordless as the Sphinx that day. My silence was my armor. But Patel didn't give up easily. He waited a moment and then came at me again.

"You seem to continue in your denial of your symptoms, Mr. Plowman. You do not acknowledge that you have very bad problems. Just because you take a bath does not mean you are well. You do not take your medication every morning like I ask you. What is to be done with you?"

I knew better than to respond.

"Take your medication or I cannot help you."

I sat there with eyes as dead as a cadaver's. But as always he wasn't going to let me go until I said something.

"Yes, doctor," was all I could muster.

"You will see improvement; this I promise you."

"Dr. Patel," my social worker, Tiffini, broke in, "Jack says that the medication makes him gain weight and feel like a zombie."

Tiffini was the case manager C.M.H. had assigned to me. Case managers are baby sitters who "monitor" head cases like me so they don't upset sane people.

"It is just side effect," Patel said in an offhanded way.

I wanted to slap him but I kept my cool. I knew how to play the game. I was a professional.

"You see, Jack," Tiffini smiled, "it's just a side effect. I told you."

A *side* effect? Those damn drugs were taking my soul away and they called that a side effect? Not for the first time, I began to wonder who the real crazy people were.

"Fine," I said.

"I do not still believe you, but your 15 minutes are almost up and I have another non-compliant patient to attend to," Patel said as he typed up the prescription that I'd never fill.

"Thank you and come again," he said with a wry smile.

I didn't get up right away. I was not anxious to leave that place even though I hated Patel. That cold government building with its neo-Stalinist architecture was actually a palace compared to the place I now called home. Concrete walls were better than the walls in my apartment, walls so porous that they were almost alive with the moving civilization of roaches that lived within them.

The apartment was a place that Tiffini had

gotten me into about six months before, and it was barely better than the mission where I'd been living. Although one nice thing about the apartment was that no one ever pissed on me while I slept at night. That had happened at the mission not once, but twice.

No, nobody was pissing on me there, at least not *yet.*

I had a new roommate and he was the kind of guy where pissing on others could not be ruled out.

His name was Johnny Chen, and he was a fellow head case.

Tiffini found me that apartment with the expectation that I would find a roommate. In spite of what a dive the place was, I couldn't afford to live there alone on my disability check. I needed someone to split the bills or I was going to end up broke and on the streets again.

Tiffini had arranged for Johnny to come over and meet me one afternoon after me and the roaches had had the place to ourselves for a couple of weeks. Tiffini and I were sitting together on my white plastic chairs in the living room when the knock came at the door. In Johnny walked, wearing a bright pink shirt, badly dyed blond hair, and speaking with an outrageous lisp. He was like some ridiculous gay stereotype that, if he had been on a TV sitcom, would have caused P-FLAG to organize a boycott.

He looked me up and down like I was a piece of meat and then gave me the world's weakest handshake saying, "Nice to meet you."

I actually longed for the mission for a second. The guy was a walking punchline but I had little choice. I needed someone to help me pay the rent on the worst place I had ever lived. What the hell had happened to me?

A few weeks later when Tiffini told Dr. Patel about my dislike for Johnny, he thought that might mean I was hiding something about my sexuality. He called it a reaction formation. He tried to explain it to me but I didn't really listen. I got the gist of it real quick. He thought I was gay.

"Jack."

It was Tiffini, calling me back to her reality.

"We need to go so that Dr. Patel can see his next patient, Jack."

I got out of my chair without a word of goodbye to the good doctor and walked into a hallway filled with other people like me, people with glassy looks in their eyes and the shuffling gait that some of the social workers called the "Haldol Shuffle." Most of the other crazies were wearing clothes stained with a world map of filth. Their hair looked like someone had electrified it. What scared me was that I knew that with a few more years of "treatment," I'd be just like them. They'd once been 25 years old just like me.

When I'd been homeless a few years back I was like them. I totally let myself go. I stunk, was dirty, and my clothes looked like they belonged in a thrift store from the 1970s. I lived like that for almost half a year before I stabilized and got my apartment. The apartment had a shower and I started to use it, stepping back from the edge. At least for now. Looking back, I guess I just felt so terrible about myself and my life when I was homeless that the effort to clean myself seemed better spent on something else, like smoking cigarettes.

The Community Mental Health Clinic was a buzzing hive of chaos as usual. The wide hallways were painted a putrid yellow that always made me slight nauseous when I looked at it too long. There were only two doctors in the clinic, Patel and a woman that I hadn't met yet. She was from India just like Patel. They served every single one of our county's poor mentally ill in the downtown location. People like me were shipped in by our social workers from all over Kent County to the clinic to get our drugs and have a little face time with our case workers.

"Jack, I need to talk to Dr. Patel for a second. Can you wait in the hallway and then we can go upstairs and work on your treatment plan," Tiffini said to me in her sweet and condescending way. Apparently, she wanted to rat me out a little more, this time in private.

With her long, silky blond hair, I often thought Tiffini must be part angel. But then she did things like this and I was reminded that she was also part demon.

It was par for the course for a social worker to gossip about clients behind their backs to the doctor. I wondered what she was saying about me as I walked back to the waiting room. "He's so angry and resentful" or "He seems to have a chip on his shoulder."

Unlike many of the social workers, Tiffini really liked to dress up for work. Whenever I met with her she had on a crisp business suit and had her hair pinned up in a bun. By looking at her you'd think she worked at a bank originating loans and not carting around crazy people. If freshman year hadn't happened, I might have been just like her.

I had to wait about five minutes before Tiffini came out of Dr. Patel's office and took me to one of the meeting rooms.

"Well, Jack," she said to me as she sat down at the green metal desk in the consultation room, "Dr. Patel wants me to start dropping off your medication every morning and watching you take it."

"Tiffini," I protested, "I am not a child."

I knew I was a few years older than Tiffini, which made her patronizing that much worse. Tiffini may have had her college degrees, but I had more mental health smarts. I saw her hair sparkle in the light of the old lamp on her desk and thought that back in high school, I would have had a shot at dating a girl like her. Of course, that wasn't going to happen in my current situation. Pretty girls don't go for mental patients.

"I know, and believe me, I'd rather not do this either. I work out in the morning."

"So, let's just forget it," I said. It was worth a try.

"No, Dr. Patel wants me to keep a med

journal, and he's going to want to see it at your next appointment, which is in three months."

The room was the dreary beige of old newspapers and didn't have a window. It did have a security camera though.

"Jack, if you just took your medication, neither one of us would have to go through this."

"I told you, I don't like the side effects and besides I'm not as crazy as Patel thinks. The voices only come once in a while now and contrary to what you people say, I am not religiously preoccupied. I'm just a very spiritual person."

"Jack, you totally stopped eating and drinking for Lent."

"So?"

"We had to put you in the psychiatric unit and force feed you through a tube."

"You over-reacted."

"You would have died, Jack," she said in that patronizing tone of hers.

"Nonsense."

"Honestly, I'm afraid this religion stuff is going to kill you someday, Jack," she said to me in all seriousness.

"I think that your lack of religion might land you in hell," I shot back.

"Well," she said, trying to backtrack, "let's just agree to disagree on that one, my friend."

Tiffini smiled at me like I was a dog that kept chewing the furniture.

"Let's talk about your treatment plan," she said, changing the subject. "You have a pretty nice apartment now and have your medication. What else do you need?"

The things that I needed were not things that Tiffini or any psychologist, psychiatrist or social worker could give me. What I needed was enough money so that I could afford my own apartment, get back into college and maybe find a girlfriend.

I was really lonely back then, still in love with a woman that no longer wanted me. Much like everything else good in my life, she was little more than a memory.

"I want to go back to college," I blurted out.

"Well, that's something we could talk about."

"What's that supposed to mean?"

"Well, Jack, you are still not very stable..."

"Now listen here!" I screamed, standing up from my chair. "I am stable! I can handle college."

Tiffini looked at me with what had to be pity. She wasn't afraid of my rage. She knew I'd never hit anyone.

"I'll put in the treatment plan that we'll explore college when you start taking your medication every day as prescribed."

We'd make a deal: this for that. Maybe Tiffini had learned a little bit more in social worker school than I gave her credit for.

"I'll take my medication if you promise to take me to Grand Valley so that I can sign up for a class."

"I'll take you after you take your medication for three months...every day."

Tiffini had the upper hand. I didn't have any money, I didn't have a car, and I sure as hell didn't think I'd even be able to take classes with all these medications fogging up my brain. But a sliver of hope is better than no hope at all.

"Okay, I'll do it," I told her.

2

Tiffini offered to drive me home but it was nice outside so I decided to walk. The clinic was on Hall Street and I lived about a mile away on a little side street called Prospect. The neighborhood was terrible. While it wasn't the worst neighborhood I'd ever lived in, it was pretty close. There were lots of drug dealers and a few hookers on the nearby street corners. The hookers often stood by one of the abandoned warehouses that littered that part of town and stared into the eyes of the men that passed by in their cars. Those women had the same kind of desperate, hollow eyes that I saw in my fellow mental patients.

It was unseasonably warm that day, for Michigan in the middle of March, that is. The sun was out and all the normal people seemed to be in a good mood. Everyone seemed to realize how lucky they were not to be freezing to death right then. It was usually so cold this time of year.

Because it was sunny and beautiful out, I decided to take my time heading home. All I had to look forward to there was Johnny Chen anyway. Johnny and his dance music at all hours. Johnny and all his strange friends.

Johnny was a little younger than me, about 20 years old, and fairly new to being in the public mental health system. He didn't know how it worked yet. If he would have asked, I could have saved him from making some of the mistakes that I'd made, but he didn't think he needed my help. Johnny knew it all already. He was a recently diagnosed manic-depressive and he tended to get out of control sexually when he was manic. He would have sex with any man that was willing, anywhere. He'd only been manic once since we became roommates and, thank God, he was staying with a friend during most of that episode.

Johnny's family had taken care of him for quite a while before giving up and throwing him to the public system. He'd told me that he'd seen private psychiatrists and gone to private hospitals since he was a teen, and that his parents had let him live at home until about three months ago. But eventually they'd gotten sick of hearing the moans of their son and strange men reverberating through their house and threw him out.

Johnny ended up on Tiffini's case load and after meeting with his family, Tiffini decided he needed to get out of the family home as soon as possible. She said it wasn't healthy for Johnny to be living there anymore, but Johnny and I both knew that was crap. This happens to a lot of us with mental illness. Our families try to help but when it becomes clear that we aren't "going through a phase" and that this is a long term situation, they bail on us.

That weird, warm winter sun kept shining down on me as I neared my apartment. I lived at 555 Prospect, a few houses down from a boarded up fish fry. If you squinted, my place looked like a stately brick Victorian house that, in its day, might have been a real palace. Unfortunately for me, it had slowly fallen to pieces by the time I moved in. The house was two and a half stories tall, with a complex roofline with lots of peaks and a big porch out front that was so decrepit no one dared step onto it. The house had been converted from a single family dwelling into apartments years ago when the area started to get rough. I knew some of the people who had apartments in the main building and they weren't bad. My apartment, though, was in an addition in the back of the main house.

In order to have more units, the owners of the house had decided to put on an addition about thirty years ago. They had some outfit build two more units as cheaply as possible and slapped them onto the back of the building. Instead of brick like the main house, the addition had white vinyl siding that after years of aging now looked like an old dingy t-shirt. If it was possible to make the addition look more out of place, I don't know how they could have done it. It was an architectural marvel of ugliness.

My apartment was on the second floor and accessible only from a rickety outdoor set of wooden steps that crawled up the back of the house. If you happened to weigh over a hundred pounds and wanted to walk up them, the steps would sway under you like a wooden ocean. God must have been watching over me back then, because I'm still alive after ascending those steps hundreds of times.

The apartment itself was...well, it was a deathtrap. There was only one entrance and one window, a picture window that didn't open. No way to get out of it if there was a fire or if those damn wooden stairs happened to fall down. Johnny and I each had our own bedrooms but shared a bathroom. The floors were all warped and I'd swear that there wasn't a level point in the whole place.

But as they say, beggars can't be choosers and I was nothing at that point in my life if not a beggar.

When I walked in, the apartment was as stuffy as usual, and dusty. I never understood why, but no matter how much I cleaned that place, it was always full of dust so thick you could see the little mites floating when the sun shone through the picture window. I was afraid to go and look, but I knew that there must be some terrible things growing in the air ducts.

Inside, the apartment was just as odd as the building looked from the outside. The front door opened directly into the kitchen. Actually the door opened right into the small stove that we had, so every time anyone opened the door, it'd make this tinny banging sound. As soon as you closed the door you were standing on the green vinyl of the kitchen, which must have looked great in the 1970s. In addition to the stove, the kitchen had a mini-refrigerator, a sink and a small white microwave that sat on top of the fridge. That was about it. There were no cupboards or any kind of pantry. We kept most of our non-perishable food in our bedrooms.

The living room was covered in a brown Berber carpet that did a nice job hiding the sloping floors. We didn't have any real furniture, just a few white plastic chairs that should have been on some suburban deck instead of in our living room.

Johnny had brought a 27-inch television along with him when he moved in and that had replaced my old 19-inch. Johnny's family was also paying for cable for us. Of course, that just made Johnny think that he could always watch whatever he wanted to.

The place was quiet that afternoon, which should have tipped me off that something was amiss. The place was never this quiet. Johnny was always screaming into the phone or playing some terrible electronic music. Looking back, I still don't know why I didn't think anything of that unusual serenity, but I didn't. Maybe I was just in a good mood from my walk home.

I sat down on one of the white plastic chairs to watch some TV, but before I could find the remote control, I heard a strange gurgling sound coming from Johnny's bedroom. I'd never heard anything like it before. It was a sick and liquid noise.

"Johnny," I called out. There was no answer.

I tried to convince myself that the noise had been the furnace kicking on, but even I knew that whatever that noise was, it came from a living thing. An animal or a person. Someone hurt.

"Johnny," I tried again.

Nothing.

I started to get scared then. My heart started beating like the relentless bass of Johnny's techno music. Boom, boom, boom.

I thought for a moment that he might be playing a trick on me, but I'd never known him to be the joking type. As I sat on that plastic chair thinking about what to do next, I heard the noise again, this time louder.

GRAWAAAA!

I started to feel it then. My vision got a little blurry, and the other white chair and the TV suddenly went out of focus. Something ran across the wall, a shadow but white like smoke. Was someone else in the apartment?

I've had more than my fair share of hallucinations, and even then I knew pretty well how they affected me. This fit the profile. When I hallucinated, most of the time I just heard things; but once in a while I saw things, usually just movements in my peripheral vision that weren't there. Most of the time, I knew what was going on and ignored it. This time I wasn't quite sure.

I decided to try and find a weapon just in case and then check out Johnny's room. I glanced around the living room, but didn't see anything that fit the bill. Tiffini frowned on her clients owning anything that could hurt someone for fear that...well, that someone would get hurt. That was probably a good policy for the Community Mental Health Agency, but it didn't do me a hell of a lot of good at that moment.

I slipped off the chair and stepped gently towards Johnny's room. The floor creaked and I froze.

jack

I thought I heard something. My name spoken softly in a murmur.

jack, we see you.

I started to sweat and my heart beat faster in my chest. Not knowing why, I took my shirt off and wiped my brow. The shirt was already soaked with my sweat.

"Keep it together, Jack. Keep it together," I told myself out loud. I was starting to panic and when I panicked all hell broke loose. I knew that I needed to calm down. I stood in the middle of the living room and closed my eyes. Then I prayed the Lord's Prayer because that helped me sometimes.

"Our Father," I said in a whisper, "who art in heaven, hallowed be thy name. Thy kingdom come, thy will be done, on earth as it is in heaven."

I took a deep breath and asked for peace.

"Give us this day our daily bread and forgive us our trespasses as we forgive those who trespass against us, and lead us not into temptation but deliver us from evil."

evil jack. we're evil.

"For thine is the kingdom, the power and the glory, now and forever. Amen."

I sat down on the floor and my breathing started to return to normal. I said the Lord's Prayer out loud again, and then a third time. Slowly clarity returned. The voice and the gurgling sound were just hallucinations. I knew that I was going to be okay. There was no one in the apartment but me. The shadow was a hallucination.

I had to sit there for another few minutes before I was back to normal. The sweat was now cold on my skin. I put my shirt back on.

This was why I was not in college. This was why my life had gone to hell. This was why Tiffini and Patel thought that I needed to take those pills. I'd been able to bring myself back to reality, but how long had it taken? I took a glance at the clock and realized that it had been about 15 minutes.

How was I supposed to attend a lecture on microeconomics when the slightest creepy noise made me lose touch with reality for 15 minutes? Maybe Tiffini had a point about taking my meds.

Although I knew that the noise that started all this had not been real, I still felt the need to go and peek into Johnny's room and make one hundred percent sure. Maybe I was OCD as well as all the other stuff they told me I had.

I got back up on my feet and walked down the short hallway to Johnny's door. It was slightly ajar.

I knocked but there was no response, so I walked in.

Johnny was there lying in the middle of his bed. His throat was slit and his neck lay open like a clumsily gutted fish.

3

The room was awash in blood. It was on the walls, on the floor, and on my hands. There was so much blood on my hands.

you did this jack.

"I'm sorry! Please forgive me!" I screamed to whoever would listen.

you'll burn in hell.

"No!" I screamed. "I'm sorry, I'm sorry, I'm sorry!"

I ran out of Johnny's room, out the front door and down the wobbly steps as fast as my feet would carry me. The air outside was swarming with black shapes that didn't belong in the afternoon sky. Sweat scorched my eyes and I knew that I was losing it. I couldn't decide whether to run or to hide but then my neighbor Gina walked out of her apartment door.

"You all right, Jack?" she asked me.

I was clearly not all right. I quickly hid my hands behind my back so she wouldn't see the blood.

"I just got scared, Gina," was the half-truth I told her.

"You want me to call Tiffini, Jack?"

"No. I'll be fine. I'm just going back upstairs."

And as if that explained it all, I walked back up the steps as calmly as I could and back into my apartment. I went into my bedroom, closed the door, and sat on my bed.

Was any of this real? Was all of it real? I

didn't know what to think. I tried to concentrate but shadows started to dance across the room like smoke from an invisible cigarette. I watched their wispy shapes float around in the daylight of my room.

I decided to try the deep breathing exercise that a former therapist had taught me. I went over it about three times and after a while, it helped me calm down. When I looked back at my hands, they were clean. The blood was gone.

When I finally felt like I had calmed down completely, I decided to take another look into Johnny's room.

I wanted to reassure myself that everything was okay.

I crept back to Johnny's door, steadied myself, and looked in. Johnny was still dead on the bed. The scene had not changed a bit. If I saw it again the same way, it was real; that was my rule. My hallucinations always changed a little bit each time I saw them. This one had not. This was real. This was really happening. The anxiety descended upon me again.

you killed him jack.

jack killed johnny.

I stepped back again and collected myself. I told myself that I hadn't done it, that I'd never kill anyone. But either way Johnny was still dead in my apartment and that was bad.

Really bad.

I didn't know exactly what to do but I knew that I couldn't stay there in the apartment. I had to get away and think. Get the voices out of my head. I

walked, calmly this time, to the front door and
locked it behind me. There was no way I wanted
anyone to stumble upon this. Down the rickety
steps and out onto the street I walked, unsure of
where I was going.

I tried to walk down the street like a normal
guy. But I felt like every move I made bore the
unmistakable mark of guilt. As much as I wanted
not to be noticed, I knew that most of my neighbors
were just like me. Down-on-their-luck losers, with
nothing better to do than peer out their windows.
Someone was going to see me leave. Hell, Gina
had already seen me in a flat-out panic.

She'd offered to call Tiffini. I told her not to,
but would she do it anyway? I checked my watch
and it was already past five o'clock. Tiffini would
be on her way home by now, thank God. She
wouldn't want to spend the first hour of her
weekend checking up on me, would she?

tiffini is coming jack

Yes, she really might be. If Gina really did call
and happened to catch Tiffini before she left for the
day, she might drive over at least for a minute. Or
maybe she'd just send the police instead! Tiffini
might just take the call and pass it along to the cops
and tell them to look into it.

That made things even worse. If the cops came
out and found Johnny before I had a chance to do
something, I was going to look guilty. I walked on,
trying to plan my next move. It was getting colder
as the sun started to drop into the horizon. I put my
hands into my pockets to keep them warm and felt a
small, folded piece of paper.

It was the prescription that Dr. Patel had written for me.

I thought about it for three seconds and then turned left at the next corner. A few minutes later, I'd made it to the drug store. The pharmacy was still open.

4

It was pitch black by the time I left the store with my prescription and a Diet Coke. The March air was growing colder; the temperature must have dropped even since my walk home earlier in the day. I took out one of the big purple pills and swallowed it with a big gulp of pop as I walked.

i'm not leaving.

These pills always messed me up. I'd been down this road before. But the way things were, I didn't see any real option. It was this or lose control completely. That was another path that I'd been down before and it was even worse than the drugs.

If I were charged with murder, I knew that being crazy didn't help you get off, at least not here in Michigan. California, maybe, but not here. I'd known a guy in the hospital that had killed his girlfriend in a psychotic rage and then been found not competent to stand trial because of his mental illness. He was shipped to the hospital and forced to take heavy doses of medication. Just as I was being discharged, he was being sent back to jail. Drugged into competency.

As I walked around downtown, it started to become clear to me who I should turn to. I had one friend that I could trust to help me with something like this. I asked a couple people I saw on the street if I could borrow their cell phone to make a call but got nowhere. Looking back, that was a stupid thing to do. We crazies always scare the normals when we talk to them. I almost gave up on calling him but then I thought about the Amway Grand Plaza Hotel.

The Amway, as everyone called it, was one of the nicest hotels in town. It was an imposing glass tower right on the Grand River and was well known for its helpful staff. I walked in the revolving door and went right up to the young man at the reception desk.

"Excuse me. I'm a friend of a guest and need to use the phone."

The young man just looked at me. I didn't look like someone who would be staying here. He must have known that I was lying.

what he knows is that you're a killer.

I told myself to ignore the voice and keep a straight face.

"I'll let you use it, but it'll cost you a buck."

The bastard. But what choice did I have? I reached back in my pocket and found the money. He gave me a glance that said he was surprised that I was actually willing to pay this outrageous charge.

"Local call only. No more than five minutes."

"Fine," I said, and dialed up my friend.

After a very brief call, I walked out of the hotel without a word. The weekend had clearly started and there were quite a few people on the streets dressed up for a night out at the bars. Young people in the prime of their lives without a care in the world besides what beer to drink or how to get home when they got drunk. They had a life that I always thought I'd have too. But my life was not carefree. Especially not tonight.

As I walked up the street, I tried to not to think about what'd happened but it just kept coming back to me. I couldn't get Johnny's bloody, swollen neck out of my mind. All that blood covering his bed, pooling in his pillow.

I passed a couple of college girls, one wearing a Grand Valley sweatshirt, as I passed Flannigan's. Based on the way they were walking and the laughter in everything they said, I was pretty sure they had been drinking for quite a while. What I wouldn't have given to be an anonymous drunken college student in that moment.

I walked up Pearl Street and saw my destination in the distance. It was right where Pearl dead-ended into Division and it looked pretty much like heaven to me that March evening.

St. Mark's Episcopal Church, in all its gothic splendor, stood out like a lighthouse beacon in the night sky. With its grand architecture, it looked like a mini version of some ancient European cathedral. The church was sandwiched between a tall office building on one side and an equally tall community college building behind it.

It wasn't the closest church to my apartment by far, and I hadn't been raised Episcopalian. I was raised Catholic; my twin brother still was.

Actually, what initially brought me to St. Mark's had nothing to do with religion or God. It was the food.

A group of the church women had made a

tradition of making lunch for everyone who
attended the 10:30 "Mission" service. The mission
service was designed for the people staying at the
homeless shelter a few blocks down the street.
When good church women start handing out free
food a mere six blocks from a homeless shelter,
word gets around quickly. I heard about St. Mark's
within a day of landing at the Guiding Light
Mission.

So my first Sunday back in GR was spent in the
back pews of St. Mark's with about 20 other guys.
The lunch program, as usual, had been successful in
filling the pews that morning. There must have been
50 people total in the church. Most of them were
homeless.

I vividly recall first meeting Fr. Chris Parsons
that first Sunday morning. He was a handsome
young man, not much older than me. He had
striking blue eyes and blond hair that was close
cropped in a monastic style. He welcomed me with
a big smile and a hearty handshake like I was
actually someone of worth.

The service was a lot like the Catholic Mass of
my childhood, so I was able to follow it pretty
easily. Everything seemed normal until Fr. Chris
started his sermon. I wish I recalled the whole
sermon but I do recall the first sentence:

"In today's readings, we hear more about the
rich, elitist first century assholes, so arrogant, they
didn't even notice the Son of God walking next to
them."

I'd never heard a priest use the word "asshole"
before, especially not in a sermon. The rest of the

sermon followed suit. It was filled with references to rap music and movies the people in the pews would relate to. It was strange, but my downtrodden brothers seemed to really get into it. I remember a lot of loud "amens" from them. The guy knew how to connect with his audience.

Fr. Chris hooked me for sure. I was a regular at St. Mark's from that day forward. As time went by, I got to know Fr. Chris pretty well after I started helping out around the church. He said he didn't get to talk to many people that were as interested in theology as I was. We also liked some of the same books. He even had me over for dinner a few times. Fr. Chris took a real interest in me. I got so comfortable with him that I started to tell him about some of the religious ideas that I had that were not exactly orthodox. He always listened patiently and no matter what I said, he never told me I was crazy or wrong.

I remember one time being really sick and talking to Fr. Chris after the service. I was explaining why I thought that cannibalism was acceptable to God because we drank his Son's blood and ate his Son's flesh every Sunday. Wouldn't it be okay to eat other people as long as you didn't kill them yourself? God didn't want people in Africa to be hungry, I reasoned; he wanted them to eat each other.

Fr. Chris just nodded, nonplussed, and said that he could understand why I thought that way, but that God intended the Eucharist to be a special meal where He shared part of himself with us. It didn't give us permission to take from anyone else.

When I approached the little church the night that Johnny was murdered, Fr. Chris was there waiting for me. His Toyota was parked in the little parking lot adjacent to the church, and the big wooden doors of St. Mark's were wide open. I could see that candles had been lit inside the sanctuary and for the first time that night I felt at peace.

Fr. Chris was sitting in a back pew facing the altar.

"Hey, Father Chris," I said as I walked into the sanctuary.

He turned around and smiled at me.

"You sounded pretty upset on the phone, my friend."

Even at this hour, he was dressed in his clericals and had a peaceful smile for me.

"Bless me," I said to him, "for I have I've sinned."

5

"Sinned? What are you talking about?" he asked. His voice revealed a hint of panic.

"My roommate is dead and I think I might have killed him."

"Shit" was all he said and looked at the floor.

The church was somber and as still as death as Fr. Chris pondered what to say next.

"What happened, Jack?"

"I'm not really sure. It's kind of a blur."

"A blur, Jack? A man is dead and it's a fucking blur to you?"

"Father, please. Stress is not something that I do well with. The voices came on and I got disoriented. I might not have actually killed him, but I might have *let* him die because I was so out of it."

Fr. Chris's posture relaxed a little bit.

"So you don't remember killing him yourself?"

"No. I was at C.M.H. this afternoon and then walked home. I was home when things got fuzzy."

"If you were at C.M.H. it's not likely that you killed him, Jack."

That made sense to me and made me feel better.

"Okay," Fr. Chris continued, "so let's assume the best case scenario for a bit. You discovered he was dead but you weren't able to help him because of your schizophrenia."

"Now, Father. I am not a schizophrenic." I hated it when people made me out to be crazier than I was. "My most recent diagnosis is Mood Disorder

Not Otherwise Specified and Psychosis Not Otherwise Specified. I've gotten a lot of labels, but no one, and I mean no one, has ever said I was a full out schizophrenic. Never."

Someone was dead and I was having a discussion about differential psychiatric diagnosis with my priest.

"Sorry, Jack. I mean no offense. This is a little overwhelming for me," Fr. Chris said. "You just called me out of nowhere, clearly upset about something. You asked me to meet you at church and then tell me that someone is dead. This is not how I expected to spend my Friday night. I was just about to settle down, relax, and watch some Netflix. A comedy. Murder was not on my agenda, Jack."

"I'm not sure if he was dead when I got there. I heard him call for help, but I didn't help him. The best case scenario is that I let him die, Father. I let him die because I hated him."

"Now, Jack. Take it easy. You responded to the best of your ability. You're kind of like a man who sees another man drowning but doesn't jump in because he can't swim and he knows that if he jumps in the water, two people are going to die."

"I could have called for help. I could have screamed. I think in the back of my mind I knew what had happened and wanted him to die. I hated Johnny, Father. I hated almost everything about him. I hated his friends, his music, everything. I let my hate take me over. I let my hate kill him." I was starting to tear up.

"Jack, God understands our limitations. God loves us where we are."

"I deserve punishment," I said as the tears dripped over my eyelids and down my face.

"Whether you deserve punishment is God's call to make. Not yours."

"What am I going to do, Fr. Chris?"

"The first thing we need to do is answer some basic questions. Like where are you going to sleep tonight and how are you going to make sure that your roommate's remains are respectfully attended to. You aren't going to get anything figured out tonight as stressed out as you are right now. Do you have a friend or family that you could stay with tonight?"

I thought about that. I could call my brother, but I hated to do that. He was always taking care of me and helping me out of jams I got myself into. During the 18 months when I was totally out of control, he made sure that I didn't get myself into anything that would permanently stay on my record. Jake was a lawyer and I didn't want to put him in a position where he might do anything illegal.

"I was hoping I could stay here at the parish house tonight; it's the only place I feel safe."

I knew that it was asking a lot, but I also knew that Fr. Chris knew me well enough to know that I could be trusted. I also knew that Fr. Chris had opened the parish house in the past to homeless men (some of them my friends) if they got kicked out of the mission for relapsing on drink or drugs. There was even a bag with clothes and toiletries that he kept in a room for just such times.

Fr. Chris paused for a second but then smiled.

"That would be fine with me, Jack. You can

stay here for the night and we'll start tomorrow with fresh eyes."

"Thanks. I suppose that we should call the police tonight, too."

A perplexed look came over my friend's face when I said that.

"What's with that look?" I asked him.

"You ever listen to N.W.A?"

"Is that one of those rap groups you like?"

"As a matter of fact, yes it is. One of the best West Coast groups of all time. They wrote a song that might provide some guidance in this situation."

"A song?"

"Yeah. It's called 'Fuck the Police.'"

6

"Fuck the Police?" I didn't understand what he was talking about.

"It's a song from their album 'Straight Outta Compton' and it's about how African-Americans in this country don't get treated fairly by the police. The police assume that anyone with black skin is a criminal. No trial or due process, just violence. The cops feel justified in acting this way because of a deep, almost unconscious racism that pervades their profession."

"And this applies to me, the young white man from a good family, how exactly, Father?"

"I think that what N.W.A is rapping about applies to any minority group. Often the people that don't look or act like everyone else get treated unfairly. Jesus knew this and preached against it. Jack, your mental illness puts you in one of these groups."

"So you think the cops will just assume I killed Johnny if I call them?" I was starting to see where he was going with this.

"Let's look at what this will look like from their perspective. A young man with a documented history of mental illness winds up with a dead roommate. A dead roommate that many people know he hates. He has motive and he has opportunity. Who do you think is going to be the number one suspect?"

I knew what he was saying was true, and it scared the hell out of me.

"Jack, the best case scenario is that you end up

in the mental hospital before they throw you in jail. The cops are never going to spend a lot of time investigating the death of a mental patient, especially when they have a suspect who has a motive right under their noses. They've got a lot of cases to attend to and they want to close them as fast as possible. The fact that you have a mental illness makes it an open and shut case."

"Maybe that's what I deserve," I said.

"If you killed him, you do deserve it. But Jack, I've known you for long enough to know that you are not a killer. But if you call the police, you'll go down for sure."

"So what am I going to do?"

"You're going to find out who killed Johnny *before* you turn yourself over to the police and I'm going to help you."

"Are you serious?" I asked him in disbelief. "In case you haven't noticed, I am not Batman and you are not Robin. I'm a mentally ill slacker and you're an inner city priest whose congregation is made up of mostly the elderly, the homeless and people like me. We have no place trying to solve a murder. That's even more dangerous than calling the police. Besides, if I disappear, aren't I going to look even more guilty than if I call the police tonight?"

"Maybe, but if you're free you can figure this out. If you're in jail or the hospital, you can't do shit."

"I don't know," I told him. I was feeling confused and lost. What Fr. Chris was saying was certainly true, but trying to figure this out alone seemed as crazy as Dr. Patel thought I was.

"Haven't you been talking about wanting to go back to college and get your life back, Jack?"

"Yes."

"Well, this might be an opportunity to take a big step towards self-reliance. You take care of yourself for a change. You take charge."

I knew that Fr. Chris had a point. The police were going to think that I was guilty as soon as they heard my story. Most of the people that lived in the house knew how I felt about Johnny and so did Tiffini and Dr. Patel. Who else had a reason to kill Johnny? In my head, I ran through the friends of Johnny that I knew. None of them had the least bit of a motive to harm him. Who else could have done this? A former lover? His shamed Asian parents?

"I need to think about this before I make a decision."

Fr. Chris gave me that understanding look of his and nodded.

"Why don't you sleep on it and I'll stop by in the morning. Whatever you choose to do, I'll support you."

He got up from the pew and bowed to the altar. I was glad that he was going to let me stay here tonight, I needed to be here. It would help me think this through.

"Get yourself a good night's sleep, a shower, and let's talk about this in the morning. We can plan your next move then."

"Thanks, Fr. Chris."

"Don't mention it. I'll see you in the morning."

"Wait," I said as he neared the big wooden

door. "There's one more thing I need from you."

Fr. Chris stopped and looked me in the eye.

"Can you forgive me for whatever I did tonight?"

"You didn't sin, Jack. You don't need to be forgiven."

"It would help me sleep a lot better tonight if I knew that God had forgiven me."

Fr. Chris looked at me for a moment. I could tell that he was tired and longed for some rest. His job took almost every minute of his waking hours and I knew he wanted to get home.

"Okay," he said grabbing a red prayer book from the pew. "I still don't think it's necessary but if it will make you feel better, okay."

He stretched his hand out to me, took mine in his and led me to the altar.

7

I was back in college in my dorm room. My roommate, a lawyer's son named Ethan, had gone out to meet some high school friends and I had the place to myself. I could hear the fall air rustle the leaves out in the quad and the other freshmen milling about outside. It was an exciting time, the beginning of a new chapter in my life.

I'd been surprised when the letter of acceptance came from the University of Michigan. I'd applied but never really thought I'd actually get in. Michigan was the best college in the state, and one of the best public colleges in the entire nation. I'd always been a good student but never a great one. My twin brother, always the smarter of the two of us, had convinced me to apply because he knew that he wanted to go there and there was little doubt that he would get in. He thought it would be great if we went to the same school. We had the type of relationship that many twins have, especially close. I never felt his pain or anything crazy like that, but we'd gone through every rite of passage together and knew each other with such intimacy that it sometimes made me wonder if I'd ever be able to be that close to anyone else, even a girlfriend or a wife.

I was set to start classes the following day and felt as prepared as I could reasonably expect to feel. I'd walked around campus the day before and found the buildings that all my classes were in, making sure that I could get from one to the other and not be late. I hated to be late.

I lay on my bed on that autumn day and tried to

just take it all in. I was a college man, four short years away from being a college graduate, something neither my father, my mother, or either set of grandparents could say they were. I was making something of my life.

A knock at the door broke me from my reverie. I hopped up and opened the door before whoever it was knocked a second time.

I'll never forget how I felt when I opened that door and saw her for the first time. She looked like the platonic form of youth and purity. Slight and small, she looked like some kind of child prodigy that had graduated from high school a couple of years early and was really too young to be in college. As she was just over five feet tall, I was almost a foot taller than she was. Her long brown hair fell over her shoulders like water over a waterfall and the glasses she wore were stylish in spite of being very much on the thick side.

"Hey," was the first word she ever spoke to me, "is Ethan here?"

"No, he went out to meet some friends from high school."

"Oh." She looked disappointed.

"I'm Jack," I said to her, "Jack Plowman. I'm Ethan's roommate. Do you want to come in and wait for him?"

"Well, I'm one of those high school friends that he was going to meet up with. I was going to try and surprise him and walk with him over to the Union."

Now, I was never the most socially astute guy. I misread people all the time. But even I could see the love in this girl's face as she talked about Ethan. She was obviously in love with him. She'd probably been carrying a torch for him since they were in middle school.

"Well, if you leave now, you can probably catch up with him," I told her.

"The thing is, I'm not really very familiar with the campus, being a freshman and all." She was so disappointed to have missed Ethan. She looked like her dog had just died. I almost thought she might start crying.

"I know how to get to the Union. I saw it when I was making a dry run of my class schedule yesterday. I hate being late to anything. I can walk you over if you want."

"I thought that I was the only one who did the practice run," she said, smiling for the first time since I said Ethan wasn't home.

"We're two of a kind…"

"I guess. Oh, sorry," she said, "I'm Anna."

"Well, Anna, let's go to the Union," I said as I grabbed my coat from the bed and shut the dorm door. As we walked through that crisp Ann Arbor air, I tried to put on a full charm offensive. Anna was not some child prodigy after all. She was eighteen and had gone to high school with Ethan back in Grosse Pointe. They met in the National Honor Society and had become friends. Just friends.

We came to a large group of people on the sidewalk. They seemed disoriented.

"What's going on?" I asked.

A young man in a Greek sweatshirt turned and

looked at me as if I was Satan himself.

you killed ethan

"What?" I said as I looked over at Anna. The crowd cleared to expose a man lying dead on the sidewalk. He had an open gash on his neck that made a familiar gurgling sound.

Anna screamed and started to run away from me as fast as she could. I tried to collect myself and follow her but before I could do anything else the guy in the Greek sweatshirt had me by the hair.

"Here's the killer! His name is Jack Plowman. He's the dead man's roommate," he screamed out to the crowd. "He killed Ethan so he could steal Anna. He's a murderer!"

I was scared and confused. I tried to speak but the only sounds I could make were gasps. The crowd started to yell in anger.

"He's a fuckin' head case and a fuckin' killer!" the frat boy screamed to the approval of the mob.

"What should we do?" the frat boy yelled to the crowd. The autumn breeze had become much colder. Snow flurries started to fall and the sky turned the color of coal.

The crowd yelled in unison: "Crucify him! Crucify him! Crucify him!"

8

"Crucify him."

I woke up mumbling it over and over like some twisted mantra.

"Crucify him, crucify him, crucify him."

I was drenched with sweat and afraid to open my eyes for fear of seeing Ethan dead on the floor. I felt hot with fever and I couldn't feel my arms.

When I eventually opened my eyes, I realized that I'd fallen asleep in the front pew and thrashed about during the nightmare, spilling prayer books and hymnals everywhere. My vision still cloudy with tears and sweat, I stumbled forward into the aisle away from the mass of open books, and looked up. The sun was shining golden morning light through the rose window behind the altar.

And above it all was the figure of Christ hanging from the cross.

9

"It was a sign from God, Father."

"Jack, you know that you have a tendency to get a little…how do I say this? You tend to get a little dramatic in your theological thinking. If you recall, I had to convince you that God was not a cannibal a number of months ago. Not to mention your extreme Lenten devotion. It was just a dream, my friend."

Fr. Chris and I were sitting on the front steps of the church drinking the coffee that he had picked up for us. It was a brisker morning than the last but clear. I'd already shaved and showered and was feeling more alive than I had been in months. I'd taken my medication right after I woke up, exactly as Dr. Patel prescribed.

"No, Father. It was a sign from God. I know now that I didn't kill Johnny. God wants me to find the man that did kill him and not go to the police. I know it. You were right."

"About that," Fr. Chris said with an uncomfortable look on his face. "I've been thinking about that. Perhaps I was a bit rash last night. I've never told you this, but I've had a few problems with the police in the past that might be affecting my judgment. I have problems with authority sometimes. I gave it some more thought last night and I think you should go to the police after all."

The traffic on Division Street in front of the church was busy. Lots of people were getting out to enjoy their weekends. I watched a few cars pass before I said anything else.

"Father," I began. "I know you have my best interest at heart. I do. But I really feel that God was speaking to me last night. I'm going to do this."

"But Jack, think about this. If you don't go to the police now, they are going to come looking for you. You were his roommate. Running away is just going to make yourself look like you have something to hide."

"You know as well as I do that the law will never give a man like me a fair shake. I'm mentally ill. Society thinks that I'm capable of anything. I'm just like Hannibal Lector and a million other crazy movie villains. You were right about them."

"But you're not Hercule Poirot, Jack. Can you really do this?"

"I can, with God's help."

Fr. Chris wasn't buying it. "This is madness," he said, putting his head in his hands. "I should have kept my stupid mouth shut last night."

"It sounds like you don't believe in me, Father. You sound like you don't believe in the power of God either."

"Damn it, Jack!" Fr. Chris yelled. "God doesn't work like that. Have you not listened to anything I've ever tried to teach you? God is not some cosmic Santa Claus that sends you secret messages and gives you superpowers. This is your illness speaking, not God."

I'd never seen Fr. Chris angry like this and it kind of scared me.

"You know how much I admire you, Fr. Chris." I said. "But I'm going to do this with or without your support. God is calling me and not even my priest is going to stop me from following."

"This is not of God, Jack. I think I need to call Tiffini and get you the help you need."

"Go ahead and call," I said to him furiously. "But as soon as you dial the first digit, I'm gone."

I could see the gears turning in Fr. Chris' head. He knew that he couldn't physically hold me here. I was faster and probably stronger than he was. If I left, I'd be out there on my own with no support. He really had no choice.

"Okay, so what's the plan, Jack?"

"I'm going to go back to the apartment and look for clues."

"And then what are you going to do after that?"

"Then I'll call someone and let them know what happened to Johnny and start hunting for the real killer."

"That sounds very simple, Jack. But you realize that this could get complicated very quickly."

At the time, it did seem very straightforward to me. I was sure that if I just looked over our apartment, I'd find some clear sign of what happened and who did it; then I'd be able to clear my name before the police ever started to see me as a suspect.

"How do I help keep you safe through all this, Sherlock Holmes?"

"I could use a place to sleep, plus some help sorting out whatever I discover."

"The place to sleep is no problem," Fr. Chris said. "You can stay at the parish house for as long as you like. I can get you some fresh clothes and food each morning."

I knew that Fr. Chris might call Tiffini and the police as soon as I left, but I decided that I'd cross that bridge when I came to it.

"I'm going to head out, Father," I said, getting up.

"I could come along, if you want," Fr. Chris offered.

"Too dangerous for you. If someone sees you walk into my place, that makes you a suspect and maybe even an accomplice. I can't let you get that involved."

He seemed to accept that and got up to shake my hand.

"Shall we meet back here tonight about dinner time?"

"Sure," I said as I walked down the steps, butterflies in my stomach. Once again, I was on my own with no one to trust and what felt like the whole world against me.

10

The apartment was just as I had left it. I walked up the weathered steps as quickly as I could without falling and shut the door behind me. Then I locked the door and checked it three times to make sure that it was locked.

I took a few minutes to steady myself before going into Johnny's room. I told myself what I was going to see and tried to prepare myself for the gore. I'd seen enough detective shows on television to know that in order to figure this out, I was going to have to look closely at everything, including Johnny's dead body.

"Don't freak out," I said out loud. I prayed that today the voices would keep at bay.

The door to Johnny's room was still slightly ajar when I walked up to it. The thought ran through my mind that maybe someone else had been here overnight. Had I shut the bedroom door in my panic? I tried to reassure myself that I had indeed shut the door. Besides, even if someone else had come in, like maybe Gina, it was too late to do anything about that now. The past was the past.

I opened the door and surveyed the room from the doorway, avoiding looking at Johnny's body for now. In the short time that Johnny had lived here, he'd personalized his room to an amazing degree. The walls were painted a soft blue color and there were museum prints without frames covering many of the walls. Most of the prints were black and white photos of flowers. I gathered they had been taken by some guy named Maplethorpe as that name was emblazoned in a black strip at the bottom of the pictures. I stepped forward into the room and looked around a little more, still careful not to look at Johnny's body that was still a fleshy lump on the bed. I'd save examining the body until the end.

Johnny had a lot of clothes. Many were in his tiny closet but quite a few dirty ones were on the floor as well. He had shirts and pants of every color hanging up in the closet to the right of the door. They looked like a rainbow all neatly pressed together. He'd always been a neat dresser, and I noticed a small ironing board up against the wall by the closet. Johnny had a little desk that was covered with papers and a few books in the corner.

I walked over to the desk, eyes never leaving the floor, and started to rifle through all the paper. I found a lot of ATM receipts. Most of them were withdrawals in sixty-dollar increments. I considered taking the receipts with me, but there were so many of them that I decided against it. I took out a pad of sticky notes and a pen that I had borrowed from the church and wrote down:

"Many ATM withdrawals."

Was that a clue or just a personal habit?

There were a few notes that Johnny had written on slips of paper. I reviewed each of them closely and tried to figure out if they were important. One said:

"dusty 9:30pm mall parking lot"

The name Dusty sounded familiar to me. Had Johnny mentioned him before? Had he come over to our apartment? For the first time, I started to regret how I had paid so little attention to Johnny's comings and goings in the months we had lived together. We hardly said a word to each other back then. What would have been different if I had paid attention? Would I be dead too? I took the note and put it in my back pocket.

Moving the papers around on the desk revealed a closed laptop computer with a few rock band stickers on the case. By the looks of it, the computer was new and a pretty high-end machine. I wondered where he'd gotten it and what was on it. Johnny's parents were pretty rich, so the most logical explanation was that they had bought it for him. I wanted to turn it on right there and check it out but decided to wait. I'd take the laptop with me when I left.

There was a nightstand on the other side of the bed and I walked over to that side of the room, looking at the colorful clothes on the floor as I went. The nightstand was obviously very expensive. It was mission style, made of solid wood, and had a rich dark finish. On top of the nightstand was a fancy mission style lamp with a colorful glass shade. What was Johnny doing with such a nice piece of furniture? Most of the other furniture in the room -- the desk, the chair, and the ironing board -- was cheap. It seemed odd that his parents would buy him only one piece of high end furniture.

I opened the drawer in the nightstand and found about five cheap paperback books. The first one I picked up was *Chain of Fools - A Donald Strachey Mystery.* There was a bookmark halfway through the book. Johnny must have read at least a little bit of this one. Below *Chain of Fools* was a book a called *Mad in America*. I had seen that one in Tiffini's office and had even paged through it once when I was waiting for her. It was a history of the abusive treatment, if you called torture "treatment," that the mentally ill had suffered through in the past. The spine of this one hadn't even been cracked. It wasn't exactly a fun read. I remember feeling sickened after just thumbing through it.

Below that was *The Courage to Heal: A Guide for Women Survivors of Child Sexual Abuse*. It was an oversized white paperback. Was Johnny trying to deal with being sexually abused? Probably. But why did he have a book meant for women? I thumbed through it. It was written in a supportive self-help style. Some of the passages that were underlined couldn't possibly refer to Johnny. Things like the number of girls who were sexually abused each year. Had he borrowed the book? I flipped to the front cover and found the name Gina Logan.

I made a note on my sticky pad that said: Gina Logan.

Johnny's wallet was on the top of the night stand. I picked it up and started to look through it but then decided to just take it with me. There was about fifty dollars in it. I knew that stealing was wrong, but then again I was a detective now and I really needed the money.

I was feeling pretty good about myself by that time. I'd uncovered some things that could legitimately be called clues. I was about to leave and consider my first day as a detective a success when I remembered the victim.

Johnny.

He was still lying on the bed, the bed that I had been so careful to avoid looking at. I told myself that I had enough to go on, that I didn't have to look at Johnny's body. What good would it do anyway? He was dead. It didn't matter how he had died, that was over. Dead was dead, whether from a gunshot to the head or an overdose of drugs. It didn't make a difference.

But what if it did?

I didn't want to look. I was afraid to look. But I knew that I had to. I remembered all the episodes of *Law and Order* that I'd seen on TV. Didn't the way the victim was killed always give an important clue? It always mattered on TV.

I turned my gaze to him.

Johnny was lying there sprawled out on the bed just like he'd been yesterday. His tee shirt was torn on the side and it appeared that he had been in some sort of scuffle. He had a few cuts and bruises on his arms but nothing major. What had killed him was the wound on his neck.

I knew that it was going to be graphic because I had seen it before, but the fear came back as I looked into the deep cut that had killed my roommate. Johnny's neck looked like the bottom of a freshly gutted fish. He had been slashed across the neck and everything that had helped him speak and swallow was now exposed to the world. Folds of skin flapped open to expose his neck muscles

that were now a deep maroon color. Had they been bright red before? I smelled death for the first time.
   death
   I'd seen enough and I knew that looking at Johnny's corpse much longer would mean that the voices would start up again. I didn't need that. Plus, if I stayed here much longer I was going to lose my breakfast.

I averted my gaze again, grabbed Johnny's laptop along with its case, and hustled out of the room. That dingy living room had never been a more welcome sight. I sat down on one of the plastic chairs and tried to forget seeing everything that I'd seen.

All things considered, my morning playing detective hadn't gone that badly. I had Johnny's wallet, his computer, and a lot to think about. I started to feel confident that I would be able to figure this little mystery out with the clues that I had. I might actually succeed at something for a change. I wanted to leave right then but then I remembered that I had a duty to call someone so that Johnny wouldn't just rot here for weeks. I looked around for the phone and found it on top of the TV.

I'd thought about who to call last night after waking from my dream and settled on Tiffini because, unlike the cops, she wouldn't be able to trace the call or get someone over here fast.

I picked up the phone and dialed her number. The phone rang and rang.

"Hello. You've reached the phone of Tiffini Ringold, Licensed Masters Social Worker. I'm not able to take your call right now so please leave me a message after the tone. If this is an emergency, please press zero now."

I took a deep breath and then pressed zero. It felt like about half an hour before anyone came on the line.

"Community Mental Health, how can I help you?" a young woman's voice said.

"I need to talk to Tiffini Ringold," I said, trying to disguise my voice by making it deeper.

"Sir, it's Saturday. She's not in the office," the woman said.

Shit. I hadn't thought of that. What kind of detective was I?

"I'm going to kill myself if I can't talk to her right now," I said without thinking. What was I doing? This was a sure way to get the police out here pronto.

"I'll patch you through to the manager on call," the woman said in a tone that suggested she had heard this line before and was not worried in the least about my threat to kill myself. A few seconds later a man was on the line.

"This is Dr. Albany. What's your name and how can I help you?"

"Johnny Chen is dead in his apartment. Send someone out to pick up his body," I said in a husky voice that I hoped sounded nothing like my own.

"Who is this?" he said. I wondered if he thought this was a prank.

"This isn't a joke. Send someone out, but not the police," I stammered out, sounding like a fool. God, please don't let anyone be recording this.

"Listen, I don't…"

I hung up and ended the call and, along with it, my embarrassment. The pride I'd had a few minutes ago was gone. I felt like I had made a crucial error that might end up costing me my freedom.

they know that it's you.

No, that was silly. No one knew anything, I was hallucinating. Too stressed.

kill yourself now and just be done with it.

I had to get out of here. Fast. I gathered up the PC case and Johnny's messenger bag, tossed them both over my shoulder, and headed for the door. But I stopped when I reached the kitchen. I'd forgotten one thing, the most important thing.

"Lord," I said, closing my eyes, "Johnny Chen was not my friend. I didn't like him and I suspect that you didn't like him a lot of the time either. But Johnny Chen was one of your children and he did not deserve to be struck down like this. Justice needs to be served, Lord, and with your help, I plan to bring justice to whoever did this. I pray that you'll help me, Heavenly Father, and protect me in this mission. Like Jonah, this is a mission that I did not ask for and do not want, but I accept it knowing that I have your support and blessing. I ask all of this through your son, Jesus Christ. In the unity of the Holy Spirit, all glory and honor is yours, Almighty Father, now and forever, as it was in the beginning and…"

I realized that I was babbling to God.

"Amen," I quickly added and walked out of the door and down the staircase.

11

The sun was out and shining down on me as I walked away from what had been my home. I knew that however this ended, I wouldn't be able to live there again.

The heat felt good on my skin, like the warmth of a mother, and it helped me relax. The laptop computer hanging over my shoulder felt lighter than I imagined it would. That was probably because I was right about it being expensive. The smaller and lighter computers got, the more expensive they seemed to be.

I walked down the street and thought about my next move. I was glad to be away from Johnny's body, but I didn't really know what to do next. The day was still young and I had a lot of time to kill before meeting up with Fr. Chris. I needed to decide what to do next. Should I find a private place and carefully look through Johnny's wallet, or should I open up the computer and check that out first?

I'd liked computers since high school and at one time I'd spent a large portion of my days in front of them, either taking notes in class on my laptop or playing games in my dorm room. I hadn't used a computer in the last year or so but not because I didn't have access. The mental health agencies always made them available to us. No, what had kept me away from computers had been a feeling of not belonging that came with my mental illness. I knew that there were lots of "normal" people out there that were using computers and iPhones to meet and stay connected to others, but since I'd become part of the mental health system, I just didn't feel like I belonged to anything besides Dr. Patel's patient list. That, and I was afraid that if I reconnected with people from high school or college on Facebook, I'd eventually have tell them that I was a mental patient. That wasn't something that you updated on your status to brag about.

"Jack Plowman is excited to be a public mental health patient in Grand Rapids."

No, computers were one of the many things I'd once loved that my mental illness had taken from me. Nature hates a vacuum, so in came confusion, regret, and a lot of bitterness to fill the void. Whenever someone told me to make lemonade out of lemons, I wanted to beat the shit out of them.

But today, circumstances had taken a turn. Here I was walking down the street with an expensive computer over my shoulder and all the time in the world to do whatever the hell I wanted to with it. At least until the cops came and arrested me, that is.

I knew that there were a few coffee shops in downtown Grand Rapids and made a half-conscious decision to walk down to the Monroe Mall towards them. I also knew that I had some cash in my pocket thanks to Johnny. Why not splurge with a nice cup of coffee and maybe even a scone?

The Three Kings Coffee Shoppe was the first one I came to when I got downtown. It was right across the street from the Grand Rapids Police Station on the corner of Division and Monroe Center Street. I was initially more than a little frightened about stopping there. I felt like my face screamed "guilty" to anyone who looked at me, especially people that happened to be cops and were trained to pick out criminals. But after a little thought, I decided that the Three Kings might be the best place in the world for me. Who expects the guy running from the police to be hanging around just outside their door?

The Three Kings was a new coffee joint in town and had an English pub theme. The outside of the building had a little wooden sign above the door and a fake English façade with aged wood and frosted glass. The real building facade was still visible on the top two floors though. It was a shallow illusion, but it seemed to be working for the place. When I peered in the window, I saw a line of well-dressed yuppies waiting to spend obscene amounts of money for something that I got for free each morning at the mission.

I snuck in the front door and ducked under the black chain that snaked around the entrance, forming the hoards of people into a manageable line in front of the baristas. I wanted that cup of coffee and maybe something sweet to eat, but I didn't have the patience to wait in line. Not when there was Johnny's computer to explore.

I moved through a dimly lit section filled with old leather couches and pictures of fox hunts on the walls. It struck me funny that the couches were probably brand new but had been made to look old in order to fit in with the décor. Every chair was taken in that section of the shop, so I kept moving towards the back. Eventually, I came across a table that a young woman was just getting up from. I avoided eye contact with her, just in case she was a cop, and as soon as her back was to me, I sat down and pulled the laptop out of the bag.

I had to feel around the base of the machine for a while to find the power button, but eventually I found it and heard the little fan start to whirl as I pressed it down.

I wondered what I would find on Johnny's computer. I sat waiting for what seemed forever as the machine went through its opening procedures. As I waited for the computer, I looked down and saw that I had goose bumps.

The screen lit up with a picture of Johnny in a night club. He was holding a drink and had his arm around a very handsome man that wasn't wearing a shirt. God rest his soul, but it seemed that Johnny had never met a gay cliche that he didn't like. As the computer finished loading, the picture became the background pattern for about fifty icons that were littered haphazardly across the screen. The man with Johnny didn't look familiar to me and so I scanned the rest of the faces in the night club photo for anyone I knew. None of the faces looked familiar. The club seemed to be a disco with lots of flashing lights and a hyper modern interior.

Johnny had a Windows machine and so I clicked on the Start menu to see what programs he had been using recently. It looked like he had been on iTunes not too long ago and had also been using Microsoft Word. I clicked on the Word icon in the Start menu to see what came up there.

Faster than I expected, a blank Word document

popped up on the laptop screen. I scrolled over to the File menu to see what Johnny had been working on. There were four documents listed. Number One said C:\...passwords.doc. I clicked it and up came a list:

Hotmail...…FabulousChen@hotmail.com...……
....69_bigdaddy_69
YouTube...…..JohnnyCCHEN...…..12587_Big
ITunes...…….ChenChenChen...……12587_Big
SelectBank...….Jchen...……………..1dusty_69
Facebook...……...FabulousChen@hotmail.com...…..
.69_bigdaddy_69

There was no doubt in my mind that I'd just hit the jackpot. Thank God for forgetful people. With these passwords, I had access to Johnny's total online life. I could feel the goose bumps starting to bristle again on my legs. My stomach felt strange for a moment. This was it. This was exactly what I had been looking for. I considered where to begin, and decided to start at the top of the list with Hotmail and work down.

The café had Wifi access, as almost all cafes did by that time, and so within a few minutes I was logging onto Johnny's hotmail account. He only had two messages in his inbox. The most recent one was from someone named Cashman19. I opened it and read:

From: Cashman <cashman19@yahoo.com>
To: FabulousChen@hotmail.com
Subject: it's all set

Hey man, everything is a go. Delete all of our emails now like I showed you. Do it now. it's very important.

-me

Whatever Johnny was into, it sounded pretty serious, and probably illegal. I checked Johnny's sent folder and it was empty. He had done what Cashman had asked and cleared out the evidence except that last message. I thought about writing a return email but then decided against it. This Cashman was probably connected to Johnny's murder if he wasn't the murderer himself. I wasn't ready to confront him yet. I needed more than a vague email to show to the police.

The second email was from Edward Chen. I double-clicked it and read:

From: Edward Chen
<Chen@brownandwallace.com>
To: FabulousChen@hotmail.com
Subject: Your Medication

John,

You win. You'll get your "medication" just like you want. It's all set. I hope you are happy. I will suffer a great deal for this, as you know. It may destroy what little pride that this family has left. Your mother and I could very well lose our home, the home you grew up in, because of this, John.

You have again brought great dishonor to us.

I never wish to see or talk to you again. I am instructing your mother to also never speak to you again. This is my last note to you. I have tried to understand you and your ways, and I believe that we have already forgiven you too many times to count. This is too much and the last time you will hurt this family. You should be ashamed of yourself.

 You are no longer my son.

Edward Chen, CPA
Brown and Wallace, P.C.
Select Bank Building
5th Floor - Suite 501A
60 Monroe Center
Grand Rapids MI
(616) 555-1295
(616) 555-7830 - fax

 Reading it made my heart ache. I'd known that Johnny had a troubled relationship with his parents but I never thought it was this bad. What had Johnny done to elicit this and what was the medication they were talking about? I felt around in my pocket for a pen and wrote down Mr. Chen's office address on a napkin. I knew that I'd have to talk to him eventually, but as there was also no way that I could tell him who I really was, I didn't know how I'd manage that. The Select Bank building was just down the mall, and I was tempted to check out the place until I remembered that it was Saturday and the office would be closed. It would have to wait until Monday.

I went back to the list of passwords and saw that YouTube was the next one on the list. I browsed over to the site and logged in as Johnny. He'd uploaded 15 videos, some of which had been viewed over 1000 times. I clicked on the oldest one, titled "New Year's Eve," but before it was loaded I heard someone close to me speak in a voice loud enough to startle me.

"Excuse me," the voice said.

I looked up and saw a man wearing an apron and a button down shirt with a name tag that said "Todd" and under that "Manager."

"You need to leave," he said sternly and then added, "Now."

Todd was stocky and still in his twenties but he clearly took his job very seriously.

"Why do I have to leave?" I asked him as meekly as I could.

"There are so many reasons, but here are just two. One, you didn't buy anything and have been sitting here using our Wifi, which is against our policy. And two, I know you." My heart froze. This was it. The jig was already up. "You're one of those homeless guys. You people are not allowed in here."

I was relieved that being homeless was all I was being accused of.

"Okay, I'm going." I powered down the computer as Todd stood staring razor blades at me while I did it.

"I know a lot of the police from across the

street," he told me. "I don't want to see you in here again. If I do, I'll tell them and they'll come over and take care of you."

"I'm sorry, sir."

"And where did you get that laptop? Did you steal it from someone here?"

Some of the other patrons were starting to look at me.

"The laptop is mine," I said. "If you want to ask everyone here if they've lost a laptop before I go, that's fine with me. You'll see that it's mine."

He seemed to consider doing just that for a minute.

"Get out of here," he said instead.

I did.

12

I still had time to kill before meeting up with Fr. Chris for dinner and so I ended up walking around downtown. Walking always helped me think anyway. What was now Monroe Center Street had once been a pedestrian mall back when I was a kid. They'd put in this road while I was crazy and out of control. I had to say I didn't like the change.

The addition of all these cars seemed to stain the childhood memories that I had of downtown. When I was a kid, my folks used to take me to see Santa Claus at Christmas time in a department store that was now the Grand Rapids Police Department. I remember big glass Christmas windows, frosted and filled with clothes, and people everywhere doing their Christmas shopping in the open air. That department store even had an elevated train that ran around the ceiling in the basement. Riding that was a yearly treat for me when we came down here to see Santa and do a little window shopping. My twin brother has a picture of us on that train in his office.

The downtown that I walked through that day was very different. The old stores that I remembered from my childhood were gone and new ones had come in. There was even a sushi place not too far from the Three Kings. That never would have survived in the Grand Rapids of my childhood. Everyone was way too conservative to eat raw fish back then. Today, the place was pretty busy, filled with people who probably lived in some of the new condominiums that seemed to be popping up everywhere down here. Those rich fools had paid big bucks to live within a few blocks of bums like me.

I walked down the sidewalk and tried to remember where everything used to be. I thought that there used to be a Chinese restaurant where the new Grand Rapids Art Museum was going in. A whole city block had been leveled for the place. It was still under construction but it looked to me like it was going to be just another big concrete block sitting on glass walls. I could see some of the workmen putting in a doorway through the transparent walls as I walked by and felt an odd tinge of loss for the restaurant that I'd never even eaten at.

I was about to turn back and head for St. Mark's when I saw the words Select Bank. Johnny's father had his office in that building. The Select Bank building had big marble columns at least three stories high that guarded the entrances, at least on this side. It was an intimidating façade. Because I had nothing else to do, I tried the brass handle on the door. It was open.

I walked through the door and into a pink marble foyer. It was marble from floor to ceiling but it felt like a crypt to me. An elaborate marble staircase ran upward directly to my right and just a little ways beyond that were two elevators with brass doors. I had a strong feeling that I was somewhere I shouldn't be. I knew where I had to go but I also knew that I wasn't going today. But before I left, I checked the directory.

Sure enough, Mr. Chen's firm, Brown and Wallace, was listed.

13

Fr. Chris and I ate Big Macs driving in his
Toyota a few hours later. He was very interested in
what I'd learned but said that he had an
appointment to visit a sick parishioner and so we
had to eat on the run.

"That's what sucks about St. Mark's," he said
as he held the steering wheel in one hand and his
Big Mac in the other. "There are just so many old
people that I'm constantly either at the hospital or a
nursing home." He took a bite of his sandwich and
swallowed without hardly chewing, careful to keep
his eyes on the road.

"You've also got a lot of mentally ill and
homeless," I added.

"Yes, that I do," he said with a smile. "And
may God bless all the sheep! So tell me about these
emails."

"Well, it seems like Johnny's father gave him
something, something that he called medication but
must be something else, not long before Johnny was
killed. Whatever it was, it destroyed their
relationship. Mr. Chen said that Johnny was no
longer his son at the end of the email."

"Man, that's pretty messed up," my priest said
through his mouthful of hamburger.

"I'd have to agree with you there, Padre. I
figure my next step is to talk to Chen."

"But how are you going to get in to see him?
The murder will probably be on tomorrow's news
and you can't just walk in and ask to talk to him."

"Oh, I'm not going to go and see him. One of

Johnny's social workers is going."

Fr. Chris flashed that movie star smile of his. "I get it. What about the other email?"

"I don't know what to do about that one. I think the author and Johnny were doing something illegal. Johnny deleted all of his previous emails at this guy's request. Whoever wrote that email is probably involved with this somehow."

"So, are you gonna email him back?"

"Not without more evidence," I said as I reached for the last French fries at the bottom on my bag. "And besides, I don't want to tip him off that I'm on the case…so to speak."

"Good plan. We're almost at the parish house. I'll let you on out and you can hang out there for the night. I'll probably be late getting in tonight. I've got a full plate of old and sick members to see. See you in church in the morning?"

"Sure," I said. "Nothing would keep me from it, Father."

After Fr. Chris dropped me off, I headed upstairs to my room, kicked off my shoes, and sat down on the bed, relieved to have my first day being a detective behind me. It felt like I'd just finished the first real day of work in my life, and in some ways that was the truth. I was tired all over and my muscles ached as if I had spent the day carrying around rocks. But it was a good tired, an honorable tired. I felt a profound sense of satisfaction and accomplishment.

I was so tired that I fell asleep not long after I lay down. I slept like the dead that night. It was a deep, blissful slumber. Little did I know at the time that this would be one of the last good night's sleep that I would have for quite some time.

14

I woke up when the sun was blazing into the room so brightly that not even my clenched eyelids could keep it out. Everything seemed bathed in radiant light; nothing and no one could escape it. I got up with the intention of getting dressed, only to realize that I had fallen asleep with my clothes on the previous night.

I wanted to at least change my clothes and so I went to the bag that Fr. Chris kept for his guests. In it I found a blue button down oxford that was only a little too big for me and a pair of jeans that fit perfectly. When I added the brown belt that was in my old jeans, I looked as good as I had in at least two years. I looked good, but I realized that I could look even better. I grabbed the grooming kit that was in Fr. Chris' bag and headed to the bathroom.

It was a small bathroom with out-of-date rose colored wall paper and the tiniest little window that looked out onto the brick wall of the community college, but it was like Buckingham Palace compared to the bathroom at my Prospect apartment. I turned on the water and it was hot in seconds, unlike at home where I usually just gave up on hot water most mornings. The grooming kit had a cheap plastic razor and it didn't take me very long to find a pair of old scissors in the medicine cabinet. I took the scissors and started to cut my dirty and unmanageable hair. It fell in clumps onto the old pink carpet that for some strange reason someone had decided would be just perfect for this rectory bathroom.

I'd started to let my hygiene go back in college just before my mental illness engulfed me for the first time. I don't remember exactly what I'd been thinking, but I slowly stopped showering and shaving about three months before the voices and delusions started. While my friends surely noticed, no one said anything. I'd also started to spend more and more time alone, so they would have had less opportunity to talk to me anyway. The only person who I spent any time with back then was Anna, who had become my girlfriend. She told me she thought it was gross that I wasn't clean and didn't want to touch or kiss me but I didn't care.

Ever since that first psychotic break, I'd dressed and smelled the part of the mental patient. Dirty and unkempt.

But this morning was going to be a clean slate.

After my hair was short enough, I lathered up and used the razor to clean off the rest of the dirty hair from my face. When I was done, I was clean shaven for the first time in months. I looked at the man looking back at me from the small mirror and thought that I recognized him. He was the man I'd once been.

Feeling full of life and still under the influence of that morning sun, I stripped down and got into the ancient shower. The water surprised me with its heat as I stepped into its baptizing flow. I wanted to get my day started so I made the shower fast. Still the shower had cleansed me enough that when I got out, I'd left a thick brown ring around the bottom of Fr. Chris's tub.

I was feeling so good that morning, almost forgot to take my medication. Almost.

By the time I was dressed I realized that I had no idea what time it was. I picked up my watch from the nightstand and realized that I was twenty minutes late for church.

"Great," I said, putting on my watch as I headed for the door. Fr. Chris was letting me stay here and I didn't have decency enough to even show up to church on time. I hoped that he wouldn't find me ungrateful.

I opened the big wooden doors of the church just as Fr. Chris was walking into the pulpit to give his sermon. I saw the familiar group of about 15 senior citizens, mostly women, sitting in the front of the church together. They were the old timers that had gone to St. Mark's for years. The guys from the mission were there as usual and turned around to look at me as I walked in. They formed a separate, much larger group in the back pews of the church. A few of the guys waved at me and gestured for me to sit next to them. I walked over and sat next to DeMarkus.

DeMarkus Williams was a big black man that looked like he should be playing linebacker for some Division I football team. He had muscles on top of his muscles and managed to stay ripped even though I knew that he'd been homeless and gym-less for at least a year. I once asked him if there was some secret gym for the homeless that he worked out in, and he just laughed that deep bass laugh of his. That morning, DeMarkus was wearing a muscle shirt and sweatpants, which was kind of like a uniform for him.

DeMarkus and I had become friends of a sort when we were living at the mission. He was in their substance abuse program and had already been there for about 6 months when I landed on their doorstep. He and I had been in line outside God's Kitchen, the place where we got our two daily free meals, and started talking. DeMarkus liked to talk and he didn't really care who, if anyone, was listening to him. He even talked to himself sometimes but he never talked back like I tended to do when I was really sick. Within a few minutes of meeting him, DeMarkus had told me that he'd been heavy into drugs, had four children from four different mothers, and wanted to get clean and become a police officer someday. He was really into getting clean and loved God as much as I did. He could quote the AA Big Book like nobody's business and whenever he saw another guy from the program, he shouted out some sort of spiritual encouragement.

I liked him instantly.

We started to eat together and discuss the Bible for hours on end after that. I carried a Bible with me at all times back then and had my favorite passages dog eared for easy reference. Between the two of us, we solved a lot of the world's problems over that table at God's Kitchen. Once I got hooked up with mental health and got into the apartment, I'd lost track of DeMarkus. After a while, I heard some people saying that he had relapsed, left the program and disappeared. But a few weeks ago, he started showed up at St. Mark's. He had a big smile on his face and said that he was back in treatment.

"I got eight days of sobriety," he'd told me proudly when we reconnected a few weeks ago.

I quietly sat down next to DeMarkus. He was with a couple of friends of his that I didn't know. One was a white guy with a scraggly beard and long stringy hair. The other guy was short and had close cropped black hair. I nodded to them and they nodded back.

Fr. Chris looked out at his odd flock, black and white, old and young, with pride. He looked like his only child had just gotten into Harvard with a full scholarship.

"Johnny Chen was killed this week," Fr. Chris said. I lost my breath.

"Killed in the prime of his life. Someone broke into his home and sent him into the next life. He was snuffed out like a flame. A priest friend of mine tells me that a family from Trinity in Kentwood lost their home in a fire two weeks ago. No insurance. Many of my brothers from the mission have been homeless for months. Lots of people are hurting, and in the reading from today, Jesus is asked if the people suffering deserve it because they are such great sinners. They point to some terrible stories that they've heard and ask Jesus if what's happened to them is God's punishment."

A number of the men from the mission hung their heads, having already asked that question about themselves many times before.

"My back row brothers, they know what

hunger is. Does God think they deserve to be hungry? Jesus says no. Those that suffer are no worse sinners than anyone else. Those that suffer know what David is talking about in the psalm from this morning. David says, 'God, you're my brother. You're like a cool drink that I find crossing the desert.' God tells us in Isaiah that God's grace is like a party where everyone is invited. In fact, God extends a special invitation to those of us that are down and out."

A few calls of "That's right" arose from the pew in front of me.

"But what's up with this? Why is God being so nice to us? Why are we getting invited to the party? We're losers, bums, and drunks! My friends in the back know that anyone who gives you something probably wants something in return. Is God any different?

"Yes and No.

"Yes, God is different because He's no crack dealer giving us a free sample to get us hooked.

"But God does want something from us. In today's gospel, Jesus tells a parable, or a little story that's meant to teach us a lesson. He tells a story about a tree. A tree whose reason for living is to grow fruit for people to eat at the big party that God is planning. If you were listening to the story, you know that the tree didn't put any fruit out for three years. Three years! The man who owned the tree said, 'Cut that worthless tree down, it's no good.' But the gardener said, 'Wait. Let me take some of the waste of my life, the dirty crap that I've got in a pile and put it on that tree. It stinks and it smells, but when you pile shit on something, it helps it grow.' The owner says, 'I'll give it another year, but if it doesn't give me some fruit by next year, we're cutting it down.'

"That tree has got to start doing what it was made to do or it's gonna be cut down. We're the tree, my friends. Joyce Madison, you're that tree. DeMarkus Willliams, you're that tree, too.

"God is saying it's time to put up or shut up. God is saying, 'You have a lot of shit in your lives but I've given you the ability to use it to make my world a better place. Get on with it!' You might not think you have much. Maybe you only have a kind heart because yours has been broken so many times before. Or maybe you only have strong hands. You might be homeless, you might be old and sick, you might even want to kill yourself most days of the week. But you know what? God still expects you to use what you do have to make this world a better place. Just like that tree was given another chance to grow fruit, God has given you another chance. A second chance that can change your life and the life of your brother and sister too.

"In today's readings, God is saying to us, 'Why aren't you using your gifts? Why are you wasting what you have?' If you are addicted to drugs, why aren't you in treatment? You can't serve God and drugs at the same time."

DeMarkus let out a deep "Amen!"

"God may want you to get clean and then help others get clean. If you're old and feel useless, why aren't you working harder to help others? That's how God will give you purpose and hope.

Fake it until you make it as they say in A.A.

"Now is the time to repent, to change your life. Get drugs behind you. Get hopelessness behind you. Get feeling sorry for yourself behind you. Get depression behind you. Grow the fruit of sobriety. Grow the fruit of hope for the future. Grow the hope of thankfulness for the gifts that God *has* given you."

The back row let out a resounding "amen" with even some of the old women joining in. The noise filled the sanctuary like the singing voice of the Holy Spirit, who was surely present that morning. Even the normal folks up front, the churchy hipsters and the blue collar guys, they were smiling too.

15

"How do you like the chili, men?" Fr. Chris asked us. DeMarkus, myself and a few of his friends had been enjoying the free lunch and catching up. There was chili and cornbread prepared and ready for us as soon as the service was over, just as usual.

"It's great, Father," the white guy with the scraggly beard said.

"I'm glad to hear it. Make sure you thank Mrs. Williams. She's the one that made the lunch today. It's her gift to us."

"We've already thanked her," I said. I could see Mrs. Williams working on serving the others, a hair net covering her white hair. It'd been a good turn out today and she was busy. I thought that I should go and help her somehow, when Fr. Chris spoke to me.

"Jack, can I see you in my office?"

"Sure," I said wiping my mouth as I got up from the table.

"Delight yourselves in rich food, my friends," Fr. Chris remarked as he left the men to walk back with me to his office. Fr. Chris had a small but cozy office in the back of the parish house. The room was covered in a deep wood paneling and every wall was covered with either rows of books or CDs. A tiny little window let in a little light but you still had to turn on the desk lamp to really see anything.

Fr. Chris had an old desk, usually cluttered

with his notes, in the center of the small room. The room was so tiny that no more than two other people could really fit in it comfortably. Its size ensured that anything that happened in the office was private.

I'd met with Fr. Chris a few times before in his office to talk about some of my religious ideas and had grown to really love the room with its scholarly cave-like feel. I wondered why he had asked to speak to me in private. Was he angry at me for being late? But then I saw the Grand Rapids Press on his desk, carefully folded to highlight one article.

"Take a look at this article," he said to me from his chair.

"It's about Johnny, isn't it?"

"Yes," was all he said in return.

Foul Play Suspected in GR Man's Death

By Rachel Baxter
Grand Rapids Press

Grand Rapids - The Grand Rapids Police Department is investigating the death of John A. Chen, 25, of Grand Rapids. Chen was found dead by authorities in his Prospect Street apartment Saturday. The cause of death is not being released at this time. Carlos Garcia, GRPD spokesman, said that the death is being considered a homicide and that the police are seeking Mr. Chen's roommate, Jackson Plowman, also of Grand Rapids, for questioning.

Garcia declined to say whether Mr. Plowman is a suspect in the case or not. He said only that he is a "person of interest." The police are not disclosing any details of the case but are asking those who have any information to call the Police Department. Chen was a life-long Grand Rapids resident and graduate of East Grand Rapids High School. Funeral arrangements are being made with Vant Hof Chapel.

"So I'm a wanted man now, huh?"

"You're a person of interest," Fr. Chris corrected.

"Same difference."

The article brought home to me what I had gotten into. This was serious stuff.

"Should I turn myself in for questioning?" I asked him.

"I wish I knew how to answer that, Jack. On the one hand, you don't want to give the police any more reason to think that you're guilty, and running from them does that. But on the other hand, if you go to the police, they'll probably try to pin this on you and I doubt whether you could get a fair trial. Look at the article. It's only two paragraphs long. Even the Press doesn't much care when someone poor is killed. I'm afraid that the police will act the same if they get ahold of you. Quickly convict you and move on to more important things."

"I know," I said ruefully.

"My offer to let you stay here still stands, though."

"Thanks," I told Fr. Chris. I knew that he was putting himself at risk now. The police wouldn't be very happy with him harboring a fugitive.

"I don't want to get you in trouble," I told him.

"Jack, I've got to bear fruit like everyone else. Maybe my fruit right now is to protect the innocent from persecution."

"You've got a lot of faith in me, Father."

"No, Jack, I've got a lot of faith in God."

Before I could say anything else, there was a loud knock at the door that startled us both. Fr. Chris looked at me with a puzzled look in his eye. We'd never been interrupted before in his office and he didn't seem to be expecting company today either.

"Come in," he said to the wooden door.

It opened halfway and a large white man stuck an unusually large head in. He was bald and didn't seem very happy.

"I'm looking for Jack Plowman," he said.

"Good day to you as well," Fr. Chris replied.

"Tell me where Jack Plowman is before I beat the shit out of you...Father," the large man growled.

The room got very cold and I felt my bladder spasm. A little urine spilled out of me.

"Didn't your mother teach you any manners?" Fr. Chris asked.

In one swift movement, the man was in the office and standing in front of the only door out. His face roared red with rage at my friend, whom I realized was just making things worse with what he was saying.

"I'm Jack Plowman," I said, wanting it all to be done.

"Come with me," he said, grabbing my shirt and hoisting me out of my chair. I didn't resist and became a terrified lump over his massive shoulder as he picked me up like I was a bag of flour. The man was starting to leave the room when Fr. Chris spoke up.

"Wait one second," he said.

"If you want me to wait, you're going to have try and stop me," the man said with a scoff and continued out the door.

I'm not sure what happened next but it seemed almost as if God had suddenly given Fr. Chris the power to fly. He launched over his desk with a strange grace and was next to my captor and pummeling him before I knew what was happening. The blows were rapid and fierce. I could tell that Fr. Chris was putting everything he had into them. The man was shocked. He recoiled in pain but continued to hold me and stepped back into the room to deal with Fr. Chris. At that moment, Fr. Chris added a violent yell to his attack while continuing to punch the man's gut.

I felt myself falling to the floor as the man dropped me in order to strike back at Fr. Chris. My head smashed onto the floor and a blinding pain radiated through my body. The room spun around in circles, and I saw the two men grappling on what seemed like the floor and then they were on the ceiling kicking and hitting. Everywhere, books fell from shelves, their pages fluttering like paper birds as they dropped to the floor.

Still dazed, I got to my feet as the room spun around me. The big man was now on top of Fr. Chris in the opposite corner, the overturned desk partially obscuring them. The man landed blow after blow. Fr. Chris lay there motionless, passed out.

he's dead

I knew that I had to do something but as I stood by the door, all I wanted to do was run. Run for as long as my body would let me. Run until I died from exhaustion. Run away from this life into the next life.

But instead I picked up a metal crucifix that had fallen to the floor.

The crucifix fit in my hand like God had designed it for just such a purpose. I held it like a knife, the bottom of the cross the blade and the body of Christ, my handle. The man had forgotten about me in the heat of violence and so I was able to move to him over the dead books on the floor without him noticing me. I worked my way behind him as he continued to beat Fr. Chris.

I paused to take a deep breath,

the body of christ

and then yelled out as loud as I could as I brought the crucifix down in a long arch into the side of the man's neck. He yelled out in pain and turned from Fr. Chris. I expected the cross to go into him like a razor, maybe killing him instantly, but it barely punctured his skin before slipping off of him and out of my hands. The pain didn't seem to be affecting him when a second later he turned to look at me with hate in his eyes. Before I could react, he hit me square in the face with a round house punch that sent me flying back to the other side of the room. Blood splattered high into the air as I recoiled like I was in some bad horror movie. I fell crumpled like a piece of wet cardboard against the wall.

The man got up and made his way toward me. I was disoriented from the blow and felt the hot blood pouring out of my nose as he advanced on me.

"Why are you doing this?" I said, my mouth now full with blood.

His reply was a fist to my jaw, and then another one. I cried out in pain and then we were joined by others in the room. Other voices that had no bodies.

you're going to die here
"hit him"
you deserve to die
"get that mother fucker"

Just as I started to fall into the darkness of unconsciousness, the man stopped punching me. It was like someone had pressed the pause button on my beating. One minute I was getting beaten and the next there was just...nothing. Nothing but a gradual blurring of my vision and encroaching sleep. I started to see shadows floating around the room that seemed to phase in and out of reality. One moment the shadow was a man and the next it was just a dark stain on the wall. I knew that I was losing control of myself, my fear and pain were overwhelming me, my demons were taking control.

I worked to steady my eyes. I imagined that I saw my attacker being beaten by a group of people. I thought it was a hallucination, but then I recognized one of the men in the group. It was DeMarkus.

This was no dream. He and some of the other men from the mission must have heard the fight and come to help. They'd attacked the man and were now holding him down on the office floor. It took three of the men to keep him down. I saw that someone was over with Fr. Chris, helping him up.

I slowly regained my footing and stood up. DeMarkus caught my eye.

"Are you okay, man?" he said as he came toward me.

"My nose might be broken."

He came over to me and let me lean on him until we were out in the hallway and then sat me down against the wall. Another man came and sat Fr. Chris down beside me. His face was purple with bruises and his eyes were rapidly swelling shut. What had I gotten him into?

"Are you okay, Jack?" he slurred out before I could speak.

"I'm so sorry, Father," I said to him and I really meant it.

"Jack," he said to me, "don't worry. I'm going to be all right. I've taken beatings a lot worse than this in my time. Besides, if I'd had a little more time, I would have kicked his fucking ass." He managed a bloody smile that I returned only half-heartedly.

DeMarkus brought me a box of Kleenex and I held my head back to try and stop my nose from bleeding. It seemed to be doing the trick and I was starting to calm down and relax when I heard DeMarkus ask one of the other men to call the police.

"No, not yet," I said loud enough for all the men to hear. They paused and looked over at me.

"Why?" one of the men asked.

"It's a long story."

DeMarkus looked at me quizzically. I avoided his gaze.

"I've got to go before the cops get here," I said, getting up off the floor. "But first I want to ask this guy a few questions."

I walked over to where the man was being restrained and looked down at him. He was still struggling to get away from them.

"Who sent you?" I asked him.

The man just looked at me with a mocking smile.

"They're going to turn you over to the police when I leave. You'll go to jail, you know," I said to him.

"You're the one the cops want, Plowman. You're a killer."

The crowd that had gathered was stilled by his accusation. I'm sure a few of them really believed every word he said too.

"That's not true. I didn't kill Johnny, but I'm going to find out who did," I said as I knelt down and felt around in the man's pockets for his wallet. He struggled but my friends held him down. I found the wallet and took out the man's driver's license.

"Bruce Daniels. 1520 Spruce Brook Drive, Kentwood," I mocked.

"And," I said, rummaging through the wallet, "it looks like you work at a hospital." I dropped his employee ID on his chest. "You have two credit cards and…"

"Put that back," he yelled at me.

"Stay away from here," I warned him, "and remember that I know who you are and where you live." I dropped his wallet and started for the door.

"Jack," Fr. Chris looked over at me, "what are you going to go?"

"I don't know, but I can't stay here. Look at what I've done," I said, feeling like a selfish monster. I saw all of the violence that I had brought into this place and it made me want to kill myself. "I got you beat up, Father, and I've scared all the old ladies. I've made a mess of things for everyone, including myself."

"Jack," Fr. Chris pleaded but I just turned and walked out.

As I walked out, one of the older women of the church, one of the kind people who always made lunches for us, looked up at me as I passed. She looked like a mother whose only child had just broken her heart.

16

I went back to the parish house and grabbed the overnight bag that Fr. Chris left for guests before I took off. I grabbed Johnny's laptop too. I didn't know where I was going, but I knew I'd need a change of clothes somewhere along the way.

Without thinking much about it, I turned left away from the church and started walking down Division Street. It was a quiet Sunday afternoon and there wasn't a lot of activity. The downtown area became a ghost town on weekends. Everyone who worked in offices down here drove home to the suburbs at five o'clock on Friday. Some came back to go to bars or shows at night, but there was none of that on a Sunday afternoon. It was just me, a few homeless guys, and the garbage that blows through city streets.

As I walked, I thought about Bruce Daniels. I was lucky to get away from him alive. Who was he? Was he the one who murdered Johnny? It didn't seem to make sense that he was the killer. Why would he come out and expose himself, in a church with at least thirty witnesses no less, if he was guilty of murder? Why not let the cops find me in their own time? Unless, for some reason, he needed them to find me soon. Maybe he needed them to pin the murder on me fast, lest something come out to implicate him.

While I didn't know much about the guy, I did know that he worked at a hospital and lived out in the suburbs. It occurred to me then that I should have paid more attention to what hospital he worked at, but I suppose I'd been too jacked up on adrenaline to think straight. Based on his actions this morning, I doubted the guy was a doctor or a nurse. I wondered what he did at the hospital. As far as I could remember, Johnny hadn't been in the psych ward and he sure hadn't been in for any medical problems. He was young and very healthy.

After about ten blocks of thought, I decided that I wasn't going to be able to figure it out right then. Besides, I had bigger, more pressing problems, like where I was going to sleep tonight. I'd been in jams like this before and knew that I had to start planning in order to keep something really bad from happening to me. My options were very limited. I had a couple of friends I could call, and I was pretty sure they would take me in. But getting them involved meant asking them to break the law and help a wanted man. My few friends here were either head cases like me, drunks or crack heads. If they got caught with me, they would be screwed too.

I thought about calling my twin brother. He'd always been the tree that bore fruit in our family. Back while I'd been running around trying to pretend like I wasn't mentally ill, Jake had been in law school. He graduated with honors. He'd made my parents proud. They couldn't say his name without smiling and couldn't seem to say my name without whispering. Jake's law school graduation was the greatest thing to happen to my family in at least two generations. My family had been farmers and laborers, and Jake was the first to graduate from college. I should have been the second Plowman to get a college degree, but the voices in my head decided differently. I had planned to be in Ann Arbor for Jake's big day, but I ended up in jail down in Ohio instead. I'd thrown a punch at some guy in a bar that I was convinced was the devil. Turns out, he wasn't the devil, he was a cop.

I wanted to call Jake just about as much as I wanted to spend some more time in a locked room with Bruce Daniels. Besides showing him once again what a screw-up I was, I worried about putting him at risk too. Jake had just started a new job with a fancy law firm in town. He sure didn't need his crazy brother showing up. Besides, he'd already done more for me than I could ever repay. I'm quite sure that I would have been sent to prison at least three times if not for him.

I thought about getting a cheap motel room. I knew of a few places that the prostitutes used. It wouldn't be the Amway Grand Plaza, but at least it'd be a place to lay my head. I reached into my pocket and grabbed my wallet to see how much money I had, but the wallet I pulled out was not mine. It was Johnny's, the one I'd swiped yesterday.

It was a nice designer wallet with an embossed logo in the black leather. I opened it up and found his driver's license and a couple of credit cards in the inside pocket. The wallet had a clear plastic insert to hold pictures and the front photo was of Johnny and his family. It was a professional studio picture that included Johnny, his mother, father and a woman that must have been his sister. Johnny's father was dapper in a black suit and a blue and

white club tie. Standing next to him was his
mother, an older Asian woman who was trim and
also dressed in black. Johnny and his sister were
seated. The sister was dressed nicely, like her
parents. Johnny really stood out. He wasn't
smiling like everyone else and had on a sports
jacket over a Nirvana tee shirt and jeans. It was
clear that he wasn't happy to be there. I imagined
how disappointed his parents must have been when
they saw that he had shown up at the
photographer's dressed like that.

He was clearly the rebel of the family, but he
also was carrying around in his wallet this picture
that he seemed to have hated sitting for. Based on
the wear on the photo, it must have been taken
several years before.

Johnny had more ATM receipts in his wallet.
All of them, at least twenty, were withdrawals for
between sixty and a hundred dollars. Based on the
dates on the receipts, they had all been made within
the past two months. On one of the receipts, there
was a small note that said: "Dusty - 555-2305." I
kept that one and balled up all the others and
dropped them into a city trash can.

He had a couple of business cards as well. One
was Tiffini's card. It had her office and cell phone
numbers on it along with the Community Mental
Health logo.   There was another card for a Gary
Desmond, who was a marketing representative for a
company called Technometrics in Grand Rapids.
More things for me to look into, after I figured out
what to do about my sleeping arrangements.

I found my wallet in my coat pocket. Between

my money and Johnny's, I had enough for a night at a cheap motel, but that would break me and leave me no money for food. I couldn't very well show myself at the mission or God's Kitchen either. I knew from my time there that the police were never far away from places like that. Whenever something happened, the cops would come down to the mission and question the same people. If the staff said that some new guy was a troublemaker they got questioned too. No, I was staying as far as possible from there.

The only place left was the street.

I'd stayed on the streets more than a few times before when I got really out of control. One time when I was on my Mental Illness Tour of the Midwest, I woke up on the steps of the post office in Gary, Indiana. I had no idea how I'd gotten there. My neck was sore for a few days but otherwise I was fine. I knew that I could survive outside for a few days. I'd done it before but certainly didn't relish it.

I decided that I'd spend a few hours looking for a safe place to bed down and then take a break and splurge on something good for dinner. Safety is the main thing you've got to worry about. There are a lot of people that will beat you up and rob you if you make yourself too visible. Those people are usually drug addicts that only care about getting money for drugs. They don't care if they have to kill somebody to get a fix. The best place to sleep is somewhere comfortable and secluded.

I walked around downtown for the next few hours scouting out spots. I found a couple of good places, but they were all taken by other homeless guys. I was getting pretty frustrated when I came upon a big dumpster behind an office building. It was labeled for paper products only and, as luck would have it, it was unlocked. Most of the places downtown that had dumpsters like this locked them, and indeed, this one had a lock on it too. Thankfully, the person that filled it last must have forgotten to re-lock it when they were done.

I opened the lid and found that the dumpster had no occupant and that it was filled half way up with shredded paper. It looked like a bed someone made for a hamster. I couldn't believe my luck. It was a primo location and I was afraid I might lose it, so I hustled back to the last restaurant I remember seeing, a little family owned Mexican place, and ordered three tacos and a guava Jarritos to drink.

When I got back to the dumpster, I hopped over the side and ate my meal with the lid open so I could hear the sounds of the city. It was turning out to be a beautiful urban afternoon. The whooshing sounds of the cars as they passed by the street out front were a lullaby to me. Even the scent of the diesel smoke from the busses was oddly soothing. When I was done eating, I just sat there in my little hamster bed and listened to the sounds of normal life bubble up around me. It made me sleepy, so I closed the lid and drifted off.

17

"Good morning, may I speak to Mr. Edward Chen?"

The receptionist looked at me uncomfortably. She was an attractive woman, probably a college student who, based on her heavy black make-up, was going through a Goth phase. She seemed lost for words and didn't say anything for a few seconds.

"Mr. Chen is not in today," she finally said through the glass window. "He's had a loss in his family."

Of course. What had I been thinking? I'd woken up excited after a restful night's sleep in my new dumpster home. That morning, I really felt on top of the world. The paper had made a great bed and I'd gotten the best sleep that I'd had in months. Total peace. I'd gotten myself looking as presentable as possible and almost skipped down the Monroe Mall to Chen's office. The pink marble entryway was still a little intimidating but I pushed through to the old elevator and up to Chen's office. I had my story straight and felt confident, like a real detective.

And then this.

I hadn't even thought about Mr. Chen not being at work, but now it struck me as so obvious. Of course, he wouldn't be at work. His son had just been killed. He was probably at home with his family busy making funeral arrangements. What a great sleuth I was.

"Of course," I said confidently to the Goth girl.

"I know about Mr. Chen's son. I was Johnny's case manager at Community Mental Health. I got the news about Johnny when I got into the office this morning. It's a terrible tragedy."

She was a little less defensive but still unsure of me.

"I came here," I continued, "because Mr. Chen has always preferred that I contact him at the office and not at home. He's such a hard worker, I thought I might catch him in this morning. You know, we've met for lunch to talk about Johnny a few times before and he was always so careful to be back before lunch hour was over."

It was a total shot in the dark, but it must have been pretty accurate. The receptionist nodded slightly in agreement.

"I'm sure that I have his home address back at the office," I continued, "but I'm really busy today and don't want to waste time going back there if I can avoid it. I know it's probably against policy, but would you mind giving me his home address, just to save me some time?"

She smiled at me.

"Let me look it up for you," she said, and then got up from her desk and walked back into the office. I hid my surprise until she turned away. I could not believe for the life of me that had actually worked.

After she'd been gone for a few minutes, my mind started running. Maybe she wasn't really going to get Chen's address. Maybe she went to get security instead. Did I even look like a social worker? I'd slept in a dumpster last night, for

God's sake! The thought occurred to me to run out of there as fast as my feet would carry me, but before I had time to build up to full panic mode and leave, the woman came back with a slip of paper in her hand.

"Here you go," she said as she passed the paper to me through the window.

"Thanks a lot. Now I have time to eat lunch today."

She was happy to have helped me and I was happy to still be a free man.

I walked over to the Grand Rapids Public Library and looked up how to get to Chen's house. I wrote down some basic directions for myself using the scrap paper that they had to write down the call numbers of books. Chen lived on Reed's Lake in East Grand Rapids. East Grand Rapids is one of the more affluent suburbs in town with lots of old money and big old houses. It's the place where Gerald Ford lived back when he was a young lawyer in Grand Rapids.

I knew from experience that it wasn't that far from downtown. One day last summer I'd gone for a walk down Franklin Street just to pass the time. It was so nice, I just kept walking and walking, past run-down home after run-down home. There were poor children playing everywhere, some nearly naked in the summer heat. The homes were all rentals and the cars out front were all run down. It went on and on like that, until I came to Fuller Street. When I crossed Fuller Street it was like I had crossed the Grand Canyon of money. The homes west of Fuller were decrepit; the homes east of Fuller were meticulously cared for and regal. The kids west of Fuller were all black and the ones east of Fuller were all white.

This was East Grand Rapids.

I knew I could walk out to Chen's but decided to go ahead and take the bus anyway. It didn't cost that much and a quick look at the bus guide revealed that the Eastown Woodland bus stopped right outside East Grand Rapids Middle School. The school was practically on the lake.

When I got off the bus, I followed my scrap paper directions, down one road after another. I was the only person walking the streets that day. It was a bright sunny day and I was sure there were housewives in many of the big brick palaces that I passed, but no one was outside. I suppose that when you have this much money, you exercise at a gym and not on your neighborhood streets. The lack of other walkers did make me worry that I would look suspicious though. The last thing I needed was for the cops to be called. I quickened my pace a little.

After about ten minutes of navigating the twisting streets, I came to the Chen house. It was modest in comparison to surrounding homes and was across the street from Reed's Lake, not on it. Chen's house was a modern brick ranch on a big lot, with a picture window facing the lake. In the winter when the leaves were off all the trees, it might even be possible to see some water from that picture window, but you'd have to crane your neck. There were a number of cars in the long driveway, all new models and more than a few were BMW's.

I made my way up the drive and tried to get my story straight in my head. Talking to Chen was the real deal. It was walking into the lion's den. I had to be convincing to him or I'd end up in the back of a police car. I hid my bag with the laptop and my clothes behind a big bush by the front door before I grabbed the fat brass knocker on the Chens' oak door.

The door opened after a single knock revealing a pretty middle-aged Asian woman blankly staring at me. She didn't say a word of greeting, she just stared through me and out towards the lake.

"I'm so sorry to interrupt," I said to her in a voice as calm and steady as I could manage. "I know that your family has suffered a great loss. You have my condolences."

She was quiet for a moment, lost in her own grief and the surrealism that comes with death. She knew in her head that it was impossible for Johnny to be knocking on her door, but I had the feeling that her heart told her to expect it and she was disappointed to see me.

"I'm one of the case mangers that used to work with Johnny," I lied to her. "I've come to pay my respects and to attend to some paperwork that has to be done." She seemed to believe me. What was so strange about death bringing with it a whole bunch of forms to fill out? Anything important that happened to you, there were forms to fill out.

"Come in," she said to me in crisp, perfect English. "I'm Mrs. Chen. I am…" she thought again, "I *was* Johnny's mother. You may come in.

What did you say your name was, young man?"

"I'm Calvin Smith, Mrs. Chen," I said as I walked into the foyer. "It's nice to meet you. I know that Johnny used to work mostly with Tiffini. She regrets that she can't be here instead of me, but she had her own family emergency to attend to."

Mrs. Chen nodded and walked into the house and I followed behind her. Mrs. Chen was a small woman with short cropped black hair. She must have been at least 55 years old but she had aged very well. She had hardly a wrinkle on her face and could have easily passed for 40. She was dressed in a tee shirt and yoga pants and wore no shoes.

I followed her into the large living room whose focal point was the picture window that I'd seen from outside. There were four Asian men sitting on plush chairs in the room. A fire was raging in the fireplace, probably for the sight of the flames more than the heat. The men were of various ages and drank coffee out of transparent glass mugs. They all stopped talking and looked up at Mrs. Chen and I as we walked into the room.

"Edward, this is Calvin Smith, Johnny's old case manager from the mental health," Mrs. Chen said to a distinguished man sitting in one of the chairs. He looked the part of a professor, with his graying temples, white oxford shirt and tweed jacket. Impeccably groomed, he seemed to have had enough strength to get dressed this morning, unlike his wife. He was handsome and trim, and rose to his feet with a smile to greet me.

"Thank you for coming," he said, with an outstretched hand. "I know that Community Mental

Health did all they could to help Johnny. You always tried to give him the best care, and my family and I are grateful for all that you did."

The other men in the room nodded in agreement, although I wasn't sure many of them knew what a mental health agency did.

"Just so you know, I don't blame your agency for what happened and I have no intention to sue anyone," he added.

"Ah, okay," I said awkwardly. I wasn't prepared for Mr. Chen to bring up lawsuits. The possibility of litigation had never crossed my mind the night before when I ran through all of the possible ways that Mr. Chen might respond to my visit. I was prepared for rage, grief, anger, and despair, but the mention of lawsuits caught me off guard for a second, but only for a second.

"I'm sorry to interrupt your grieving, Mr. Chen, but it would help me tremendously if we could talk for a few minutes."

"Sure, Calvin. Why don't we step into the den where we can have a little privacy," Mr. Chen said as he motioned for me to follow him down the hallway.

"It's not that I don't appreciate your visit, Calvin," he said to me as we walked down the hall side by side, "but I thought that Tiffini was still assigned to Johnny's case."

"Oh, she is, sir. It's just that she had her own family emergency to attend to and the agency wanted someone to come out and meet with you right away due to the manner in which Johnny was found. I'm sure Tiffini will be in contact with you as soon as she is able."

Chen seemed to be buying my story and didn't seem put off by my visit. About halfway down the wide hallway, Chen turned into a room on the right and I followed him in. The room was very dark and didn't seem to have any windows, but then Mr. Chen turned on a light that illuminated the wood paneled den. It wasn't large but it was nicely decorated in a nautical theme. There were boat diagrams on the walls and a few model ships were nestled in with the books on the bookcases. I noticed a number of photos on the wall. There was a larger version of the family photo that I'd found in Johnny's wallet in the center and three other pictures clustered around it. There was a picture of a young, very attractive Asian woman in academic regalia receiving a degree and an old photo of what must have been a young Mrs. Chen. There was also a photo of Mr. Chen at what looked to be a casino poker table. He had a big pile of chips in front of him and a huge smile on his face.

Chen sat down at his cluttered desk and motioned for me to take a seat across from him. Although the rest of the room was neat and tidy, the desk was strewn with paper a foot high and Chen started to absent mindedly move piles so that we could see each other clearly. He tossed two or three newspaper sports sections that were heavily inked into an invisible bin behind his desk. There was also a large stack of spreadsheet documents that he moved to another area of the desk. The header read "Davidson" and they were filled with hundreds of boxes with numbers in them. I silently cursed myself for not taking accounting in college before my psychotic break. Maybe I would have been able to understand what they meant.

"What can I do for you, Calvin?" Mr. Chen said after he had rearranged his desk.

"Well, I've got a few questions I have to ask you about Johnny and his passing. Most of them are related to this form we have to fill out."

"Sure. What's the first question?"

"Well," I said to Chen, "The first thing that I need to ask is if you know whether Johnny was taking his medication as prescribed."

"As far as I know, he was," Chen said. "Johnny had a lot of problems, as you know. We tried to love him and care for him the best we could, but he so often would push us away. We tried to protect him from the ugliness of the world, but as time went on Johnny fell deeper and deeper into it. When he lived at home, I watched him take his medication every morning before I went to work. He never refused it. Once he chose to move out on his own, I stopped by and saw him at least two or three times a week to check on him. Frankly, he always seemed to be doing fine to me."

"It's a shock to all of us," I said honestly. "I'm sure you've heard that the police haven't been able to locate Johnny's roommate."

"That's what Detective Robinson told me on the phone. Do you think..." Mr. Chen said very seriously, "that this man had something to do with Johnny's murder?"

"The police want to question him. He's also a consumer of ours, so we don't know what to think."

"What is this man's name again?" Chen asked me.

"His name is Jack Plowman."

"Plowman, huh," Mr. Chen grabbed a pen and wrote down my name. I kicked myself inside for telling him my real name. What was I thinking?

"Besides this guy, is there anyone else you know that could be behind Johnny's murder?" I asked.

"Calvin, there are a number of people that might have wanted to hurt my son. As you know, he hung around a lot of dangerous people, people who would not think twice about killing someone. These were the people that my wife and I tried so desperately to protect Johnny from, the ones that he ran back to time and time again. Apparently, he loved drugs more than he loved us."

"Did you ever help Johnny get his medication, Mr. Chen?"

"No, he did that himself. He was more independent than most people thought. He just acted helpless sometimes to manipulate people. One Friday night not too long ago, he called and told me that he needed a ride to the pharmacy to pick up his pills and so I went over to his apartment, picked him up, and drove him there. I waited in the car for him and when he came out, he had a couple boxes of cigarettes and a case of beer but no bag from the pharmacy. When I asked him about it, he just said that the pills weren't ready yet and he'd get them later. Johnny was sly as a fox and I fell for his manipulations many times."

Chen seemed amused by his story and smiled a

wry smile.

"You said that Johnny was a drug user. Was he using when he was murdered?"

"I would bet my life on it. We got him into treatment a number of times but he never followed through with it. Last fall, we spent thousands of dollars for the best residential treatment for him when he told us that he wanted to get off of drugs for good. It seemed like things might be turning around for him, but we found out that he had left the program after only three days. I was very angry and called the facility as soon as I heard that he had left. Can you believe that they would not give me one penny back?" Mr. Chen was aghast. "I gave them a down payment of five thousand dollars for long term treatment and Johnny left after only three days. I paid $1666 a day for that treatment."

"What a waste," I said.

"I don't even know where he got the money to buy all those drugs. We certainly weren't giving it to him and I know for damn sure that he didn't have a job. The boy never worked. He hustled but he never worked. Not a day in his life."

Chen looked at me with a mix of anger and frustration. I half expected him to sigh or hang his head. I'd never seen Johnny use any drug, not even pot. He never left anything around the apartment that led me to believe he was doing drugs either.

"Do you think that Johnny's mental illness played a role in his death?" I asked him.

Chen met my eyes but didn't say anything. He seemed to be sizing me up.

"I'll be honest with you, Calvin." He started

slowly, "This mental illness stuff has always made me a little suspicious. I never thought, and to this day do not think, that my son was mentally ill. Troubled, yes. Mentally ill, no. I mean no offense to you, but I think that some of your psychiatrists over there at Community Mental Health want to call every problem under the sun a mental illness. A person isn't shy, they have a social anxiety disorder and so on. I'm in business. I understand the strategy. The more disorders there are, the more potential patients; the more patients, the more money in the doctors' pockets. From a business perspective, it makes perfect sense. That doesn't mean that I think it's the truth, however."

"No offense taken, sir."

"I'm glad," Chen said with a smile. "Any more questions for the form?"

He looked at me and I realized that I hadn't taken out the piece of paper that I'd planned to say was the form I needed to fill out.

"Ah," I said, fumbling my hands into my pockets. I eventually found the sheet of paper and unfolded it across my lap. From the corner of my eye, I saw Chen look at me with raised eyebrows. I knew that I looked silly and felt my armpits start to fill with sweat.

"Yeah, so…you said…ah… what do you think happened?"

Looking back, it was a strange question to ask but in the moment, I thought that I'd made a brilliant recovery. At least in the second before Chen said something.

"What exactly do you mean, Calvin?"

I didn't know what I meant, and I was at a loss for what to say next. I started to feel strange and was aware that my face was starting to fill with icy sweat. I opened my mouth to say something, to say anything, but nothing came out except a child's whimper.

"Calvin, is something wrong?"

Something was wrong. I had walked into this man's house under false pretenses to question him and was very close to being caught for the fraud that I was. If I got caught, I'd go to jail and from there to trial. A quick guilty plea would drop me in prison for murder. I started to imagine what prison would be like for me. I was weak. They'd take advantage of me. They'd use me. I started to feel like an animal backed into a corner. I wanted to run away but the door was blocked.

"I have to have diarrhea right now," I said loudly enough for someone in the next room to hear me.

Chen looked at me, taken aback and alarmed for the safety of the leather chair that I was sitting on.

"The bathroom is just across the hall."

18

I bounded out of my chair, rushed into the bathroom like my legs were on fire and then slammed the door behind me. The sweat was pouring out of me like I was back helping my dad blacktop our driveway in the middle of August. I looked at myself in the large mirror that covered the wall. It looked like I had taken a shower with my clothes on.

"Cool lake breezes," I said under my breath as I closed my eyes.

I'd had a therapist a few years before that had taught me visualization to help me relax. He'd helped me create this vivid picture in my head that I could recall when I got overwhelmed with stress. It'd helped me before when I was stressed out and I hoped that it would work this time. As I tried to settle myself, I heard that familiar small, whispery voice.

he knows.

The image of myself in the mirror was saying it. Ignoring it, I tried to go deeper into the vision in my head. I was on the Lake Michigan beach with Anna. It was twilight and a golden sun was setting over the water. We were snuggled up on a blanket by the dune. We were all alone. Everything was still and peaceful and I was with the woman I loved.

he's going to come in the bathroom and get you.

Anna was pressed against me and I could

smell the baby powder scent of her perfume getting rubbed into my clothes. The sound of the waves falling gently against the wet sand of the shore was like a lullaby that God had written especially for me. I was not mentally ill, I was totally clear-headed and totally sane. I had a future and was a top student in Ann Arbor. I could do anything that I wanted with my life and Anna supported me in all my wildest dreams because she wanted the same dreams that I did. I felt a feeling of peace start to come over me and felt my muscles start to relax. The sweat that had been pouring out of me now felt cool on my skin, as if my body temperature had changed.

I could feel myself starting to regain my composure. I was going to be okay. Chen might think that I was a little strange but he wouldn't think that I was a killer. Things were going to turn out just fine here; no one was going to call the cops because I got the runs.

My confidence at least partially restored, I opened my eyes and started to clean myself up. The bright lights and the large mirror seemed to magnify how terrible I looked. I grabbed the hand towel and tried to pat the sweat off of my forehead and straighten my clothes. At least my buzzed hair wasn't a mess.

I went over to the toilet, flushed the empty bowl, and then opened the door.

Mrs. Chen was standing in the hallway waiting for me. Her face was that of a kindly mother. I could tell that she'd dealt with much worse than this in her years as a parent.

"Would you like some tea? That always helps me."

"Yeah, that would be great, Mrs. Chen. Thank you."

"Oh, don't mention it," she said. Helping to take care of me seemed to have momentarily lifted the veil of grief that had been covering her.

"I'm really embarrassed about this," I told her. "I've never gotten sick on the job like this before and I have no idea what did this to me. Did I scare Mr. Chen off?"

"No, he just stepped out to the living room to catch some sports scores on television. He loves sports very, very much. He'll be back in a minute if you have any more questions. Why don't we go into the kitchen? I'll get you some tea and we can wait for him there."

"Sure."

Mrs. Chen and I sat next to each other at the table in the breakfast nook and sipped tea. She'd brought out some cookies that someone had made when they'd heard about the death in the family, and we munched on them as we drank tea from dainty china.

The Chen kitchen was big and modern. It had shiny steel appliances and black granite counter tops with an island in the middle where all the pans hung from the ceiling. It was the kind of kitchen that people on television had.

"Thanks again, Mrs. Chen," I said taking a sip of black tea.

"Don't mention it, my dear. We've all had

those days. It must not be easy for you to come here on a day like this. Frankly, I don't even want to be here. I love my family but they never really understood Johnny. I know they blame Edward and I for this. They all said something like this would happen and it looks like they were right."

Mrs. Chen looked down into her dark tea as if she saw someone drowning in it.

"What do you mean, 'something like this'?" I asked.

"Johnny's problems have been very difficult for the family to understand. I'm proud to say that our family is filled with very successful, bright people. Edward's brother is one of the best cardiologists in Seattle, my sister is the president of a small liberal arts college in Vermont. They couldn't understand what we had done to have a child that was so…" she paused and tried to choose her words carefully, "different. Johnny was very different. He had problems that my family thought only other people had. Maybe it was snobbery. It probably was, but we never imagined that we could have a child with a mental illness."

It was a speech I could imagine my mother giving her hair dresser, except in place of cardiologist and college president, she would have said "union job" or "skilled tradesman."

"It didn't help," she went on, "that Johnny treated people the way that he did. He used people to get what he wanted from them and didn't think twice about who he hurt in the process. He thought only of himself, not of his family or friends. It is something that people of my culture do not look upon with approval."

I knew what she meant. I remember once when Johnny ate a big box of granola bars that I'd bought for myself. He didn't even try to hide the empty box and the wrappers. When I confronted him about it, he said that it was my fault because I didn't put my name on the box. I started keeping my food in my bedroom after that.

"Mrs. Chen, I know from being a case manager that lots of my consumers get into trouble because they have money problems. Do you think Johnny got involved with drug dealers or other dangerous people to make ends meet?"

"No," she said, "we paid his share of the rent, paid for his food and utilities and even gave him a modest allowance. He had more than enough to be comfortable. We even gave him money for cigarettes. He had everything that he needed. Now, we knew that he did drugs sometime. I'm sure you knew as well. Crack cocaine was what he liked and I know from the sessions we had with the substance abuse therapist that crack is very cheap."

"Do you think that he dealt drugs?"

"He always denied it to us, but who knows really. He might have."

"Did Johnny have a boyfriend that was violent?"

Mrs. Chen sighed. This was not something she liked talking about.

"Frankly, I never asked about this area of his life. It was not something that I wanted to know about. When Johnny lived at home and had a manic phase, he did tend to get very sexual. He was not very…how should I say this, not very selective with his partners. It was a significant problem for us but I never felt like the men that he brought home were dangerous. Some were dirty and some were loud but the ones that I met never seemed violent to me."

"Was Johnny sexually abused?" I asked.

Mrs. Chen's face froze as I said it and I knew that I had asked the wrong question. The catatonic woman that I'd met at the door was back and the loving mother gone. I was about to apologize when the pretty young woman from the picture in the den walked in.

"Mother," she said.

I looked up and our eyes met. When I'd seen her picture, it was clear that she was attractive, but seeing her face to face, she was absolutely stunning. She must have been about 35 years old with flowing jet black hair and a graceful manner. She was dressed in a tasteful black pantsuit that was somehow the slightest bit sexy. She was long and lank with eyes as deep and dark as the tea in front of me. I had to stop myself from staring.

"Mother, are you okay?" she asked.

"I'm fine, dear," Mrs. Chen said, breaking the spell. "This is my daughter, Missy Chen."

I stood up from the table and reached out to shake her hand.

"I'm Jack," I said to her.

"Missy Chen," she said as she put her hand in mine. She was so lovely.

"I'm from Community Mental Health," I explained. "I just stopped by to make sure everyone was doing all right."

"Thank you, Jack," Missy said to me. "That is very kind of you."

"It's a terrible thing that happened," I said again.

"Yes, it is. Mother, I'm so sorry but I have to go for a few hours. I've got an important meeting at the court that I can't miss. I'll be home as soon as I can."

Mrs. Chen nodded.

"It was nice to meet you, Jack."

"Likewise," I said.

As Missy started to walk away, I saw that Mr. Chen was standing in the kitchen as well. He must have come in with Missy, but I hadn't seen him.

"I thought you said that your name was Calvin," Mr. Chen said to me.

Shit. Shit, shit, shit.

"Jack's just a nickname," I tried to explain causally as dots of sweats appeared on my forehead.

"I've never heard of that before," Chen said. I could feel the heat building inside me and the panic coming at me like a freight train.

"Yeah. Well, I've got to get going. Lots of crazy people out there, you know. They need me." I tried a fake laugh but no one was buying it. Mrs. Chen looked hurt and Mr. Chen seemed to be getting angry.

I got up and briskly walked towards the front door, and was shocked when Mr. Chen didn't try and stop me. Glad for my luck, I walked past the men sitting quietly in the living room and out the front door, grabbing my bag hidden behind the bushes as I left.

I walked briskly down the driveway to the street, and then I started to run. I ran full out and tried to zig and zag through the streets around the lake, not even paying attention to where I was going. As I ran, I imagined Mrs. Chen watching me despondently from the big picture window and Mr. Chen next to her cursing and holding the phone. How fast would it take for the police to respond? Where should I go?

After about a mile, I started to get tired and felt the stitch in my side grow more and more painful. I couldn't keep running like this. I'd collapse. I had to find a place to hide. A place to rest for a while. The adrenaline was pumping through my veins and it made me feel like a cornered animal.

Kill yourself

I tried to ignore the voice but a part of me wanted to do what it said. If that meant death, it seemed like a fair trade in that moment. All my hope drained out of me like the buckets of sweat that I'd left back in the Chens' bathroom.

drown yourself in the lake

While that voice usually sounded like Satan to me, as I ran from the Chen's house that day the voice didn't sound evil, it sounded like the voice of a wise counselor. It felt like God was talking to me. It was like I was receiving a revelation, like the voice was the voice of an angel leading me. Or maybe it was the Holy Spirit calling out to me. Guiding me.

I listened closely and then - without me having any control in the matter - my mind was filled with an image of my body lowering itself into

Reed's Lake, my mouth opening to fill with murky lake water. I swallowed it, gulp after gulp, and was filled with a blazing euphoria. It was like the water was the body of Christ. It transformed me. I could breathe the water. I didn't need air anymore. I could live in the lake. No one would chase me ever again. I thought I saw the outline of a white robed Jesus at the bottom of the lake with his arms stretched wide. He wanted me to come home. He wanted to grant me a new life, a resurrected life under the water.

drink this all of you: this is my blood of the new covenant

I followed the call into the front yard of a stately modern home. A home that, unlike the Chens' home, was right on the lake.

19

The water of the lake was cool on my face as I knelt before it in prayer, feet folded beneath me, my bag on the lush green lawn beside me. In that moment I knew that all of my life had been leading up to that moment. This was the great moment where God finally opened my eyes to Truth. Everything that had happened with Johnny had been leading me to this. His death suddenly made sense to me. Johnny had to die so that I would be led to his parents' home and to Reed's Lake from which I would be reborn.

Wasn't Moses put into the reeds of the river Nile? That's where his story began, by the reeds and by the water. My new life was going to begin alongside reeds as well, and along water. God put Moses in a river and was going to put me in a lake. God was speaking in symbols. I was going to be America's new Moses, just like Jesus was Israel's new Moses. I was going to set the captives free, just like Moses did. I was going to rescue God's people.

Why hadn't I seen this before?

When I looked deep into the lake, I was still able to see the man. He was dressed in long flowing robes and his outstretched arms were aching to hold me and transform me. He wanted to baptize me with water and the Spirit. All I had to do was walk under the water and receive His grace.

receive your baptism, Jack. conquer death

Yes. I had to get to Jesus. There was no

time to lose.

I got up and started to wade into the water. It was freezing cold, but I barely felt it in my frenzy of devotion. I waded farther and farther out into the lake, the sun a ball of fire above me and the water freezing my body. I don't know how long I had been out there before I started to hear the scream.

"Get out of there!" the voice called.

I tried to ignore it, tried to focus my attention on my savior, but it was no use. The yelling seemed to be making Jesus disappear. His image was drifting off with each scream from the shore. I started to cry, feeling that I had lost my chance for a new life.

"I'm going to call the police," the woman yelled. "You can't be out there!"

I turned around and saw a middle-aged woman standing at the shore. She must have seen me walk into the lake from her house. It was clear that she was angry but I didn't know exactly what to do. I knew that the Lord was still in the lake but this woman was making him invisible to me. Maybe he'd retreated because the vision was just for me and not for others. That woman had scared him away.

I decided that I had to leave for now but I would be back, at night this time when no one could see me. I turned around and walked back towards the shore. The woman, seeing me advance on her, stepped back and started to run back to her house. She was going to call the police. Before long the whole East Grand Rapids Police Department would be after me.

When I reached the beach, I started across the woman's lawn back to the street but before I got there I saw the police car. It was racing down the road with its lights and siren off. It was strange to see a police car like that. They usually had their lights and sirens blazing when they were going this fast. This was a tactic they'd use if they wanted to catch someone unaware.

Someone like me. I froze my feet and tried to pretend like I was a piece of life-like statuary in that rich woman's lawn.

As it got closer, I noted that the police cruiser wasn't slowing down.

Thank God for protection! The car must have been responding to another call, maybe from the Chens'.

I couldn't go back to the road, so as soon as the cruiser rounded the bend, I took off down the narrow beach, struggling to get my footing as I ran on the wet sand.

I got a few feet before I remembered my bag. It had everything in it. I ran back to snatch it and then took off down the beach.

I ran and ran down the sand in my soaking wet clothes. Every so often I would take a glance into the lake, hoping to see Jesus beckoning me. But each time I looked, he wasn't there. I knew he wouldn't leave me for good though. It was just a matter of time before he came back. But when? I prayed to God as I jogged down the beach, asking that the door would be opened for me again, but I didn't hear a reply.

I started to get winded just as I reached a

small brick building. I figured it was some sort of commercial building because it had a decent sized parking lot attached to it. A tall chain link fence separated me from the parking lot, so I stuck my fingers into the mesh and quickly scaled over it and fell over to the other side. The asphalt was soothingly warm on my palms.

When I looked more closely at the small brick building I saw that it was the East Grand Rapids Public Library. God had given me a sanctuary.

I walked in as inconspicuously as possible and found a quiet corner near the periodicals. There weren't a lot of people in the library but there were enough that I didn't stand out. No one seemed to pay any attention to me and no one seemed to notice that I was soaking wet.

The library was nice. I felt safe from the police while also still being close to the lake. I browsed through the magazines which were protected under plastic covers, but none of them seemed very interesting. I was still elated from the experience I'd had by the water. It had a lingering effect, kind of like I used to feel after I'd been with Anna.

Sitting there alone at the big round table, I realized that I'd thought more about Anna in the past few days than I had in months. She'd been so important to me for so long, and then I went crazy and everything fell apart. I'd never known happiness like the kind of happiness that I had known when I was with Anna. She'd been the bright guiding star of my life B.C., Before Crazy.

Anna didn't give up on me in those terrible early days. She came to see me in the hospital after my first breakdown and told me that things would get better now that I was on medication. She called me to offer support but I never wanted to talk. I brushed her off like she was lint on my sweater but she just kept on calling. I still loved her, of course, but I pushed her away because I felt like my life was over and I was all but dead. All the psychiatrists were telling me that I'd have to take these medications for the rest of my life, that my mental illness was like diabetes and the pills were my insulin.

I remember how much I hated those pills. Sure, they made the voices go away and helped me to calm down, but they also deadened all the other parts of me too. It was like getting a shot of Novocain directly into my brain, except this Novocain didn't wear off. I might look normal but I always felt numb all over. But all through it, Anna stood by me.

Until I pushed her too far.

But I didn't want to think about that, especially now, so I got up and grabbed the *Grand Rapids Press*. There wasn't much going on in the city that day. Just more of the same things that you read in any newspaper in the world. There had been a car crash on the Ford Freeway that killed the driver. A man tried to rob a bank in Wyoming but the police caught him before he could get out of the parking lot. Humanity and its foibles. I'd almost

made it through the entire front section of the paper
when an article on page A8 caught my attention.

Chen Announces Congressional Bid
Staff Writers

Grand Rapids - Local attorney Melissa Chen
announced today that she intends to run for the Third
Congressional District seat being vacated by
Congressman Dale Matthers. Chen's entry into the
already crowded Republican field was not unexpected.
According to WOOD TV's Rick Albin, Chen had
been expected to announce her candidacy before this
time and her late entry into the race puts her at a
distinct disadvantage.

Ms. Chen is currently a senior partner at Brinks,
Rankin and Chen, P.C. She is a former Kent County
Republican Party Treasurer who ran for a judgeship
three years ago, only to withdraw from the race two
months before the election, citing personal reasons.

I wondered why she'd dropped out of the
judicial race. Did her personal reasons have
anything to do with Johnny? The article didn't
mention if she was married or not, but I couldn't
recall seeing a wedding ring on her finger. Maybe
she was divorced and dropped out because of
marital problems. Or maybe she had some sort of
illness? I looked around to make sure that I was
still alone and then tore the article out of the paper
and stuck it in my bag.

Why had God drawn me to that article? Was
He trying to tell me something? I could still see

Jesus under the murky water looking up at me. He wanted me to come down and join him. I knew that the Lord had a special destiny waiting for me. Maybe God wanted me to finish finding Johnny's killer before he called me home? Was that why Jesus disappeared when the woman came out of her house? Was that why I'd found the article on Missy Chen?

I felt very sure that God was speaking to me but I was also having a hard time understanding Him, so I browsed the aisles of books until I found where the Bibles were shelved. I picked out a sturdy King James and sat down right on the floor with it in my lap. Thumbing through the old book, I stopped at a random page, then I closed my eyes and stabbed my index finger into the middle and read the passage. It was Psalm 18, verse 38: "I pursue my enemies and overtake them; I will not turn back till I have destroyed them."

20

I waited in the library for a few hours to let the heat die down and then I boarded the bus to go back downtown. There was hardly anyone else on board and the trip was quiet and quick. The sun was back out and its light seemed to settle my mind. Since I had a few hours before it was dark and I could return to the lake, I decided to call Gary Desmond. I felt called to call him, really.

I'd found Gary's card in Johnny's wallet. It said that he was a marketing executive. I figured that it would be easy to just call him up at work and ask some questions. If things started to go bad or he was suspicious, I could just hang up.

I wasn't in the mood to be taking any more risks today.

When the bus let me out on Division, I walked around until I came to a beaten up pay phone by a liquor store. It always took me a while to find a pay phone when I needed one and this one was pretty close to my house on Prospect. It made me nervous to be so close to where I used to live but at least I knew the area pretty well. DeMarkus used to hang out around here too and this had been his favorite place to buy booze.

Gary answered the phone on the second ring.

"Hello, Technometrics, this is Gary."

"Hi, Gary," I said into the cold receiver. "My name is Detective Jones of the GRPD. Do you have a few minutes to talk?"

"Ahh," Gary stammered. He seemed frightened. "Just a minute." I heard him get up and close his door, "Okay, what can I do for you, detective?"

"What can you tell me about John Chen?"

The question just hung there.

"Mr. Desmond, are you there?" I asked.

"Yes, I'm here."

"Did you hear my question?"

"Yes, I just don't know what to say. I knew someone would be calling me, but I didn't do anything wrong, I swear," he pleaded.

"I'll be the judge of that."

"Of course. I'm sorry, detective."

I have to admit, I enjoyed the fear that I raised in him. I liked the power.

"Tell me what your relationship was with Mr. Chen," I said in my most authoritative voice.

"We were friends. I didn't know him that well. We hung out together a few times on the weekends but I had absolutely no reason to harm him. I liked him."

"Who said anything about you harming him? Do you have something to confess?"

I knew that I was pushing him hard and that he might get scared and hang up. Then again, I liked being the person doing the pushing instead of the one being pushed around for a change. I was starting to see the allure in being a bully.

"No, sir. It's just that my relationship with Johnny was not something that was public knowledge. If it came out that I was connected to him, it could really hurt me."

"Then you have a good reason to be totally honest with me so that I don't have to pay you a visit at work."

He didn't say anything for a second. I had him exactly where I wanted him.

"Please don't do that," he whispered. "No one knows that I'm gay here. This place is super conservative and if they found out about me, I wouldn't be able to stand it. I'd lose my friends and maybe even my job."

Gary's voice cracked a little and I started to feel a little bad for him. "I used to spend time with Johnny and party with him," he continued. " It was always a rush being with him. He was so free and … uninhibited."

"I don't need to know about that," I said and really meant it.

"Sorry. He was great to be with. We had great times together and I started to develop… feelings for him. When I told him about how I felt, Johnny just stared at me. He didn't want that kind of a relationship with me. It really broke my heart because I thought that he felt the same way I did. But he didn't." Gary went silent. "When I tried to tell him that I was falling in love with him, he told me that all he wanted me for was my money and the sex…"

"Okay," I said, feeling uncomfortable and not wanting to hear any more, "I get the picture."

"Oh, I'm sorry. So anyway, after that I tried to stay away from him at the bar. He was always with someone, so I just ignored him, but after a while I started to get worried about him. He was hanging out with people that were deep into drugs. I saw him come out of the bathroom with white powder under his nose more and more often. We never did that stuff. I started to worry about him. I just wanted to help him. That was it. I was over what had happened between us. After I reached out to him, we had coffee a couple of times and he told me that he was mixed up with some bad people. I asked him what he meant but he wouldn't tell me anything specific. He said that it would be dangerous if I knew anything.

"I tried to get him to go to rehab but he refused. He said that he couldn't leave Grand Rapids again. I really wanted to help him, detective. I called him once a week to check in, but he stopped returning my calls about two weeks ago. I was worried and then I read the paper yesterday and…"

I heard his stifled weeping in my ear.

"I'm sorry, Mr. Desmond," I said to him. "I'm going to find out who did this to Johnny. God's justice will be done, that's my solemn vow to you."

"Thank you, officer."

"Do you know any of the other men that Johnny was…involved with?" I asked.

"Not really. The only guy that I knew was Johnny's most recent boyfriend, Dusty Ramerez."

For some reason, the named sounded familiar to me.

"Do you have Mr. Ramerez's phone number?"

"No, but I know that he works at a men's

store in the Woodland Mall."

"All right. Thank you for your time, Mr. Desmond."

"Are you done with me?" he asked.

"For now, but I might need to ask you some more questions in the future. We can just talk on the phone for now."

"Thank you, sir," he said and I hung up the phone.

Because the name of Johnny's boyfriend sounded so familiar to me, I knelt down to my bag and rummaged through it until I found the scrap of paper that I was looking for. It was the one I'd found in Johnny's wallet. It said: "Dusty - 555-2305."

I knew that I needed to talk to Dusty, but I needed to call someone else first.

"Hello," the man answered.

"Hi, Fr. Chris. It's me."

"Jack, how are you?"

"I'm fine," I said, breaking the ninth commandment.

"Where are you?"

"I can't tell you that. I'm obviously in pretty deep here and I don't want to put you in any more danger than I already have. I'm very sorry about what happened at the church. I didn't know that people were after me. If I had, I wouldn't have involved you at all."

"Jack, you don't have to apologize," he said. "It was a little scary but we made it out in one piece. Bruised, but in one piece."

"Did you have to go to the hospital?"

"Just to get checked out. The paramedics looked me over and said that I should be examined to make sure I didn't have a head injury. So I went over to the hospital and after a quick exam they told me that I'd be fine. How about you?"

"I feel okay. Just got a bloody nose and some cuts. I'm going to live."

"Listen, Jack," he said, turning very serious. "I know that I'm the one who told you not get the police involved in this, but things are very different now. This is bigger than I expected and I really think that you should go to the nearest police station and tell them everything. It's just too dangerous to do this on your own and I see that now. I was wrong about the police. They were very helpful when they came to arrest our attacker. I think we can trust them."

Standing by the pay phone at the liquor store, I thought about what my friend was saying. This really was bigger and more dangerous than I thought it would be when I initially decided to try and solve Johnny's murder. I never thought that I'd be physically attacked like I had. I couldn't remember ever being more scared in my life either. But in spite of these things, my experience at the lake had convinced me that God wanted me to continue.

"Thanks for your concern," I told him, "but I have to continue down this path, and do it alone. God has spoken to me and He wants me to find Johnny's killer before he calls me home."

Fr. Chris didn't say anything.

"What are you talking about, Jack?"

"I had a vision, Father. Jesus was calling me to be the new Moses. I have a mission and then I am going home to glory!" I almost screamed the last word, I was so elated.

"Father, Jesus has been living at the bottom of Reeds Lake, and no one has ever seen him until now. Can you believe that? He revealed Himself to me this afternoon. I've been chosen to bring vengeance to the wicked. I think I've been called to be God's Executioner, Father."

"Jack," he said very slowly, "you sound sick. Where are you? I can come and get you."

"I'm not sick, Father. I'm anointed!"

"Please, Jack, listen to me. I'm your friend, remember. This doesn't sound good to me. Have you been taking your medication?"

"Father, relax. I've been taking my medication. I know that I need it. But I'm not crazy. Things are clearer for me than they have been in years. Everything is starting to make sense to me. God is speaking so clearly to me."

"Do you hear his voice?"

"I hear it, I smell it, I feel it. It's everywhere."

"Jack, that's not God talking to you. It's your mental illness. Maybe the stress has been too much for you. I never thought this would happen. You need to go to the hospital or to the police, right now. I'm not kidding."

His tone said he was very serious. More serious than I had ever heard him.

"When I finish my mission, I will," I promised.

"Listen to me, go right now!" He was getting angry. "Hang up this phone and walk directly to the hospital. Do it now, Jack!"

"That's the devil talking through you. I have a mission," I said, getting angry myself.

"Don't be a fucking idiot! You are in way over your head!"

"I can't believe this," I yelled into the phone. "You of all people should understand what God is calling me to do!"

There was silence from the other end of the phone. I was about to hang up, write Fr. Chris off as an agent of the devil and forget that I had ever known him. I was about to tell my only friend to go to hell.

"I'm sorry," he said into my ear, "I shouldn't be so short with you. It's just that this is very serious and I'm very worried about you and...I'll be honest with you, Jack. I feel responsible for this, and if you get hurt, I couldn't live with myself. Do this as a favor for me, man. Let me take you to the hospital, if for no other reason than to ease my mind. I don't want to be responsible for anything bad happening to you."

He wasn't a devil after all. He was my friend.

"Thanks, thanks for everything you've ever done for me, Father. You just don't know what you mean to me. I don't know how to even express it, but...I know you've treated me better than my own family has. You've fed me and...."

"I know, Jack."

"But," I continued as a car horn echoed in

the valley of buildings around me, "I can't lock myself up right now. I just can't. This is bigger than I thought it was, but it's bigger because God has made it bigger. He's called me and I can't run from my destiny even if I wanted to. Remember Jonah? He tried to resist God's call, but in the end God made sure that he ended up in Ninevah anyway."

"I know the story," Fr. Chris said with a chuckle. "I know that one well. Lots of days, I think that I'm living it."

"So you understand?"

"Yes," he said gently, "I understand how you feel. I do. You're very passionate about this, and I admire that. You hunger for justice. That's wonderful. But I think that God might allow you, or even want you, to have some help with your mission. Maybe I'm being called to be your help, here."

"I don't know," I said.

"Just meet me. We can get a burger or something and talk."

"Thank you, but no."

"Jack, are you sure…"

"I love you," I said, and then I hung up the phone.

21

I walked around for a long time after that. I walked over to the Calder Plaza and looked at *La Grande Vitesse*, the huge abstract sculpture in the center of the plaza. It was a bright orange-red and wavy like the river that ran through this city. I walked around it, touched it, and let it make me feel small.

I knew that I had to continue. I knew I had a calling that could not be denied.

My mind turned to Dusty Ramerez. He'd been Johnny's boyfriend, probably closer to him than even his parents were. I had to talk to him next. I had his phone number and thought about calling him right then.

go and see him

The Spirit was calling me.

take vengeance

There was a good chance that Dusty was the killer. He could have killed Johnny after some argument. Maybe someone was cheating. That kind of thing happened all the time. Husbands killed wives, wives killed husbands. But if Dusty was the killer, going to see him would be dangerous, very dangerous.

I decided to walk back to the Three Kings before doing anything else. For one thing I needed to figure out where Dusty lived, and there was no better tool than the Internet if you wanted personal information about someone. Google knew more about some people than they knew about themselves. Plus, I wanted to check out what else Johnny had been doing on the Internet. There'd been a lot of other sites that he had been on that I hadn't had time to check out before.

I walked into the Three Kings a wiser man. This time I was going to buy a coffee *before* I sat down.

The Three Kings wasn't very busy. There were a few college kids sprinkled around the place, eyes glued to their laptops, but it was nothing like it'd been during my previous visit. The whole place had a more relaxed vibe. It was probably the lack of business people. Those hard-driving young professionals that schedule out every second of their life gave the shop the same harried feeling that I saw in their eyes.

I ordered a tall latte and found a table away from everyone else. I'm sure that the latte was good, but I only took a few sips. Too much caffeine made me nervous and I didn't need to be nervous now.

I opened my bag and booted up Johnny's computer. Once it powered up, I was like everyone else in the place, a young man mesmerized by the screen in front of him. Anyone that walked in would have mistaken me for the college student that I'd once been.

I decided to check Johnny's Hotmail first. I opened the browser and went to the Hotmail site. When I logged on, I saw that he had a new message. I felt a little flutter in my stomach when I saw that it was from cashman19. The subject header read "I

See You Jack Plowman."

> From: Cashman
> <cashman19@yahoo.com>
> To: FabulousChen@hotmail.com
> Subject: I See You Jack Plowman
>
> Hey Jack,
>
> I see what you're doing and if you're not careful, it's going to get you killed. You will never find me and even if you did, you have no proof of anything.
>
> Do yourself a favor and turn yourself in. You deserve punishment, but if you admit what you've done, they just might go easy on you.
>
> You don't want to fuck with me, Jack.

I tried to stay calm as I read the words. Cashman knew what I was up to, but how? Was Bruce Daniels Cashman? Was he watching me now? I took a quick glance around the café and eyed the other customers. None of them was paying any attention to me. Everything *seemed* normal.

he's watching

I knew that it was true. He was watching me, if not now right then at other times, but there wasn't a lot I could do about it. I closed the Hotmail tab, and surfed over to YouTube. I logged in as Johnny and then clicked on his uploaded videos.

I spent the next fifteen minutes watching all 18 of them. Most were filmed in a nightclub, on a camera that didn't have the greatest resolution. All the videos were grainy and it was hard to make out anything that was not directly in front of the camera. Most of them were of people that were drunk or high and dancing frantically. I couldn't even make out what most of them were saying over the pumping beat of the music.

There was one video that was interesting though. Johnny had titled it "Dusty Morning." When I clicked to play it, the screen displayed the hallway of an old house as someone walked down it. The cameraman was laughing under his breath. The man behind the camera opened a wooden door and entered a room that was bare, except for a bed with a man sleeping in it.

The cameraman said, "How does it feel to be this close to a soon-to-be-rich bitch!"

The man in the bed propped himself up. He was a young Hispanic who was handsome and very thin. He could have been anorexic. He said, "Who is that?"

"The man that is going to make me fabulously wealthy!"

A smile came across the Hispanic man's face.

"I thought that would make you happy," the cameraman said. "What should we buy first?"

"How about a red convertible?" the man in bed said.

The cameraman laughed gleefully. I thought that laugh sounded like Johnny.

"That would be awesome!"

The cameraman started to spin the camera around in circles and I saw the room blur around on the screen like pixilated paint splatters. Both of the men were laughing and in the spinning I caught quick glances of the Hispanic man's face. He looked very young to me, but maybe that was just his boyish looks and thin features.

I heard Johnny say, "Oh, shit," and then the camera broke out of its tight spin into a looser rotation. The perspective changed; it was now higher. Johnny must have accidentally thrown the camera up in the air. As the camera recorded on its own, I saw the man's face in the bed change to panic during one sweep.

The camera came down spinning on a dresser and the men collapsed into uproarious laughter.

"I cannot believe that," Johnny said as the camera stopped its spinning to create a perfect frame of the two.

"Oh, my god," the other man said. "That did not just happen! I've got to see that, man."

The two were still laughing as Johnny walked over to the camera and stood in front of the lens. "This shit is going on YouTube," he said.

I logged onto Johnny's Facebook next. He had a few new messages. None of the people seemed to know that Johnny was dead. One of the messages was from a guy who had the same taste in music as Johnny. He mentioned a bunch of bands that I'd never heard of and asked about getting together to see a band in Chicago. Another message was from a guy from Detroit that invited Johnny out to some club in Motown. Johnny had 559 friends on Facebook. I spent some time looking at the pages of some of his friends. Most of them lived in either Chicago or Detroit but a lot of them didn't list a hometown, so it's possible that they were local.

Johnny was a member of a group called "Abuse Survivors" on Facebook so I checked out the group. There were a lot of postings where people talked about how being abused had messed them up emotionally. I didn't see that Johnny had ever posted to the group. I read a few of the postings all the way through, but then started to skim them. There was just too much pain in those postings for me to bear.

I navigated over to Johnny's page, so I could see what it would look like to someone who visited. His page had a bright pink background. It made me smile a little when I saw it. Before I even opened it, I knew that his background would be pink. I was getting to the point where I could anticipate what he would do. It was strange and a little sad to get to know my roommate only after he was dead.

Johnny's page had a link to the video with the flying camera, and a bunch of photos of him and his club friends. I looked for pictures of Dusty but couldn't find any. Johnny's profile said that he liked to go clubbing and dancing for fun, that he liked Donald Stachey mysteries and that he wanted to be a psychologist someday. That was something that I'd never known about Johnny. He wanted to be a shrink. I checked out Johnny's sent messages before I logged off. All of his outgoing messages seemed pretty innocuous to me.

The last part of Johnny's online life that I had the password to access was his bank account. I logged onto the Select Bank website and then checked Johnny's password document to get his username and password.

When I logged in, a pop-up splashed onto my screen. It said that Johnny's account had an "administrative lock." I didn't know what that meant exactly, but I figured it meant that someone thought there was something fishy going on. I wondered if this lock had been attached to Johnny's account before he died or only after.

Worried that the bank might be able to trace my attempt to access Johnny's account to the Three Kings wifi, and then maybe to me, I closed the window and decided to end my surfing for the day. I was about to power down Johnny's laptop and leave when I remembered one more thing that I needed the Internet for.

In a few clicks, I had the directions to Dusty's house and left the Three Kings, nervous about the danger that might be waiting for me when I got there.

22

The Spirit spoke to me all the way to Dusty's house. It was a gentle voice that murmured to me constantly, soothingly as I walked the broken sidewalk. He told me everything that I needed to know, teaching me lessons that a man like me needed to learn. He even told me which side of the road to walk on. The left side was where serpents walked, so I kept to the right. As I looked across the road at a group of men walking by, I could see the vague twist that some of them had in their stride. To move in such a serpentine manner, there was no way they were not snakes in disguise. I was surprised that I had ever *not* seen it.

I started to get tired about halfway through my walk and stopped to buy a Coke at a small barbecue restaurant called Moe's Pit. The front windows were covered in rose-colored plastic blinds that would have looked very much at home in Marcia Brady's bedroom. The blinds kept out the light of the late afternoon and filled the place with an eerie dark red light. Moe's Pit was nothing but a dirty storefront on Division Street, in a mostly Hispanic neighborhood. Thick dust covered all the window sills.

dirty place for dirty souls

I walked up to the old counter but there wasn't anyone there.

I looked around the dining room and saw one black couple eating the last bits of food off their plates. They weren't talking and didn't seem to care about me. I was tired and thirsty. I could see the plastic bottles of Coke in the refrigerator just behind the counter.

"Hey," I said loudly towards the kitchen that was partially visible in front of me. "Can I have a Coke?"

Nothing.

"I've got somewhere I've got to be," I said to whoever was back there in the kitchen. "How about some service out here?"

The couple just sat there not saying a word.

"Come on, somebody has got to be back there," I said again, this time screaming at the top of my lungs and banging one of my fists on the counter for emphasis.

There was still no sound or movement coming from the kitchen.

go ahead its fine

I jumped up and started to crawl over the counter. It was higher than it looked but I was able to get my weight adjusted and pull myself up to stand upright on the counter. The new higher view let me see deep into the kitchen. There was no one there.

"What are you doing, man?"

I turned around and saw the black man who had been finishing up his meal standing by the counter. He had crept up on me somehow. It was strange. I didn't know how that had happened. Seeing a conflict coming, the man's girlfriend started to walk to the door.

"I'm just getting a Coke," I told him.

"Get off the fucking counter before I pull you off," the man said.

He was young and looked strong enough to do it if he really wanted to. Another man would have been afraid of him, but not me, not that day. I felt infused with the Spirit of God. No man, regardless of how strong he was, could stop me from doing God's will. I had a mission of vengeance to complete, to find Johnny's killer, bring justice to him and then meet my Lord face to face. No one could stop my mission because my mission was God's mission. Right now, God needed me to be refreshed. That meant getting a drink of something. No man was going to stand in my way.

"Get behind me, Satan," I screamed at him in rebuke.

"You drunk?" he asked me, suddenly puzzled.

"Drunk on the blood of the Savior."

He just stood there not sure what to do next. I took the opportunity to jump down behind the counter, landing with a thud as my big shoes hit the concrete floor. I opened the cooler and took out one of the plastic bottles. The man just looked at me.

"I'm no thief. I'll pay," I told him as I took a dollar bill out of my wallet and laid it by the cash register. He watched me put my wallet back into my pocket and then open the Coke and drink it down in one long gulp. It was cold and sweet, just what I needed.

The man stood silent and we glared at each other. The standoff was broken by a deep voice from the kitchen.

"What's going on out here, Danny?"

Suddenly, a man in his fifties was standing a few feet from me. He had on a white tee shirt and a big stained apron. He was built like an ox and the look he gave me made me feel like I already needed stitches. I scrambled back on top of the counter so he couldn't grab ahold of me.

"This guy jumped over the counter, Moe," the younger man explained. "I thought he might be trying to rob you or something. I think he's just drunk or high though. He's acting really weird."

Moe looked at me and tried to size up the situation that had developed in his little restaurant. Neither of the big men moved. I could see that they'd never encountered a true prophet before.

"I come in peace, and I bring you peace," I told them as I stretched out my arms.

"I think you need some help, young man," Moe finally said.

"There's nothing that any mortal man can give me, my friend," I told him. "I am on a divine mission. A mission to bring vengeance to the demons that kill the innocent. A mission to bring justice to the downtrodden. I'm on a mission to rid the world of the evil of murder and to avenge those whose throats were slit on their own bed. A cold-blooded killer should prepare to meet his God! After this last blood is shed, the killing will end and then I will lead you all into the arms of the Lord. He's so close! You can't imagine how close he is…"

They both looked as if they were trying to hide how afraid they were.

"Danny," Moe said in a soft voice. "Do you

have a cell phone?"

"Yeah, Moe."

"Why don't you call 911. I think this white man has some problems."

They were talking like I wasn't even there, like I wasn't worthy of being spoken to. They were talking about me like I was a child who couldn't understand them. Danny fished around in the pocket of his jeans and pulled out his phone, tapping the tiny device three times in a staccato rhythm. I stood on the counter and planned my exit. There was no way I was going to be here when the police pulled up.

"Why don't you come down from the counter, man," Moe said to me and took a step closer. I didn't move but I also didn't react to him. I just stood there like I was a stack of clean dishes.

"We can get you some help, man," he said as he inched closer to me.

"Yes, this is an emergency," Danny said, "I'm at Moe's Barbecue on Division. There's a guy here who's acting crazy. He's standing on the counter and was trying to rob the place."

It was now or never.

From the countertop, I leapt as far as I could into the dining room. Danny moved out of the way and when my feet hit the floor they were already churning as fast as they could. I dodged around the tables and made a bee line to the front door.

"Hey," Moe screamed at me as I hit the front door and dashed through it like a lightning bolt thrown by God Himself. Out of instinct, Danny started to chase me but I heard Moe call him back as I ran down the road.

I didn't hear what Moe said back but I could guess pretty well. "Don't follow that crazy white guy, Danny. Crazy people are dangerous."

23

I ran full out down a side street and then slowed to a jog when I was a few blocks away from the restaurant. I kept moving, trying to feign being a jogger out for his daily run. I acted casual and tried to not look as beat from the running as I really was. Sweat was pouring off me like I'd just walked through a rain shower. I doubt anyone watching would have believed that I was a jogger, though. There were a lot of things that I'd been in my life but God knows, I've never been a jogger.

run the good race, run for righteousness sake

After a few more blocks, my side started to burn with pain. It was as if the running had torn a massive gash into my skin. I knew that I couldn't keep this up. I had to stop. I decided to keep it up for just one more block. I used my memories of the jails I'd stayed in to motivate me.

Finally, I got the point where I felt like if I didn't stop I would collapse into a pile on some poor old woman's lawn. When it got to that point, I stopped.

I stopped and just stood on the sidewalk panting like an old dog for a few minutes. I started to feel like I was going to hyperventilate, the air was going in and out of me so quickly. I worried about passing out on the sidewalk on some street that even I didn't know the name of. I tried to focus on my breathing, the in and out rhythm, getting it back.

"Cool ocean breezes," I said out loud.

I willed myself to regain my breath. I thought of Anna, of Anna when the times had been good. When I was sane. Slowly, my breath returned to me. The air was so sweet and clean. I swore that I'd never take breathing for granted again.

When I felt rested, I walked until I found a main street and was surprised to find that I was very close to Dusty's house. It wasn't more than a block or two away. God had been guiding me even in the panic of my running.

trust in the Lord your God

As I walked down Dusty's street, I thought about what I was going to say to him and how I should approach this. Should I act like I was somebody else? A friend of Johnny's or a case manager? I wondered if the police had connected Dusty to Johnny and if they'd been out to see him. I knew Johnny's murder wouldn't be a major priority. When the cops find a dead gay guy who is a known nut case, the department isn't going to assign their best detective.

the root of all evil

Dusty's house stood out from the others in the neighborhood. It was a neat and tidy Cape Cod with a manicured lawn. Dusty's neighbors lived in homes that hadn't been painted in 25 years and more often than not had a couple cars in the driveway that hadn't seen the road in years.

In contrast, Dusty's place was so well kept that it looked like it was newer than the other houses on the street. Maybe it was the bright blue paint job. The paint was still sharp and glossy, like it'd just been done. If you picked up Dusty's house and moved it over to Mr. Chen's neighborhood, Dusty's would have been noticeably smaller but otherwise, it would fit right in.

I walked up the driveway and then up the two cement steps to the front door. There was a freshly washed white Camry in the driveway. Did that mean he was home? I gave a quick knock on the door.

I heard someone moving around inside but whoever it was didn't come to the door.

I decided I should say something. "I'm a friend of Johnny's," I spoke into the keyhole like it was some kind of microphone. "I'm trying to figure out what happened to him. Please open the door, Dusty. I need your help."

I heard more movement behind the door and then from the corner of my eye, I saw something move in the window. I looked up but whatever had been there was already gone. Only the gentle movement of the curtain remained, the wake of whoever was inside.

I didn't know if I should say something else to try and prove who I was or just stand there. Whatever I did, I wasn't going to stand out in front of his door for very long. People would see me and maybe even remember me. I didn't need that attention.

"Dusty," I tried again, "please listen to me. God has sent me to find Johnny's killer. I'm here to bring justice. Please open the door. I come in peace."

There was more movement behind the door, but louder now. I could hear the lock disengage, and the door opened an inch.

blessed is he who comes in the name of the Lord

"Who are you?" a male voice asked me. I could see the chain dangling between the door and the frame but I couldn't see anything else inside the house. All the lights were out and the man speaking hid behind the door.

"My name's Jack Plowman. I used to be Johnny's roommate, over on Prospect. I'm the one that found him. I'm not going to hurt you, Dusty. I'm on a mission from God."

That day my name was like the Lord's Himself because at the sound of it, the door opened and a tall thin man in pajamas whisked me into the house in one elegant movement. Any lingering fears that I had that Dusty might be the killer evaporated when I saw how scared and frail he was.

It was dark inside and I was disoriented. I felt the panic start to rise in me, felt the old familiar sweat start to rise. Then the lights came on and the room filled with multicolored light.

Dusty, at least six feet tall, was standing in the living room next to an exquisite lamp that sat on an end table and was the source of the rainbow. The lamp was what I later learned was called a Tiffany Style lamp. The shade was made up of hundreds of small glass pieces of differing colors that cast multihued light all over the room. For a moment, I felt like I was in Oz.

"Thanks," I said to him.

Dusty stared at me for a moment. He had on a blue and white pajama set that looked like it had been ironed. His thick black hair was styled in a fashionable mess atop his head and his beard had at least two days of growth on it. He looked like he was dressed up to go to some swanky Hollywood pajama party.

"Why did you come here, Jack Plowman?" he asked me.

"I told you. God sent me."

Dusty's eyes rolled. "God? I don't believe in God."

"Why did you open the door, then?"

behold the man!

He smiled at me.

"No one talks like that," he said as his grin grew. "I knew you must be who you said you were when you started talking like a religious freak."

"Why don't you believe in God?" I asked him sincerely. I really wanted to know.

"Because your God hates gay people."

"God sent me to bring justice for the killing of a gay man, Dusty. The Lord is coming again and his kingdom will have no end. I have been sent to lead the sinners back to Jesus, Dusty. Jesus has come back. He's in East Grand Rapids."

Dusty let out a little laugh. "Are you serious, man?"

"Yes."

"Then you must be even crazier than Johnny."

"What do you mean by that?"

Dusty sat down on his blue pinstriped couch.

It matched the pajamas that he was wearing. Did this guy coordinate everything?

He motioned for me to take a seat in a big chair with an elaborate tapestry across from him. The room was small but it had been carefully decorated. If it'd been bigger, it could have been in *Architectural Digest*. I sat down in the chair. It was soft and yielded to my body, almost hugging me.

"First, tell me how you found me," Dusty said.

"God led me to you."

the Lord your God

"How about you drop the God talk and give me the real story, Jack."

"I found your number on a scrap of paper in Johnny's room but I didn't know who you were until I talked to Gary Desmond. He told me that you were Johnny's ex-boyfriend. God told me that you might know what happened to Johnny and so here I am."

"Gary Desmond, huh?"

"Yeah, what about him?"

Dusty looked up at the multi-colored sky his lamp was making on the ceiling.

"Gary Desmond was one of Johnny's playthings before he and I got together. Hell, maybe I was just one of Johnny's playthings, too. You never knew with Johnny. He used people. Sucked them dry like a vampire and tossed them aside when he was done with them. Gary fell in love quickly and became obsessed with Johnny. Johnny told me all about it later. How Gary would call him every day and beg to see him. It was sick how Johnny treated Gary. I even told him so once after he played one of Gary's desperate messages to me on his cell phone. Johnny laughed but the way he was treating Gary turned my stomach."

Dusty put his legs up on the matching ottoman.

"Gary couldn't accept that Johnny didn't want to be with him. He couldn't let go. Even after we were together, Gary kept calling. I told Johnny to change his number but he wouldn't. He liked knowing that he could call Gary day or night and he'd come running. He even threatened to go to Gary to get new clothes when I finally put an end to him stealing from the store I work at. I let that go on for too long. I guess I got sucked in just like Gary."

"What about drugs?" I asked. "Gary said that Johnny was really into drugs."

"Oh, yeah," Dusty said with a smile. "We partied hard for a while. That's how I initially met Johnny. We were at the bar one night and one of my friends bought some crystal from a guy there. Johnny was waiting to make a buy too and the two of us struck up a conversation. We hit it off right away and ended up using together that night…"

"So you're into drugs too?" I asked.

"I try not to use as much anymore. It got really crazy. I'll tell you what, Jack. Crystal meth is one of the greatest things on the earth. It heightens everything. If you take it before you have sex you can…"

"I don't need to hear about that," I

interrupted.

He laughed out loud at that. "You're quite a prude, aren't you, Jack?"

"Fornication is a sin, Dusty. So is drug use."

Repent and be saved

"Okay, okay. I won't talk about how intense the meth makes it when you…"

"Please stop," I told him again.

he's a sinner, jack

"Okay, man," he said, chuckling. "I'm just having some fun with you. But to answer your question, yes, Johnny and I used a lot of drugs when we were together. I got into it when I started doing the club scene. Someone just passed it to me when I was drunk and I was off!"

Dusty stretched his arms out like he was an airplane. "Johnny told me that a friend of his got him going on it too. The drugs were great, at least for a while."

"What do you mean?"

"Well, when Johnny and I started using together, the drugs just made everything more intense. We had fun without the drugs, but with them it was a hundred times better. After a while, it started to be all about the drugs and it wasn't any fun anymore. I told Johnny I wanted to stop, and he said that was fine, but he was still going to party. It made me really angry. The drugs had gotten ahold of him in a way they never got to me."

"So Johnny was an all-out addict?"

"Yeah, he became a big addict. When using wasn't cool anymore, I just quit and that was it. It wasn't that hard. I just stopped using and stayed away from clubs that I knew had drugs in them. Johnny had gotten arrested a few times before he realized that he had to quit too but it was too late. He tried going cold turkey like I did but that didn't work for him. He went to counseling but that didn't work either. He kept telling me that he wasn't using but then he'd go behind my back and use. It drove me crazy. I eventually talked him into going into rehab, but then we couldn't put together enough money for it. Johnny even asked his dad for help but of course he refused. His dad is a fucking hypocrite."

"Mr. Chen?" I asked.

"Yeah, Mr. Chen. He isn't as clean as he wants everyone to think. Johnny told me that his dad has been to rehab at least five times himself for 'various addictions,' whatever the hell that means. Johnny made his old man sound like he has a major addictive personality. Like the guy couldn't brush his teeth without getting addicted to toothpaste. A real mess, but when his son comes asking for help to get clean, he just slams the door in Johnny's face."

"Was he just using meth? I never saw him do any drugs when we lived together."

"He used everything that he could get his hands on, except he never used needles. Needles scared him. Mostly it was just meth and crack. Those were his favorites."

Dusty stopped talking and tried to clean a blemish off the bright lamp. Whatever he was trying to clean wasn't coming off though, so he rubbed at the lamp harder and harder.

"I've got to get that smudge. I'll be right back," he said to me as he got up and went into the kitchen. From where I was sitting, I could see that Dusty's kitchen was small but immaculate, just like the rest of the house.

He came back with a washcloth and went at the smudge with gusto. I could tell he got the spot that he was trying to clean when he smiled.

"That's sure a nice lamp," I commented.

"It is. Actually it was a gift from Johnny. It's the only nice thing that I have left from him. When his dad refused to pay for rehab, it really was hard on Johnny. He started using every day. It ruined our relationship and eventually I just quit talking to him. That was about a month ago."

Dusty held the blue wash cloth between his hands, nervously twisting it around his left hand.

"How could he afford all the drugs?" I asked.

I knew that Johnny was living on disability checks just like I was. My check was enough to pay for my half of the rent and some food, but beyond that I never had much left.

"After he got into drugs hardcore, Johnny started to make…friends. They were giving him money all the time. He always denied that he was doing anything to get that money but I don't know if he was telling the truth. Plus, near the end, whenever Johnny and I would talk on the phone, he'd go on and on about making 'a big score.' I asked him what he was talking about but he wouldn't tell me anything."

As he spoke, Dusty twisted the blue wash cloth in his hands into a thin snake.

beware, it's the tempter from the garden, jack

"So why are you so nervous?" I asked him. "You're sitting in here with the blinds closed and hiding out. You think the person that killed Johnny is going to come for you?"

"I don't know what to think, man. I guess I'm just scared. The police called me yesterday and left a message on my answering machine. I didn't call them back and then I called in sick to work again today. I don't want the cops showing up at the store and questioning me about a murder. I had nothing to do with this, but I'm not so sure that cops would believe me if I told them that."

"No," I told him. "you can't trust the cops. If it makes you feel any better, I'm pretty sure the cops think that I'm the one that murdered Johnny. I was his roommate and I'm the one who hasn't been heard from since Johnny died. I'm sure that I'm the number one suspect."

Saying it out loud made me realize what a mess I had gotten myself into.

"Why don't you call and talk to the cops?"

"I thought about doing that after I found Johnny," I said, "but it's too late for that now. Besides, ultimately the police and the courts have no authority over this. God has jurisdiction when one of the Ten Commandments is broken, and God has called me to bring justice. Do you think Johnny was killed because of the drugs?"

"I don't know. He usually bought all his

stuff from Randy, and Randy is very cool. I can't see him doing anything like this." He seemed pretty sure about it. "You know, Jack, I think you should talk to the police."

"Why do you want me to do that?"

"Well, listen," he said, looking me directly in the eye, "I want to just move on with my life and I can't do that with the police nosing around my business. If you just talked to them, even over the phone, and told them that you don't think I'm involved, that might allow me to get back to normal."

"So you want the police to focus their attention on me?"

"No, that's not it at all. I just need someone to put in a good word for me. Someone who knows the whole story. I've told you what I know, Jack. I've been honest with you. Can't you return the favor?"

"Before I can do that," I said, straightening myself in my chair, "I need to know who killed Johnny. I'll tell the police the whole story after justice is served. I'll do it before I go to glory in the lake."

For a brief second, his eyebrows raised, but then he was back to normal.

"That's cool," he said. "Will you promise me, swear to God, that you'll talk to the police?"

I didn't see the harm in making that promise. I could call them after Johnny was avenged and then walk into Reeds Lake to be with my Lord.

"Yes, I give you my word before Jesus

Christ and all the saints."

"Good," Dusty said to me and smiled.

I hadn't suspected that Dusty had anything to do with Johnny's murder until he started asking me to go to the police and put in a good word for him. Why was he so interested in that? It seemed strange, and I didn't buy what he said about going on with his life. Dusty was putting almost as much effort into avoiding the police as I was. Maybe he was just worried about being the subject of an investigation. I couldn't be sure just what his motives were.

"Well, Jack," Dusty said, getting up from the couch, "I've enjoyed our little discussion but I really want to clean up the house tonight before bed. The place is a mess. I'm embarrassed that you even saw it like this."

If Dusty's house was a mess, I lived like a dirty pig every day of my life.

"Thanks for your help, Dusty. God is grateful for your help."

"Let's hope *someone* finds out who did that to Johnny. Who knows, maybe you and your imaginary friend will be the ones to break the case wide open."

Dusty laughed and walked me to the door.

I heard the words of the Spirit come into my head just as Dusty shut the door behind me.

he won't be laughing on the judgment day

24

It was close to dusk when I left Dusty's house and started the walk back to my dumpster home. The night air was cold on my face as I walked into it.

"Have mercy on him, Lord," I said as I walked down Dusty's driveway and into the growing twilight. "He knows not what he does."

he is a sinner and sinners deserve judgment

"Please, Lord. I beg of you, show him the fullness of your grace. He did try to help me, your loyal servant."

you are being called, follow the call

"I will heed your call, God." I said as I stared up into the darkening sky. "I am your humble servant."

I knew that God would grant Dusty the mercy he deserved. God was loving and forgiving. Dusty would have to take his punishment, but then the Grace of the Lord would fall upon him like a heavy load.

Just then, I heard the ruffle of paws on the concrete and turned around to see a middle-aged man behind me walking his little dog. He was about twenty feet back and looking at me with caution in his eyes. He stopped walking when I turned around and our eyes met.

"The Lord be with you," I said to him.

He turned into a statue. Even his dog became nearly motionless, sitting on the sidewalk.

"I said, 'The Lord be with you,'" I repeated, with more emphasis this time.

"And also with you," he said, with a question in his voice like he was unsure of the answer.

"That's more like it!" I said and took a few steps towards him. The little dog cowered between his owner's feet.

"So you believe in God?" I asked him.

The man was bald and short and as we stood there in the darkening night I could see that he was scared of me.

"I'm a Christian," the man said meekly.

"Don't be afraid," I said to him as I walked towards him. "I come in peace, with tidings of great gladness. A king has been born of water and the spirit. At the bottom of Reed's Lake, the Lord has been born again in East Grand Rapids. He will bring terrible judgment to the wicked and salvation to his servants. I am his holy prophet. I am Jack Plowman."

The man didn't say anything.

"If you are one of God's children, you should join me," I said, touching his shoulder. "Come, leave all your worldly possessions and follow me. I am to lead the believers to glory. Come and listen to my teachings, come and be my apostle."

In a hundred years, I never would have expected what happened next. Not from a man out walking his dog. From a woman in a dark, deserted parking lot, sure. That would've made sense. But I didn't expect it here, not in this situation. But sure enough he had it.

Pepper spray.

It was like the spray somehow came directly

out of his fingertips. I looked away from him for just a second, saw his fingers move and then the pain engulfed me as if my eyeballs had been covered in gasoline and then lit on fire. I fell to the ground with a yell as the pain from the spray seared me. I heard the man run away as I fell to the sidewalk. Everything seemed to be burning. I wanted it to stop.

satan, he was satan

I called out to God to save me, from the pain, from Satan, but nothing changed and the agony just continued. I felt abandoned by God and alone in a cold world. It was a feeling I'd felt before

I don't know how long I writhed around on the ground, the cold concrete scraping my hands as I moved. It could have been ten minutes, it could have been fifteen. Eventually, the fire in my eyes died down to a cinder and I was able to get up. My vision was still blurry and tears still ran down my face in streams but I was able to stand up and start walking again. About a half a block down the street it hit me.

The devil that had blinded me might call the police.

run, run, run

I didn't need to hear it twice. The Spirit had returned to guide me. I broke out in a sprint down the sidewalk, running for my life once again. I ran north, towards downtown, but didn't pay any attention to the streets as I ran wildly. I just wanted to get away from that neighborhood. In my panic, I never thought that my running might draw attention to me.

I was running down the middle of a side street, when I saw the black and white car drive slowly past the street in front of me. There was a man in the passenger seat looking carefully out the window. He was looking for something, or someone. I heard the wail of the siren a second later and for a minute I thought that the squad car had been called away to an accident or something more important than me.

I was about to let out a loud shout of praise when the car turned around and appeared in front of me. It was barreling down on me, lights blazing and siren blaring, and I was running right towards it.

I turned on a dime and fled into the yard of the first house on my left, a little white ranch. The owner had fenced in his back yard with a simple chain link that jutted out of the garage, boxing in his property. I dashed for the fence and frantically started to climb over it. I heard the door of the police car slam behind me and saw the red lights from the top of the cruiser flash across the white siding.

With a giant leap, I cleared the fence and ran across the yard. The grass was patchy, more dirt than grass really. I ran until I reached another fence. It was the fence on the back property line. I cleared it and landed in someone else's back yard.

I looked back and saw that the cop had cleared the first fence and was running towards me and gaining fast. He looked mad. Like a bull in a uniform.

There was no fence in this yard and I could see the street ahead of me. I ran for it with my heart beating in my throat. I could almost feel the cop's hot breath on my neck as he gained on me. The officer was fit and fast and I wasn't either.

I burst out onto the sidewalk just in time to see another squad car make the turn onto the road in front of me. I bolted across the street into yet another yard before the car could reach me. As I ran, I heard the car blaze past, going around to the next block.

I felt the stitch in my side start to scream again. The cop behind me continued to gain on me. I could hear him behind me now. I was going to have to give up or try and stand and fight.

i'll be with you, my son

My chest heaved as I hit a thin line of flowering bushes that separated one lawn from the next. I dove into them. They were dense but there was a small open space at the base of the bush that once I got into it, I was able to crawl sideways along.

I closed my eyes and willed myself to be somewhere else. If I could have, I would have teleported back to the lake. I wanted to be there with my Lord. I wanted to be anywhere besides here, cowered under a bush like an animal. My breath was heavy and came out of me in gusts that moved the leaves near my face. I willed it to slow down.

As the police officer burst through the line of bushes, his shoe brushed against my back. It was a light brush, but if I'd felt it there was a very good chance that he'd felt it too. That knowledge shocked me into perfect stillness.

The cop must have known something was wrong when he didn't see me in front of him anymore because I heard him stop dead in his tracks.

He stood still, breathing lightly. I didn't move.

I could only see his legs, but I guessed that he was looking around, scanning the long line of bushes for signs of movement. The normal sounds of the city seemed to fade way and night grew silent. There were no birds, no crickets. The cop stood and then his legs slowly began to move away from me. He was walking to my left, rustling the flowers on the bushes as he went.

go

It was my only chance. The cop was searching away from me. He'd chosen to go left down the line of bushes instead of right. If he'd gone right, after a few steps he would have been able to see me huddled there.

I was lucky. I had to get up and run now.

run

But for some reason, I didn't. Instead, I tried to make myself smaller by curling up into a tight ball there in the dirt. I thought that if I tucked myself up small enough eventually I might disappear. The police would call my escape a miracle because it would be a miracle. God would take me away from here. All I had to do was call out to Him.

"Save me, Lord," I said in a whisper to the yellow flower rubbing against my nose. "Deliver me from evil, for thine is the kingdom, the power and the glory, forever and ever."

I shut my eyes tightly, sending the prayer skyward.

Waiting on the Lord.

In a flash, I felt myself being lifted up into the air, heavenward. The strong arms of God pulling me up through the bush with violent force. The yellow flowers brushed past my eyes as I went upward, little yellow blurs of oil paint on a green canvas. I flew up and started to open my arms to fly, but before I could unfold them, I felt myself start to fall.

I opened my eyes just before I crashed back down head first into the dirt. I was disoriented and a throbbing pain exploded in the middle of my forehead.

"Stay on the ground," a man's voice demanded of me. Was it God?

I blinked furiously and rubbed my eyes, trying to get the sand out of them. My vision was just starting to clear when I felt the stab in my back as a crushing weight came down on top of me. Something grabbed my right arm and pulled it behind me and held it there. Then my left hand was pulled back and glued to my right. I tried to pull them apart but no matter how hard I tried, I couldn't free myself.

I was lifted onto my feet.

"Walk," the man behind me said.

I did what he said, putting one foot in front of the other.

"I can't see," I said. "Please help me."

The man stopped. The next thing I knew, a

cloth was wiping the remainder of the sand from my eyes. The first thing I saw when my vision returned was the police officer that had been chasing me. He was a young man with steel eyes. He looked at me dispassionately.

"Officer," I said to him, "there's been a mistake. I've been sent by God to bring justice. You must let me go immediately. I am doing the Lord's work and there is no time to waste."

With God's help, I thought it might actually work.

"Keep walking," he told me and marched me out to the cruiser that was waiting on the street. The cop in the car had a sheepish grin on his face. The cruiser's red lights flickered like flames across the houses, making them look like they were all on fire, like everyone was in hell.

25

The cell I ended up in was small, but at least I was the only one in it. Walking in, I saw a number of large cells that held upwards of fifteen people. I don't know what I would've done if they had put me in one of those cells.

My cell was at the far end of the hallway, off by itself. I could hear other prisoners calling out and yelling from time to time but I couldn't see anyone else. Even the cell opposite me was empty.

The cops hadn't talked to me much on the ride to jail. I tried to explain my mission and told them that they were agents of Satan for holding me.

That went over really well.

I prayed to God as the squad car drove through the streets of the city, my hands held behind my back in handcuffs. I called out to my Lord.

But there was no reply.

I laid down on the jail cot and tried to sleep. I was tired from all the running and the chase but I couldn't get to sleep no matter how hard I tried. I just tossed and turned, my mind racing. Once an hour, a man in a brown uniform would slowly walk by my cell. He never said anything to me, he just peered in and looked at me for a moment like I was some animal at the zoo. Then he turned around and walked back the way he came. I could always tell when he was coming because the prisoners down the hall would get very quiet when they heard his shoes clacking on the linoleum.

I knew it was all over for me. They would charge me with killing Johnny and then they would find a way to convict me and throw me in jail for the rest of my life. They'd treat me the way they've treated so many other prophets of God.

Eventually by some miracle I finally drifted off to sleep, probably from sheer exhaustion more than anything else. I dreamed about Anna. She was an angel in my dream, an angel with big transparent wings folded behind her shoulder blades. It seemed totally natural to me that she should have those wings jutting out of her favorite U of M sweatshirt. In the dream, I was walking with her down a set of abandoned railroad tracks in a hot and windy desert. The parallel rails were the only thing my eyes could see; the rest of creation was just endless oceans of sand that went off in every direction.

Anna walked on one of the rails and I walked on the other. They were smooth from being ridden over for so many years, so smooth that they reflected the sky above us.

I looked over at her and she smiled. Her wings shuddered a little.

"I don't know where I'm going," I said to her.

"That's okay, Jack."

I reached out for her hand and she took it.

"Jack," Anna said to me, her eyes on the distant horizon. "You know that I'm with you always. I've never left your side, never."

For some reason that made me angry.

"What's the matter?" she asked me. I took my hand back and stood rigid on the rail.

"You just don't understand, Anna. You don't get it. You never have." I felt hot with anger.

"Just leave me alone. I don't want you around."

"But, Jack," she pleaded.

"Get out of here."

She didn't say another word to me or even react to what I'd said. I wasn't looking at her, but I could see the wave go through her body as her wings gracefully unfolded behind her and she stepped into the sky above me, circling upward into the blue.

I kept walking alone.

I woke up the next morning and saw that the guard had already been by with my breakfast. A small plastic plate was lying on the floor just inside my cell. There was a small cup of orange juice and a bagel. The pad of butter was melting in a yellow pool on the floor. They hadn't given me silverware.

I got up, picked up the tray and brought it back to my cot. The food tasted good to me although the bagel tasted stale. Halfway through my solitary breakfast, I heard the clicking of footsteps coming down the hall, but these weren't the familiar steps of the regular guard. Someone else was coming.

The man was well over six feet tall and very thin. Although he must have been in his thirties, his face was still pockmarked from what must have been severe teenage acne. He was dressed in khaki pants and an oxford shirt, not the usual uniform the guards wore.

"Mr. Plowman?" he asked. As he said it, he looked me in the eyes. He was the first person who'd done that since I got here.

"Yes, that's me."

"My name's Robert Miller. I'm the mental health clinician here at the jail. Do you mind if we talk a little bit?"

The mental health clinician for the jail. It may have taken half a day, but they'd finally gotten around to calling in the psych squad. It always came back to the psych squad. Whenever something significant happened in my life, someone made me talk to a shrink.

"Sure," I said. "What do you want to talk about, Dr. Miller?"

"I'm not a doctor, Mr. Plowman. I'm a social worker from Community Mental Health. I'm stationed here at the jail to help inmates who may have mental health issues. I was asked to speak to you based on some on the things you said when you were being arrested."

he's not real

"If you check your records, you'll see that I'm a consumer at C.M.H. Tiffini Ringold is my case manager," I told him.

"Okay," he said through the bars. "I'll let her know that you're here. I know Tiffini and I'm sure she'll want to come and see you." He seemed sincere.

"Oh, I'm sure she will."

Miller stood in the hallway and made a note in a little pad that he was holding.

"Do you know what you're being held for?" he said when he was done writing.

"For being too much like Jesus?"

Miller looked down at me sympathetically.

He was so tall that he could have lorded over me even if I'd been standing up.

"What do you mean by that?" he asked.

"Jesus was arrested for following the will of God, just like I was. Jesus sought nothing but to bring the love of God to others, just like me, but he was stripped of his clothes and questioned by the authorities. Look at this orange jumper they've given me. Look at you standing there questioning me."

"It says here that you were arrested for disturbing the peace and that you've been wanted for questioning about the murder of your roommate. How is that following the will of God?"

"What do you know about the will of God, Mr. Miller?"

"Not very much," he admitted. "What does God want you to do?"

"God has called me to assist Him in bringing justice to the sinner that murdered Johnny. I'm a prophet sent by God, Mr. Miller, but I can't go home to the lake until Johnny is avenged. Your Roman police force has arrested me and now you plan to crucify me. I am being called to offer my body as a holy sacrifice like so many prophets before me. I will die, but I prophesy to you today, Mr. Miller, that on the third day, I'll rise from Reeds Lake and give all of Grand Rapids the gift of the Holy Spirit before I return to be with Jesus forever."

"I see," he said. "Have you been hearing things that other people can't hear, or seeing anything that other people can't see?"

"I see the will of God, which apparently you and your Roman friends refuse to see. That doesn't make me crazy though, Mr. Miller. It just makes you blind."

"Right. In the past week, have you used any drugs or alcohol?"

"I never do drugs," I told him. "It's a sin against the temple of the body."

"Have you ever been in a psychiatric hospital?"

"Yeah, a few times."

"When was the last time?" Miller asked.

"About a year ago. Tiffini had me petitioned for following the will of God during Lent. Essentially, I was persecuted for making a commitment to God during Lent. Apparently, Tiffini was taken over by Satan for a few days."

"Okay," Miller said as he made notes. "Do you take any medications? Have you been taking them?"

"I see Dr. Patel at Community Mental Health. He has me on the meds that were in my bag. The cops took my bag away. I can't very well take my medication when my pills have been confiscated."

"I'll see what I can do about that."

Miller made a few more notes in his little pad. His brow was furrowed as he wrote, his pen moving over the paper furiously.

"Have you ever felt like you wanted to harm yourself?" Miller continued.

"That's a sin, but...yes, a few times. When my life gets dark, sometimes I give in to the darkness for a little while."

"So," Miller probed, "when was the last time you felt like harming yourself?"

"I don't know. A while back. I don't want to kill myself now, if that's what you're getting at. Is that what you're getting at?"

"Yes. I suppose that is what I'm getting at. Are you a cutter? Have you ever done that?"

"Not since I was a teenager."

"Good, good," he said to his pad. "Have you ever felt like you wanted to hurt other people?"

"Again, that's a sin," I said with authority. "Jesus commanded us to love the Lord our God with all our heart, mind and strength and to love our neighbor as ourselves."

"But we all sin, don't we, Mr. Plowman?"

I thought about that. He was right. I'd sure done more than my fair share of sinning in my life. I'd hurt people, usually the people that I loved the most. Sometimes I'd even meant to hurt them.

"Yes," I told him, "we do all sin, Mr. Miller, and I suppose that it would be another sin for me to not admit to you that there have been times when I've wanted to kill. I've felt the urge a few times in my life, but I've never acted on it. I'm not violent."

"Of course," Miller said as he wrote.

Miller wrote in his pad as I sat there on my cot and waited. Talking to Robert Miller was the first time I'd felt like a man, not an animal, since they put me in this pen.

"Mr. Plowman," Miller said, "is it okay if I call you Jack?"

"Sure, as long as I can call you Robert."

"You can call me Rob. I like Rob better."

"Okay, Rob it is," I said to him and we both smiled.

"Jack, I think you need to go to the hospital," my new friend said to me.

26

I didn't want to be angry at him. Rob Miller was a gentle man that was just doing his job. He'd treated me with compassion, unlike everyone else inside this Godless pit. It wasn't his fault. But I still felt the burn of anger in my stomach. Those words struck a rawness in me. They were like a kick in the nuts.

"What do you mean?" I said to him through the bars, trying my best to maintain my composure. "Are you saying you think I'm crazy?"

He looked at me gently but for the first time I thought I sensed a bit of condescension.

"Listen, Jack," he said slowly, "I've read your chart. I know your history. When you're put under stress, you tend to become religiously preoccupied. It's happened before. I don't know what happened with your roommate or how you're involved but what I do know is that you were involved with something very traumatic. Even the most stable and resilient person would have been deeply affected. You've been deeply affected, Jack, whether you know it or not. I think you need to be evaluated, and the hospital is the place to do that."

"You don't think I'm really hearing the Holy Spirit, do you?"

"I think that your recent religious experiences might be... amplified, shall we say, by your mental illness, but that's all I'm saying," Miller said sheepishly. "I don't pretend to understand the Holy Spirit. They didn't teach me about that in social work school." He thought he'd

179

told a funny joke.

"I'm not crazy, Rob."

"Never said you were, Jack. What I said was that you needed to go to the hospital. I didn't say anything about being crazy."

"But that's what you meant. You say mental illness but I hear, 'He's batshit crazy.'"

I could tell that his patience was starting to wear thin. Now it was his turn to force himself to remain composed.

"Listen, Jack. I could send someone else, like your case manager Tiffini, to come in and screen you but I can guarantee you that they'd say the same thing. You need immediate treatment, Jack. That's very clear."

I knew he was right, not about the treatment part but about the second opinion. I'd been in this situation before. Once in Ohio and once here in Michigan. There was no way around it, no talking them out of it. I was going back to the hospital whether I liked it or not.

"I'd like you to sign a voluntary admission form. That will make it easier for both of us. I don't want the hassle of petitioning you against your will and you don't want to come out of the hospital on a court order, am I right?"

"Yeah, I suppose." He'd defeated me already.

"So you'll sign?" he asked me.

"I'm going in one way or the other, right?"

"That's the sad truth, my friend." He really did seem disappointed for me.

"All right. I'll sign. When do I go?"

Rob seemed relieved that he wasn't going to have to petition me. I'd saved him from more paperwork.

"I'll talk to the deputies," he said, "and we'll work out the transportation. They'll probably want to take you over themselves, as you still have a pending charge. You'll also have to talk to Detective Robinson."

"Detective Robinson?"

"He's the detective that's investigating your roommate's murder."

I sat in silence as the social worker finished writing his report. When he passed the voluntary admission form through the bars I signed it.

"I really do wish you well, Jack," he said to me as he took back the form.

"Yeah, thanks."

After Miller left I was left alone in my cell to ponder what came next. On one hand, I always dreaded going to the hospital. They'd just label and drug me there.

On the other hand, the hospital would be a lot nicer than the jail. Mental hospitals are no Grand Plaza Hotel, but the One-Flew-Over-the-Cuckoo's-Nest picture that most people have of them isn't true either. The ones that I'd been in had all been reasonably clean and the food wasn't even that bad. They gave you a fair amount of free time to socialize with the other patients too. They thought it was therapeutic.

Plus, there was always a big screen television.

Just then a new deputy walked down to the end of the hall and made sure that I hadn't found some creative method to off myself and then walked back to his station.

He made two more trips before I heard three men coming down the hallway, their distinctive footfalls clopping on the floor. When they reached my cell, I saw that two of them were brown shirted deputies, but different ones than the ones that had been watching me, and the other was an older man in a rumpled shirt and black polyester pants. The old man had a bulbous nose and was rather obese. One of the brown shirts used a key to open up my cell but it was the older fat man that spoke.

"We're taking you to Pine Rest, Mr. Plowman. I'm Detective Robinson. I need to talk to you on the way."

Nothing more was said. One of the deputies handcuffed me and then I was wordlessly marched down the long hallway to a corridor that I hadn't been able to see from my isolation cell. We turned down this hallway and were buzzed through a door by a deputy behind a thick window, and we were suddenly outside.

The sun was hot on my skin. It felt good after being stuck inside for a day. The deputies had an idling squad car waiting for them at the curb. They opened the door while the detective helped me into the back seat. Once I was in, the detective got in the back of the cruiser with me and shut the door.

No one said anything until we'd left the jail grounds, but as soon as we passed the gate, like magic, the detective started talking.

"Okay, Plowman," he said, still looking forward, "tell me why you were running. What were you trying to hide?"

"Nothing," I said to him.

When I turned to look at him I couldn't help but stare at his prominent red nose. He had what they called a gin blossom nose, like some of the drunks down at the mission. "I didn't do anything wrong, detective. I found Johnny when I came back to my apartment from the doctor. His neck had been slit and he was already dead. I got scared and thought that you guys would try and pin it on me because I'm mentally ill, and so I ran."

"I see," he said, still looking forward. "Did it ever cross your mind that running from the police would just make you look more guilty than you already looked?"

"The thought did cross my mind."

"And yet you still ran," he said stoically. "That sounds crazy to me."

"Guilty as charged."

I tried to make a joke but it fell flat with Detective Robinson. He didn't react at all.

"Why did you visit Johnny's father?" he asked.

"I was trying to solve the murder and clear my name. I figured that if I discovered who really did kill Johnny, then you wouldn't suspect me anymore. I know you think I'm just crazy, but once I started to investigate, the Holy Spirit spoke to me and commanded me to find Johnny's killer. You see, I have to find the real killer before I assume my role as high prophet. Christ himself called me,

detective. He's in East Grand Rapids. Isn't that
funny?"

Robinson didn't seem to see the humor in
that either.

"You can drop the crazy act, Plowman. You
got what you wanted."

"What do you mean?"

"Don't play dumb with me," he said, turning
his stern fat face to look at me at last. "I've been on
the force long enough to know the crazy act.
You're going to make a go at the 'not guilty by
reason of insanity' defense. I've seen it before. It
hardly ever works, you know."

"Detective, I'm not trying…"

"It works," he continued, "less than one
percent of the time. You ought to know that before
you start plotting with your cheap lawyer. It's a
losing strategy. It won't work, Plowman. I'll make
sure of that."

I didn't say anything for a moment in case
he wasn't finished. I didn't want to make him
angrier than he already was. When I was sure he'd
had his say, I looked him in the eyes and said, "I'm
not playing games with you, sir."

He held my gaze. His eyes looked deep into
mine.

"If you didn't kill him, who did?"

"I don't know that yet. I was just getting
started when I got picked up. I think I'm starting to
put together the puzzle though. Johnny was
involved with some pretty dangerous people. This
guy I'd never met before came and tried to kill me
at church. He's got to be involved. Johnny took

drugs. Did you know that? And he was a homosexual too."

Robinson didn't seem impressed with my investigating skills.

"I know all of that, Plowman. Is that all you got? Maybe you should leave the police work to the professionals and focus on whatever it is that you do. This isn't some movie or a video game, you know. This is serious. People that try to play junior detective can get into a lot of trouble."

"I was just trying to clear my name and follow God's will."

"If that was your goal, you failed miserably," he said, looking forward again.

I thought about telling him about Missy Chen or Johnny's talk about making a lot of money but decided against it. When all was said and done, Robinson was right. All my detective work hadn't done any good. I'd just made myself look more guilty and in spite of everything I'd done, here I was, getting a ride to the mental hospital, just like all the times before.

Robinson didn't say much else. He seemed to have grown tired of me. He was an old veteran cop that had heard people tell the story that I was telling, or variations of it, a hundred times and he didn't want to hear it again. I wasn't a person to him anymore, just another example of a particular category of scumbag. The Insanity Defense Scumbag.

We got to the Pine Rest campus a few minutes later. Pine Rest was out on the edge of town, in Cutlerville. The campus was aptly named.

Tall pine trees covered the entire property, obscuring most of the buildings from the road. If I hadn't known better, I would've thought they were taking me to some nice private college instead of the loony bin.

The car drove deeper and deeper into the campus. We passed building after building, each with its own little parking lot. I saw a few professional looking people out walking the paths but I didn't see anyone outside that looked like a patient.

Eventually, we came to the end of the road. There was a modern brick building sitting where the road ended and two large men in scrubs were waiting in front of it. My escorts. One of the men looked oddly familiar to me. He was big and brutish and had a black eye. As we got closer to him, it became clear. I felt the prickly fuzz of panic come over my skin.

One of the men was Bruce Daniels, the man who'd attacked Fr. Chris and I at the church.

27

Bruce smiled at me as the car stopped and one of the deputies got out to open my door. This was the hospital that he worked for. He must have known that I was coming. He'd been waiting for me.

get away!

I knew that I had to do something, and fast. I tried to distance myself from the panic that was growing within me. I started sweating and my heart began to pound like a hammer in my chest.

"Detective," I said as the deputy opened the door. "Could we talk some more privately? There are some other things that I need to tell you about Johnny. I have other information that you might not have."

He tried to hide his puzzlement, but his eyes gave it away. He hadn't expected this.

"What?" he said. "You suddenly don't want to go to the nut house?"

"No, it's not that; I just remembered some more things you should know."

"Like what?" he asked.

The deputy stood guard at the car's open door. Bruce and his friend were a few steps back waiting.

"I was attacked," I said, making eye contact with Bruce. "That man over there tried to kill me and my friend at church. He's involved with Johnny's murder. You have to arrest him."

Robinson smiled.

He nodded his head slightly and I felt the deputies grab my shirt and pull me violently out of the car.

"No!" I screamed. "You can't give me to that man! He'll kill me!" I started to struggle against the officer but he was much stronger than me. He had me in a bear hold before I could even get my footing. He flipped me with one quick movement and I found myself being carried fireman style towards the door. I screamed as loud as I could and kicked him. My kicks landed but he didn't deviate from his path.

"Help me, God!" I yelled.

Robinson had gotten out of the car himself and he and the other deputy grabbed my feet so I couldn't kick. I tried to lash out with my arms but Bruce and his friends grabbed them. I could feel Bruce dig his fingernails into my skin and I roared in pain.

My screaming brought a crowd of assistants whose job it must have been to help with people like me. They carried me into a room just inside the front door. A woman barked an order, and I was pinned on the ground face up. A flood of faces looked down at me. I kept screaming but my shouts seemed to be absorbed into the walls. Someone stabilized my arm and I felt the prick of a needle. It moved around under my skin releasing a cold liquid.

Stunned, I felt the icy liquid spread up my arm. It felt like the injection was turning my arm into frozen steel. My head began to swim and the room started to spin, the faces above me smearing into one another. All my senses twisted, then started to slowly dim. I was still screaming but I couldn't hear it.

Then I blacked out.

I woke up strapped to a bed and feeling the hangover from whatever medication they'd given me. I'm not sure how much time had passed, but based on the blazing sun outside my window, it must have been the next day about noon. As my eyes adjusted to being open, the view from my window started to come into focus. My window looked out onto a garden that, as it sharpened, surprised me with its beauty. Blooms of all shapes and sizes formed a ring of color right next to the building. All the rooms, on all four sides, seemed to look out onto this green space. It was like an oasis in the harsh desert of the hospital. Outside the ring of flowers, a green plain of perfect grass extended to the center where a fountain threw water into the air. The fountain was surrounded by a deep circle of daffodils, their yellow blooms full in the sun. A floral bullseye with the flying water as its center. The grass must have recently been cut, because I could smell its wet scent.

It was quite a sight, not something you usually see in a mental hospital.

I must have gotten lost in it, because I didn't hear the man walk up beside my bed.

"No way in there," he said.

I turned to find the source of the rich baritone of that voice. It was deep yet gentle. He was an older black man, probably in his late fifties, with sparse graying hair. He was thin and dressed in a gray sweatshirt and sweat pants. It was hard to believe that such a big voice came out of such a small man.

"It's a beauty to behold, all right," he continued, "but ain't no patient ever been in there. Not once. Staff don't even get to go in there. Only people go in are the gardeners, and they just go in to tend to it. They got an iron bench over there," he said, pointing to the opposite side of the garden, "but ain't no one allowed to sit on it."

"That's how the world works," he said with a sigh.

"I'm Jack Plowman," I said, introducing myself. "Forgive me if I don't shake your hand."

He looked down at my securely strapped hands and gave a little laugh.

"I'm Walt," he said, "Walter Westmoreland. I'm your roommate."

I turned my head to the left and saw that our room was divided by a green floor-to-ceiling curtain. Walt had pushed it open a little ways to come and visit. I had the garden view, and Walt was closest to the door. I figured that I had the better part of that deal. Walt moved to sit on a chair at the foot of my bed. He moved slowly, shuffling across the tiled floor. He looked out at the courtyard with me.

"How long have I been unconscious?" I asked him.

"I don't really know. They brought you in here last night. This is the first that I've heard you move. They must have given you some major drugs. I started to worry that you was dead."

"They must have. My head's still a little fuzzy

even now. My admission didn't go that well."

"I guess not," Walt said, shaking his head. "You know, I've been here going on a week now, and you're the first roommate they've put in here with me."

"Sorry to crowd your space, Walt."

"Not at all," he said. "I'm glad to have the company. I was getting pretty tired of being alone after the treatment day was done. One of the reasons I ended up here was that I was so damn lonely, and what do they end up doing but locking me up all by myself so I can sit and stew. How's that gonna help me? Don't make any sense, if you ask me."

"You got a point there."

"Yep, I say I do. Some of the stuff they do in the name of treatment here is more crazy than any of us are. Lots of stuff that does more harm than good. But I know they mean well, they really do. All the doctors and the therapists and the nurses, deep down, they real nice, kind people. Sometimes they even kind to me. But I think seeing all the pain they see make a lot of 'em act different."

"Yeah, I've seen that too," I said. "They're afraid of what they see in us; they're afraid it'll happen to them. Those people can be really cruel."

"You're right about that, man. One time I was in the state hospital down in Kalamazoo, and the doctor there…"

Walt was interrupted by a familiar female voice.

"Hello, Jack. I'm glad you've finally woken up. I've been waiting to talk to you."

Tiffini was lovely as ever, her long hair a little lighter than the last time I had seen her. It must have been from all the artificial sun she was getting. By the looks of her fake tan, she must have gone to the tanner at least three times a week. Next to Tiffini was a man I didn't know, wearing a suit.

"Hi, Tiffini," I said to her. "What's going on?"

"Nothing compared with what you've been up to." She looked at Walt.

"Can you give us some privacy?"

"Sure," he said and shuffled out of the room and into the hallway.

"Hello, Ken," he said to the man with Tiffini as he left the room.

"Jack," Tiffini said, as she and the man moved into the area by my bed and the man closed the door. "This is Ken Albany. He's my supervisor at Community Mental Health."

The man stepped forward and went to shake my hand, then realized that I was strapped down and just nodded at me.

"Nice to meet you, Jack. I'm Dr. Albany," he said. His cologne was so strong, I could smell it from my bed.

"We came by to see how you were doing, buddy," Tiffini said, smiling at me.

"I'd be doing a heck of a lot better if I wasn't strapped to this bed."

"Oh," Tiffini fumbled, "I don't know if…"

"I'll go talk to the doctor and see if we can get Jack out of that bed," Dr. Albany said and winked at me as he walked out into the hallway.

"So what's going on, Jack?"

It was a stupid question. She knew very well what was going on. Her cutesy "ain't we great pals" routine always drove me crazy. We were not pals now and never had been.

"Well, Tiffini. I have obviously gotten myself into a whole heap of trouble, haven't I? They think I'm the one that killed Johnny when all I was really trying to do was follow the Lord's wishes for me. I was trying to bring justice to the killer and I wound up in the nut bin. Just like Jesus. Jesus comes and tries to save souls and they slaughter him. Compared to Jesus, I guess I'm lucky, huh."

"You poor man," she said to me. "I can see that your religious preoccupation has intensified. That really stinks, doesn't it?"

"Tiffini," I said, trying to be patient with her. "I don't know why you continue to think my devotion to God is a sickness. Have you ever stopped to consider that maybe you're the one that's sick? You can't see God anywhere."

It was the truth, she really couldn't. She wouldn't recognize the Lord if he'd come down from heaven in a flaming chariot and landed on top of her fancy little sports car.

"Jack, we've been through this. Religious preoccupation is part of your illness."

she's a demon

"With all due respect to you in your lofty position as my social worker, I think you're the one that's sick here. Not me. I read a while back that new studies say humans are hardwired to seek God.

Yet you mock me for seeking God because you don't think He exists. Based on these studies, Tiffini, maybe you need an MRI to see why your brain isn't working right. If you get tested, maybe we could get a diagnosis and then treat you. Maybe psychosurgery would fix you up and after it's done I'd be happy to be your spiritual social worker."

I knew that all this poking would frustrate her but that was exactly what I wanted.

"Jack, we've been down this road, I don't know how many times before, but I'll say it again. My personal beliefs about God have nothing to do with helping you manage your mental illness. In order for you to manage your mental illness, you have to recognize when you are decompensating. You decompensate with all this religious stuff. You think you hear the voice of God, but it's really just a hallucination."

"Then we agree to disagree," I said to her.

"Whatever."

Silence descended on the room like the Holy Spirit on Pentecost. Tiffini tried to talk to me but I wouldn't say a word to her. I kept a holy silence.

28

I perked up when Dr. Albany came back with an orderly to unstrap me.

The orderly unbuckled the leather straps around my chest, arms and legs and then stood back. I felt like a butterfly coming out of its cocoon. I moved my arms around and then started to sit up.

"You better take it easy for a little bit," the orderly said. "When you haven't moved in a while your muscles get a little loose."

"Loose?" I asked. It sounded bad.

"Just take it slow and don't try to walk for at least a half an hour," he said as he walked back to the hallway.

"Well, Tiffini," Dr. Albany commented, "it looks like we have a captive audience for a while."

He was trying to be funny, but I was in no mood for jokes that were even remotely at my expense. I thought about telling Tiffini about how Bruce Daniels had attacked me. It was a crazy story but Fr. Chris had witnessed it and could back up what I said. Of course, he'd back me up if they contacted him, which they probably wouldn't. I was crazy. Everything I said would be considered suspect. I decided to keep my mouth shut about Bruce and pray that he didn't show up on the unit.

Besides, he wouldn't dare to do anything to me while I was a patient here.

"So, Jack," Dr. Albany started, "I know that it might be hard to talk about, but Tiffini and I would really like to chat about what happened with Johnny. I'm sure you're aware that he was also one of our consumers. We want to make sure that treatment issues surrounding his mental illness didn't play a role in his untimely passing."

"You mean, you don't want to get sued."

Albany didn't miss a beat. "No, of course we don't want to get sued. But our first concern is the well-being of our patients. I know you did some sleuthing. Did you uncover anything that leads you to think his death was related to his mental illness?"

"No."

"That's good to hear," he said.

Tiffini had sat down in a chair by the window that looked out onto the garden. She was getting lost in its beauty just like I had. My conversation with Albany was just background noise to her. She knew this was above her pay grade.

"I'm going to ask Tiffini to document that this is your opinion in her progress notes."

Tiffini looked over to us and nodded.

"That's fine by me," I said.

"Good, good. I'm glad that you agree."

"Is that it?" I asked him.

"I suppose it is. My understanding from the police is that you were questioned by them already. Did you mention to them that you felt Johnny's mental illness was not related to his death?"

"I can't remember if I mentioned that or not. I just told them the truth. About how I found him dead and was inspired by the Holy Spirit to find his killer."

Dr. Albany nodded. "So what did you learn about Johnny's killer in all your sleuthing?"

It seemed like an odd question to ask. Why did Albany care what I'd learned as long as his ass was not in the frying pan. I was beginning to not like this guy at all.

"I didn't really learn anything, Dr. Albany."

"I see," he said, nodding his head. "Well, I think you should probably leave the detective work to the police from now on. They're the professionals, you know."

"That's what they tell me."

He laughed politely.

"If you wouldn't mind," Dr. Albany added, "could you mention to the police the next time you talk to them that you don't feel Johnny's mental illness or C.M.H. played a role in his death?"

"Sure."

"Okay, terrific. That's all that I have for now. Would you like to have some more private time with Tiffini?"

It was Tiffini that answered that question for me.

"I think we've made as much progress as we're going to make today," she said.

"Fine. I'm going to ask Tiffini to come and see you each day while you're in the hospital, Jack. I want her to keep a close eye on you during this difficult time. For your safety, of course. If you need anything, please feel free to call me anytime."

He took out his card and handed it to me. I put it on the nightstand without even looking at it. Dr. Albany shook my hand and then got up to leave. He had to clear his throat to snap Tiffini out of her garden-induced reverie. As they reached the threshold of my door, I heard Tiffini say to Albany, "I don't think there's any way into that beautiful garden."

Walt came back to our room a few minutes after Tiffini and Dr. Albany left. I'd just taken my first shaky step away from my bed. The orderly was right. My muscles felt weak and loose like the Jello that passed for dessert in places like this. I felt like a baby taking his first steps.

"How'd your meeting go?" he asked me.

"Fine, I guess. Dr. Albany was just trying to make sure that Community Mental Health doesn't get sued. He sounds more like a businessman than a psychiatrist."

"He ain't no psychiatrist, Jack."

"What do you mean?"

"Ken Albany used to be my case manager not that long ago, until he got promoted to be a supervisor. He's just an arrogant prick, if you ask me, and he sure as hell ain't a real doctor. He's just working on a Ph.D. at some online school. He started to call himself Dr. Albany when he finished up his classes last year."

"Really?"

"Yeah. He has to write some book before he gets the real degree but that hasn't stopped him from calling himself 'doctor.'"

"I didn't like the guy at all."

"He's a piece of work, man. A real piece of work. He's always dressed fancy, like he was going to work at some bank or something, even when he was just a case manager. The guy has issues. Big time daddy issues, if you ask me. His dad's some bigwig businessman with all kinds of money. When Ken was my case manager, he used to talk about how he was going to start his own clinic someday and be real successful and famous. He was always trying to act bigger than he is."

"I could see that," I said. "Being a case manager isn't the most prestigious job in the world."

"It's better than being the mental patient, Jack."

I laughed. "That's the truth."

"So tell me, Jack," Walt said seriously. "How'd you end up in here? You know, there was a big commotion when you got admitted. Lots of staff running around. You were the talk of the unit, coming in all strapped down and shit."

"Not the best way to make an entrance, huh?"

"Well, you certainly made an impression. People been saying some pretty wild things about you, man."

"Like what?" I asked him.

"Well," he mumbled. I could tell that he was afraid to say.

"You can tell me, Walt. It's okay."

"It's just... some people say you mixed up in some deep shit."

"I'd be lying if I said I wasn't."

It was the God's honest truth. I tried to take a few steps over to Walt's side of the room, but my legs were so shaky that I had to lean on the bed.

"Some people say you killed a man," he said

somberly.

I glanced out to the garden. The birds were still frolicking in the water. They sprayed the daffodils with beads of spray. They were free.

"I did not kill anyone," I told him. "No matter what anyone says, Walt. I didn't do it. I swear to God."

"I believe you," he said.

The silence that fell between us was a holy one. I'd just met Walt but I felt a special kind of kinship to him. To this day, I still don't understand it. Maybe it was the stress of the situation and my need to have someone to confide in. Things weren't looking that good for me and Walt's companionship meant a great deal to me then. It still does.

"Mary asked me to tell you she wants you to come and see her," he said, ending the silence.

"Who's Mary?"

"Mary's one of the social workers for the unit. You'll like her. She's nice. Her office is down the hall to the left. You'll see her name on the door."

"Do I go right now?"

"I guess."

I stuck out my hand to Walt and he shook it. I looked him in the eye and he nodded. I did too and then we both laughed.

29

The name plate on the door said, "Mary S. Winslow, ACSW." I tried the door and it was locked, so I tapped lighted on the dark wood of the door. I heard her chair move across the carpet and then the door opened.

"Hi," she said, still sitting in her chair, "you must be Jack Plowman. Sorry I couldn't get down to talk to you when Tiffini and Ken were here but I had a client that was being discharged. I never miss a discharge. The last words I say to a client are sometimes the only ones they remember."

Mary was in her fifties, with a kind face and a welcoming smile. She was a little heavy and was wearing a flowing animal print dress that hid her middle age paunch. Her office was small and didn't even have a window; it was just her desk and two chairs, one for the patient and one for her.

Mary motioned for me to sit down as she rolled back to her desk. She moved one chart from the top of her desk and brought out one from a drawer. I saw my name on it.

"So, Jack," she began, "can I call you Jack?"

"Sure. What do I call you?"

"I like Madam Social Worker, but Mary will do just fine." She glanced down at a page in my chart. "It seems that you come to us from the jail. Being held for disturbing the peace and…" she paused to read something. "And it looks like you are wanted for questioning in regard to a murder."

Mary looked concerned; I started to explain, not wanting her to get the idea that I'd really killed

Johnny but she just kept on reading, nonplussed.

"You've been with Tiffini for less than a year and you see Dr. Patel at Community Mental Health. They had to sedate you to get you in the door, I see. You're 25, single and you've got no children. You've been inpatient before but never here." She looked up at me again. "Does all that sound right to you?"

It was just another day at the office for her. I wondered how many cases like mine she'd seen before. Did she have a category in her head for people like me?

"Yes, all that sounds right," I said.

"Good. I hate to find errors in records."

She put the chart down on her desk and looked at me kindly, like she was my mother.

"Jack, we're going to work together to try and get you well. What do you think you need?"

"I don't know," I said. I was still a little groggy from the shot they'd given me and my mind wasn't as sharp as it usually was.

"Well, let me make a suggestion," she said. "I'm not sure if you're aware of it or not, but you have some pretty serious legal issues."

"Yeah," I said, "I know."

"There's a detective named Robinson that wants a daily progress report on you." She turned to her desk and handed me a piece of paper.

"This is a release on information. It gives me permission to communicate with the detective about you. Now, I don't like this anymore than you do. I hate to see anyone interfering with my patient's recovery. But Robinson was very clear to me that he would make sure you were discharged immediately and sent back to jail if you refused to sign this…"

"That's fine. I don't have anything to hide."

"I'm glad to hear that." Mary shot me a little grin. "But you need to know that I'm going to have to divulge to him what we talk about during our sessions. I hate to start a therapeutic relationship like this but in this case, I don't see any other option. Jack, you have my word that I won't tell him anything he doesn't need to know, but he seemed very interested in you."

I took the form and signed it. I didn't care what Robinson knew about my treatment. If anything, it would help me prove that I wasn't guilty. When I was done, Mary took the form and put it in my file. I wondered if Robinson would call her for a report today.

"So, Jack," Mary continued, "do you have a lawyer yet?"

I hadn't made that call yet. I'd been dreading it. When they offered me my phone call at the jail, I'd turned it down. Sure, I knew exactly who I *should* have called, but it was the one person that I wanted to call the least.

My twin brother, Jake, the lawyer.

Jake had pulled me out of countless messes before when I was following the voices all over the Midwest, leaving a trail of wrecked cars and angry women behind me. Back when I first got sick, the voices that I heard told me to drive my car all night and to have sex with any woman that would have me.

Fortunately, I failed at that like I've failed at most everything else I've done in my life.

Jake was there for me the entire time. Getting me out of jail countless times, even when he was in law school. He must have tried his professor's patience with his requests for them to help me. Although I knew I'd probably be in prison without him, I'd grown to resent his help. I said terrible things to him and tried to push him away, but it never worked.

He was the good twin, and I was the evil one. And the good guys just never give up trying to save the bad ones.

Fortunately, for the last year or so, I hadn't needed his help. Jake and I were starting to develop a normal relationship, like we were equals. I even went over to his house for dinner sometimes. We watched the Lions getting massacred on Sundays.

But now there was this.

I knew I had to call him, probably should have called him as soon as all this had started. But I hadn't and now I was in very serious trouble and needed Jake like never before. I'd been charged with a lot of petty crimes before, but never murder.

"I've got someone I can call, but..."

I thought about what to say next.

"Then maybe," she said, "you should call him."

There was no putting it off anymore. I'd waited as long as I could.

"Can I use your phone, Mary?"

After I left a message for my brother at his firm, Mary had given me my treatment schedule. They kept the patients busy with individual therapy, group therapy, art therapy, and psychiatric appointments. Apparently they thought idle time was not good for the soul. Mary told me that I would start treatment in earnest tomorrow, but she wanted me to have a little time to adjust to the unit before throwing me into it full on.

I decided to take a walk around the unit. I went more out of curiosity than to get a feel for my new temporary home. I'd been in a number of different hospitals and I liked to compare the units. Some were dumps and others were almost like the dorms back in Ann Arbor. As I walked out of my room and down the empty corridor, it became clear to me that this unit was one of the nicer ones I'd been to. The halls were carpeted with a nice speckled blue design. There wasn't a stain in sight. All the walls were white and clean. They were cinder block, a wise choice. I'd been on units that had drywall and those walls were filled with massive gashes that looked like a bomb had gone off in the wall. Seeing those holes always scared me. They implied a kind of chaos that was dangerous in a cage like this.

I saw a few staff members walking around. They were clean and all dressed in matching blue scrubs. They didn't seem angry. That was another good sign.

I was stopped by a large metal door when I came to the end of the hall. There was no point in even trying to open it. It would be locked. There was a small window in the door that I had to stand up on my tippy toes to look through. On the other side was the geriatric unit.

A few old men were shuffling down the hallway in their thin hospital gowns. One of the men was so pale and gaunt that he looked like he might drop dead at any minute. He was looking at me, but I knew he wasn't really seeing me. He was mouthing something under his breath as he walked. His eyes were glazed over from all the drugs. He walked up to a dry erase board that announced the date, the weather and what season it was. There was a plastic Easter bunny cling at the top of the board. The man looked at the board for a second, nodded, and then turned around and walked back the way he came. His gown wasn't tied in back so his backside was exposed as he walked away from me and I could see the shit that was smeared down his right leg in long streaks.

I turned away, disgusted, and started to walk back to my room.

The rooms were very nice compared to some of the other places I'd been. They even had cable, something I didn't have at home. I watched it for about 10 minutes until I heard Walt come in.

While I turned the TV off as soon as he walked in the room, Walt didn't talk to me at first. He just sat down on his bed and stared at the wall. Something in therapy must have upset him.

"Hey, Walt," I said.

"Hi, Jack."

"You doing okay, man? You seem upset."

He was fighting the urge to cry. His brown face still glistened with a wet trail of tears cried a short time ago. The lines wound down his face and then disappeared under his chin.

I wanted to say something. Something that would make him feel better.

"Walt," I said, "whatever it is, no matter how bad, you've got to remember that God loves you."

It always made me feel better to hear that, but Walt didn't reply. He just continued to stare at the orderly white blocks of our wall. I thought about saying something else. Maybe I could remind him that Jesus also loved him. Maybe I could tell him about the lake and how Jesus was living there, planning to come back and finally make everything right with the world. Maybe Jesus had a job for Walt too.

"Walt, Jesus is coming back very soon. He's been living in…"

"I want to die, Jack."

His words stopped me in mid-sentence. Walt was one of *those* people, one of the suicidally depressed that flooded units like this.

I knew a lot of depressed people. Heck, I was depressed myself much of the time. But my depression was never like the depression that people like Walt had. I'd never tried to kill myself. I didn't have a plan or stockpile my pills. I knew people that did both those things. Those people thought about suicide all the time and actually tried to do it. Sometimes they really messed themselves up. Back in Ohio, I'd met a man that had tried to kill himself by driving his car into a tree. He lived, but was paralyzed in the process. Of course, when he was medically stable, they brought him to the psych unit and made him do therapy with us. I went to groups with him for a week, but he never said a word. Not one word.

I didn't know Walt's story. Some of the suicidal people I'd known had always been depressed. They couldn't remember a time in their whole lives when they'd been happy. Some other people had been pretty happy most of their lives and then something bad happened to them, a death of a loved one or an addiction, and they fell into a darkness that had never lifted. Those people scared the shit out of me. Anyone could end up as one of them after a bad trauma.

I looked over at Walt and fought for the right words.

"Man, we all feel like that sometimes," was what I finally said.

"You don't understand, Jack. For me, it's not just sometimes anymore."

He couldn't hold the tears back any longer; they started down the trails on his face one after the other.

"I wish I could just die and end it all. I can't bear the pain of this world anymore."

"God doesn't want you to die, Walt. If you're alive, he's still got something for you to do. Now, I don't know what you're supposed to be doing, but I know God speaks to us if we're willing to listen. Have you tried to listen, Walt? Before they put me in here, God gave me a vision and spoke to me. He'll speak to you, too, if you'll listen."

Walt nodded but still didn't look at me.

"Maybe it's just not time yet, Walt. God does things in his own time, not ours. Maybe you need to be patient. Be patient and wait on the Lord."

"I been waiting a long time," he said.

"I know. Believe me, I know. It ain't easy for people like you and me, Walt. No one sees us, we're like invisible men. It seems like no one sees our pain. People are cruel and selfish. But that's not the way God is, Walt. He cares."

I don't think he was convinced, and my words were certainly not as magical as I wish they'd been, but Walt did look at me then and smiled.

"Thanks for trying to help me, man."

"It's not working very well is it?"

"Nope," he managed a tiny laugh. "But like I said, thanks for trying. You're a good guy."

That was it. He laid down on the bed then and closed his eyes. Feeling tired myself, I did the same. Although it was still early, sleep descended on me almost immediately. I didn't realize how tired I still was. The drug-induced sleep that had been forced on me hadn't allowed me to get the kind of rest that I really needed.

Now it came, dropping like a black curtain over me. My sleep was deep and dream-filled. I dreamed of playing football with a group of friends I had from college and I dreamed of meeting Anna's parents. They were vivid dreams, but they were all pleasant and I was always happy in them. I was dreaming of walking around one of the quads back at college when suddenly everything started to fade. The blue sky darkened as if a massive rainstorm had appeared out of nowhere and then the next moment, it was night. Everything was black. I tried to speak but couldn't. I opened my mouth but nothing came out. I tried to breathe in but I couldn't get enough air into my lungs.

It started to feel less and less like a dream. I was floating up into that odd space between being awake and asleep. A part of me thought that it was all in my head, that my pleasant dreams had given way to a terrible nightmare. A nightmare where I was being held underwater in the middle of the night. Cold and alone. There was no Jesus in this lake, just the blackness of the grave. Panicking, I tried in vain to move my arms. Nothing. When I tried to move my feet, they failed me as well.

No, I was not dreaming. Someone was trying to suffocate me.

30

My lungs ached for air. I could feel them strain and beg for oxygen. My brain started to ease back into a final sleep.

I tried to fight it. I moved wildly. I screamed in silence. I moved and hit and kicked.

But nothing changed.

Still the darkness. No sounds. No light. I felt myself fall in slow motion. I just wanted to go back to sleep then. Nothing else mattered. I gave up for the last time.

I was dying.

But then I wasn't.

I heard something. Someone was crying out, pleading. The deep bass of his scream was pulling me back into the world of the living. The longer it went on, the more I woke up. I opened my eyes and saw the hospital room. Walt was standing next to my bed, gasping for air. He was wailing in his deep voice and his head was covered in blood.

I lifted myself up to help him. Everything was spinning, like I was drunk.

"I'm okay," I managed to say, my voice straining.

He looked at me, his eyes filled with panic. I could tell he was surprised that I was alive, not to mention able to talk. The gash on his head slowly dripped blood onto the bed sheet, making a splatter pattern like some Jackson Pollack painting.

He tried to speak, but couldn't get the words out of his mouth. Maybe it was shock. Whatever had happened must have been terrible. Waking to see your new friend being suffocated would have been hard for even the strongest person to deal with, and Walt was not in the best frame of mind back then.

Although I assumed his inability to speak was related to stress, it occurred to me that his inability to talk might actually be related to a physical injury. Based on the blood, he must have taken a heavy blow to the head. Was his brain damaged? Did he need medical attention?

I tried to shake off the dizziness and stepped out of bed. I heard commotion in the hallway. The door to our room was open and I could hear the frantic steps of someone coming towards us. Worried about the blood loss, I took the pillow case off my hospital pillow and, walking drunkenly to him, pressed the pillowcase against Walt's wound.

I'd never seen a wound quite like what I saw on Walt's head. Just above his temple was a cut like a crevasse, red and gaping. I didn't want to look at it. Within a couple of seconds, the blood was seeping through the thin fabric of the pillow case. It was warm and moist on my hand. I fought the urge to throw up and kept my hand in place.

"You're going to be okay, man," I said to him.

Just then Walt's eyes started to close.

"Somebody help us!" I screamed with all the voice I could muster.

Just then, as if they had been waiting for me to call, three orderlies came rushing into the room. The shock on their faces stopped them in their tracks. All three of them just stood there, shocked by the blood and the severity of Walt's injury.

"Help," I pleaded.

My voice shook one of them out of their shock and she rushed to Walt's side.

"Sir," she said with medical authority that I didn't expect, "can you hear me?"

Walt was silent.

"Code Red," she barked at the other two, who ran out of the room and down the hallway in opposite directions.

The woman took the pillowcase off of Walt's head and examined the gash. Without missing a beat, she reached for my pillow and then used it to try and stop the bleeding. I saw something flicker out of the corner of my eye and turned my head to see a red light flashing on the wall. It covered the room in intermittent red flashes that were so much like the ones cast by the police car that, for a minute, I seriously considered whether this was all some vivid hallucination.

The reality of the situation was reinforced when a full medical team with a rolling bed ran into the room and proceeded to treat Walt. I moved back and sat down with my back against the wall.

The group moved Walt onto the bed and the doctor, a middle-aged man with thinning hair, said something very loud, and the group started to move en masse out of the room. They were like different parts of one body moving together and responding to each other like they shared a single mind. In a few minutes I was alone in my room, my bed awash in the bright blood that had been shed to protect me.

It had happened so fast. One minute, I'd

been dreaming and the next I was being suffocated. How could that happen? I was in a hospital. I was here to be protected. I was here so that nothing bad would happen to me; so was Walt. But I knew who must be behind this.

Bruce Daniels.

He worked here and had given me a good beating at admission. He was also the one who'd tried to beat the daylights out of Fr. Chris and I back at the church. He had to be Johnny's killer, or at least the trigger man. Why else would he try to kill me, not once, but twice? The fact that he worked here made me think there was a mental health connection. If Daniels was the killer, maybe he'd known Johnny from when he was a patient here.

At that moment, I had a thought that I'd never had before. It was this: maybe getting sent to the loony bin was the best thing that could have happened to me.

I was surprised that the police officer who came to talk to me seemed to believe my story. He questioned me for a few minutes about what I remembered, but never pressed me too hard.

I told the cop all about Bruce Daniels. I told him about how Daniels had showed up at the church and beat up me and Fr. Chris. I told him how he was an orderly at the hospital and had been rough with me when I was admitted. The cop, a young guy with a severe face and a buzz cut, just listened and nodded. I asked him if he knew Bruce but he just asked me another question about the attack. After a few minutes he left and I tried to sleep.

I tried for over an hour, tossing and turning, but for the life of me I couldn't get even a few minutes' sleep. I kept running over it again and again in my head. Was Bruce the killer and, if so, what was his motive? Were he and Johnny friends? Was he the one that was going to make the "big score" with Johnny? They didn't seem like the type of people that would become friends, one a gay manic-depressive and the other a big brute orderly. Plus, Bruce didn't strike me as the brightest guy in the world. He was all brawn and no brains. Johnny was no dummy, but there was no way that he was smart enough to pull off any sort of "big score." Something didn't add up.

When the sun started shining in the garden outside my window, I gave up on sleep. I sat up on the bed and watched the sun spray its golden light over the big circular beds of flowers outside my window. There were a lot of other windows that looked out into the garden but I couldn't see the people in the rooms because all the glass was reflective.

A woman came with breakfast and my pills about 7:30. An English muffin with jam and a tiny cup of orange juice along with a small cup containing three capsules of various sizes and colors. I didn't even ask, I just swallowed them with a swig of O.J.

I asked the woman about Walt and she told me that he'd been transferred to Spectrum Health downtown, but that his injuries weren't life threatening. I was so happy. I wouldn't have been able to contain my sorrow if something really bad had happened to him. The news came as such a great relief to me that I ate my muffin with gusto and even allowed myself to watch a little mindless television before treatment started at 8:15. My schedule said that I had group therapy in room 155 and I made my way down to the big room with about five minutes to spare.

31

After group, I was walking back to my room when Mary stopped me in the hallway.

"Your brother is here to see you, Jack."

My twin brother, Jake, was waiting for me in the conference room. His back was turned to me when I walked in but I could smell his cologne as soon as the door opened. It was a clean scent, and knowing Jake, very expensive.

When Jake and I were growing up, and we were too young to protest, our mom always dressed us in the same clothes and made sure that our barber, John, gave us identical haircuts. She loved the double fun of having twins. This was back when the Wrigley's Double Mint Twins were popular advertising and our mother bought into the craze. She even planned to take us to an audition for one of those commercials when we got older. Thank God that never happened. Jake and I were the little baby dolls that all the other mothers were jealous of, or at least Mom always thought so. The twin thing went on until we became teenagers and started to demand our own identities. I grew my hair long like Jon Bon Jovi and Jake went preppy. Mom was not happy.

Mom's twin mania compensated for Dad. He never had the same sense of excitement about us that Mom did. He just seemed frustrated with both of us. To this day, I'm not sure what it was about the two of us that exasperated him so much. As we were growing up, all he seemed to do was sigh whenever we were around. Jake and I talked about it a lot when we were teenagers and the best we could come up with was that we were too expensive. Dad had been an only child and had hoped to have just one child himself. He worked in factories all his life and in spite of his constant work, we never had much money. Everything we had went to Jake and I. It was either Jake's football helmet or my music lessons. Dad always said he didn't want any hobbies, but I figured out later that the truth of it was he just couldn't afford to have any.

But when I walked into the conference room that day, it was nothing like the Double Mint days. Jake looked nothing like me anymore. He was dressed in a suit like he wore every single day since the day he graduated from law school. That day's suit was a black double-breasted, tailored in a way to accentuate his runner's body. Thin and lithe, Jake had taken up running in law school and now ran 10 miles three times a week. His resting heart rate was half of mine and I had fifty pounds on him, easy. Jake kept losing weight and I kept gaining it. He ran marathons while I took anti-psychotic medications that made me fat and a borderline diabetic. Like I said, yin and yang.

Jake turned around in his chair and smiled. He had a new haircut since I saw him last. It was messy but in a very intentional and fashionable way. It actually looked a little like how my hair used to look when I was staying at the mission.

"Hi, Jack," he said, smiling.

"Jake."

"I can leave you alone," Mary said, "to talk

privately if you'd like."

"Thank you, Ms. Winslow," Jake said sweetly as Mary went to close the door behind her. "Thanks for watching out for my little brother."

Mary smiled her grandmotherly smile and left Jake and I sitting across the table from each other.

"Little brother? Really, Jake?"

"It's true."

"You're three minutes older than me, Jake"

"Which makes me your *older* brother, Jack."

"Maybe, but you don't have to make it sound like you taught me how to shave."

He sighed but then laughed under his breath.

"This is a real mess you've gotten yourself into, Jack. Even for you, this is pretty serious. You've never gotten caught up in a murder before."

For once, he was right. I'd had more than my fair share of legal troubles but it was always for minor things. I'd been caught panhandling in Ohio a few times and arrested for disturbing the peace, God knows how many times. I'd seen the inside of a jail before too, but it was never this serious. It was never felony serious. But this time was different, this time it was murder. Murder was about as serious as it came.

"Do I have to say it before we can move on?" I asked him.

"What do you mean? Say what?"

"Do you, my one and only brother, think so little of me that I have to say it out loud? Do I have to actually say that I didn't kill my roommate?"

I knew that a part of Jake resented my very existence. It was disturbing for him to know that there was an identical copy of himself that had turned out like me. Maybe he secretly worried that he'd end up just like me someday.

"No," he said, sounding tired. "In spite of all your issues, I don't think you're a murderer."

"Good," I said smugly.

"My plan is to get all the interested parties in the same room," he went on, "so we can have an open discussion about this. Why are you even a suspect in the first place?"

I explained how I'd found Johnny dead and had decided to try and solve the murder on my own rather than trust the police. Jake nodded as if he understood. Even though I tried to explain to him countless times, he couldn't understand how the legal system treated people like me. He couldn't understand that there were groups of people that almost never got a fair shake. He was a real idealist when it came to the law.

"So, you essentially ran from the police. That doesn't make you look like you have nothing to hide," he said when I was done.

"It was the right thing for me to do at the time," I said. I still believed that.

"Well, I suppose that we can't go back and change it anyway," Jake said as he scribbled a few notes on his legal pad and reviewed them before saying anything else. When he started talking again his tone was friendlier. It was the way he used to talk before he became a lawyer. "So are they treating you all right in here?"

"Fine," I said. "If you don't mind getting suffocated within an inch of your life during the night."

"What?" he said, not sure if I was exaggerating.

I told him about the events of the prior night and about how I was sure that Bruce Daniels was involved. Then I told Jake about what had happened at the church and how Bruce had given both me and Fr. Chris a beating.

"So," I told him, "this bastard Bruce Daniels has beaten two of my friends up. Fr. Chris and Walt. He's either the killer himself or he works for him."

"That may be, Jack. But my concern right now is making sure that we clear your name. Finding Johnny's killer will have to wait for another day."

"Doing justice should be our primary concern, Jake. It's even more important than what happens to me. God has put it upon me to bring his killer to justice. Everything else is of secondary importance."

Jake was a practical lawyer and he didn't understand my religious zeal. It was another thing that he didn't get about me. Jake went to his wife's Catholic church because it made him look good and a couple of the partners at his firm went there. He never missed a Sunday but I don't think he ever listened.

"Okay, Jack. I'll see what I can do about clearing you so that the police can focus on finding the person that really did this. Does that work for you?"

"Yes. When you put it that way, I'm totally on board."

Jake looked at his watch then and got up to

leave. He was young and ambitious. Pro Bono work didn't get you a partnership and I was nothing if not the Pro-est of the Bono.

"How's Lisa?" I asked him as put his notepad in his briefcase.

"Fine, I guess."

"You guess?"

"She's been spending a lot of time at the country club."

Country club? Jake was certainly a man that was going places, but he was months, not years, out of law school. He wasn't rich yet.

"You joined a country club?" I asked him incredulously.

"It's a long story. All of Lisa's friends are members and..."

"I get it, Jake. I get it."

Silence descended over us then. Lisa never liked me. I'd been praying that the marriage wouldn't go through up until the very last minute.

"Can you do one more thing for me, Mr. Power Lawyer?" I asked him.

"What's that?"

"Can you let Fr. Chris at St. Mark's Episcopal Church downtown know that I'm here. He's probably worried about me."

"Sure. I'll call him when I get back to the office."

Jake opened the door and waved at Mary, who was sitting reading a magazine in the hallway. She had the key to release him into the normal world.

As he shook my hand and walked out the door, I realized that, at the end of the day, I was blessed to have a brother like him.

     After Jake left, Mary took me to her office for an individual session. As we walked down the hallway, Mary went on and on about what a nice brother I had and how kind and handsome he was. About how lucky I was to have such a caring brother who was a lawyer to boot.

I didn't argue with her.

When we got to her office, Mary offered me some coffee, which I accepted. I always drank my coffee with a lot of sugar and I think Mary was a little taken aback when I emptied seven little packets of the stuff into my Styrofoam cup. Mary's office felt like a closet after being in the big conference room with Jake.

"How are you feeling, Jack?" Mary asked me as I threw the empty packets of sugar into the waste basket.

"Pretty good," I said. It was true. As much as I hated to admit it and in spite of the events of the night before, getting put in the hospital had already done me a world of good.

"I'm glad. We need to come up with some things you'd like to work on while you're here. I know there's a lot to talk about, but if it's okay with you, I'd like to start by talking about what happened last night."

"With Walt, you mean?"

"Yes. How are you doing handling what happened?"

Knowing Walt was going to be okay had helped me feel much better. I'd been so relieved that I hadn't thought much about it since last night.

"I'm glad that Walt is going to be okay," I told Mary. "Did anyone find Bruce Daniels yet?"

"Who's Bruce Daniels?" Mary asked.

I explained about the attack on Fr. Chris and I at the church and how I knew that Bruce worked here because he'd been waiting for me when I was admitted.

"I know the guy you're talking about," Mary said. "He's a big brute. Kind of distant. He's been here about six months but he's always been cordial to me. You're sure he's the one who attacked you and Walt last night?"

"I didn't see his face, but I don't see who else it could have been. Bruce is involved in Johnny's murder, and he's already tried to stop me from investigating. Apparently, he's so scared that he's decided to move beyond a good beating to trying to kill me outright."

"That's a serious accusation, Jack."

"Murder is a serious crime, Mary."

I could tell that my seriousness made her uneasy. The last thing she wanted to do was get caught up in something like this. Her world was safe, clean, and predictable, the opposite of the way my life had been since my first breakdown.

"Jack," Mary said, leaning forward, "we've got to keep in mind that you have a history of auditory hallucinations and, according to what Tiffini has told me, occasional visual hallucinations. Is it possible that you are mistaking your fears for reality? As far as I know, Bruce has never worked the overnight shift, and I'm sure someone would have seen him if he came onto the unit when he wasn't working."

Who else would have tried to suffocate me in the middle of the night if it hadn't been Bruce? Was there more going on here than I knew about?

"When's Walt coming back?" I asked her.

"No one has given me any specific time, but he should be readmitted here sometime today. It says in the chart," Mary wheeled over to her desk and picked up a green file, "it says here that once a nurse got a look at him, it was clear to her that the wound wasn't anything serious. Walt is just a bleeder. They wanted to keep him overnight at the hospital for observation. It would have looked a lot worse than it really was."

What it looked like was Walt dying right in front of me.

"Were you scared, Jack?"

"I've felt more guilt than anything else. Here's this guy I just met, he saves my life in the middle of the night and then gets the hell beat out of him for it. I didn't deserve what he did for me. It was so selfless. I mean, he barely knew me at all and he could have died saving me."

"Why don't you think that you deserved to be saved?"

"Same reason as the rest of your patients here, I guess," I explained to her. "I don't like myself very much. I haven't met many people with a mental illness who do like themselves very much. It's hard to feel good about yourself when you drop out of college to go into the psych ward."

"So you didn't have any symptoms until you went to college?"

"Naw. Everything was fine with me. I've met other head cases who are abused as children or are raised in some ghetto or trailer park with drugs or lived in foster home after foster home. That wasn't me. Those people at least know what the hell went wrong for them. What started it. Not me. My parents loved me and my brother, and there was no perverted uncle who put his hands down my pants when I was a kid."

"Current research," Mary said, moving from the caring mother to the professional effortlessly, "strongly suggests that much mental illness is caused by errors in our genetic makeup. It doesn't have to be caused by abuse or a distant mother. It's not your fault, Jack. You aren't to blame."

"See, this I don't get," I said to her, getting a bit angry, "I hear all this genetic error stuff spouted off by you people all the time. I know you're trying to make us feel better, and I appreciate that. You don't want us to believe that our emotional weakness or inability to deal with trauma is responsible for how messed up we are. That's fine. But do you really think that it helps to tell us that, at the level of our genes, we are riddled with 'errors'? What you're saying is that at my very core, I am nothing but a defect."

Mary nodded. "I'd never thought about it that way before. You make a very good and articulate point, Jack."

That was a compliment, something that I hadn't

heard directed to me in a long time.

"It's just how I feel, Mary."

"You feel like you're somehow broken at your core?"

"Yes, that's exactly it. Something happened to me my freshman year. A crack started inside me. It was really subtle at first, but then it started to spread until parts of my personality shattered and I didn't even notice. Do you know what it's like to be so sick that you don't even know that you're sick? When those pieces shattered, they shattered for good. I lost me, Mary."

"It must have been terrible."

"It was, and is, terrible. I feel like I'm not even the same person that I was before my first break. I used to be a college student full of potential, but now I'm a shell of a man. The old Jack is like a guy that I used to know."

"You don't like the Jack Plowman you are now?" she asked, giving me the empathic therapist gaze. I'd seen it many times before. They must train them to do it that way. They almost look like little kittens with eyes that are too big for their heads.

"If you're trying to make this about self-esteem, you're barking up the wrong tree, Mary."

"I never said that it was *only* about self-esteem," she said to me. "But I think that self-esteem is a part of what's going on with you. You seem to think that the man you are now has no value."

"I never said that," I challenged.

"Not in so many words you didn't, but you

certainly idealize your college self. Even if you'd never developed a mental illness, that young man you were talking about would still be gone by now. He would have grown up just like all people do. Hell, I wish I was as thin and full of life as I was back in college too, but I also grew up."

"I know what you're saying," I said. "But you've got a job and a family and a life. I don't have any of that. I can't keep a job, or a girlfriend. Not to mention being a total outcast and riddled with poverty. Now, to top it off, I'm wanted for murder."

"You're not wanted for murder, Jack."

"What do you mean?" I said, shocked.

"I've spoken to Detective Robinson. They want to question you some more, but you're not considered a suspect at this time. The police have checked out what you said about Bruce Daniels. They know that something else is going on here."

"I'm not a suspect *at this time*. I know how the cops think, Mary. Lord knows that I've had enough run-ins with them. They're just telling you what you want to hear. Trust me, they're not ruling me out. Mark my words, if nothing really breaks in this case, they'll end up pinning it on me, in spite of what Robinson told you. The cops want a happy ending, even if it's a lie."

"You're pretty cynical about the police, aren't you now?" she said to me a little testily.

"I've got my reasons. There's a lot of crooked cops out there."

"Maybe so, Jack. But if I were you, I'd take Detective Robinson at his word. I've known him for 15 years, and he is about as straight as they come. Besides, what you need to do now is try to get yourself healthy."

Mary knew Detective Robinson? That made me a little nervous. I knew all about patient-therapist confidentiality but I also knew that people love to talk about other people behind their back.

"I am feeling better," I told her. "I hate the hospital, but I have to admit that at least this time, it's done me a world of good."

"I'm glad to hear that."

I didn't say anything else and so Mary and I sat in silence for a while. It didn't bother me. Therapists let you sit quietly all you wanted with them. I'd learned that from Dr. Prinster at the University of Michigan. He was my first shrink, the guy that I saw after my first break. He was a soft and effeminate man, with out-of-style gold rimmed glasses and a tidy office. I was angry at being in the nut house and refused all of his attempts to engage me. I just sat there mute as he talked. On the third day, he asked how I was feeling and when, as usual, I didn't answer, he just let the question hang there for the rest of the hour. Total silence. When our time was done, he opened the door and I left. We had two more sessions like that before they discharged me.

Later on, I told another therapist about the experience and he told me that he did the same thing with patients sometimes. Instead of fighting the resistance, you just go with it. That could have been it, but I always thought the real reason was that Prinster was a lazy prick.

It was Mary who finally broke the silence between us.

"It's almost time for you to see Dr. Patel, Jack. Is there anything else you want to talk about before we finish?"

Apparently, Dr. Patel worked at this hospital too. It was like he was the only psychiatrist in Grand Rapids.

"No," I told her. "Thanks for listening to me, Mary."

"Well, it's what they pay me for."

32

Patel was waiting for me at the door of his
office. He wore a black suit, white shirt, and a
black tie. He looked like an undertaker.

"Well, Mr. Plowman. Nice to see you again,"
he said, his teeth a blazing unnatural white. "I
suppose that I do not need to ask how you are
doing, now do I?"

The wise Dr. Patel. He thought he had all the
answers, but he didn't. I mean, the man was a
pagan; he didn't even worship the true God. If
that's not the very definition of wrong-headed, I
don't know what is.

"Hello, Dr. Patel," I said.

I was surprised that his office was no different
than Mary's. There were no windows and the walls
were white painted cinder block. Like his C.M.H.
office, Patel had added little in way of decoration.
The only thing that he had on the walls was a print
of Seurat's "A Sunday Afternoon on the Island La
Grande Jatte." I doubt Patel had even picked it out.
The print and the ornate frame had "institutional
art" written all over it. Someone probably thought
the serenity of the scene would calm us nuts down.

I sat down in the shabby chair and Patel took
his appointed seat. His chair was rich leather,
cordovan like the penny loafers I used to wear when
I was a kid. It was the only extravagance in the
room. Unlike the Seurat, he probably brought that
in himself.

I waited for Patel to start down the list of
regular questions but he didn't. He just sat there

studying the blue screen on his computer.

"You've gotten yourself involved in quite the mess, haven't you," he finally said when the screen had given up everything it was going to tell him about me. "You ended up in the jail after you ran from the police because you'd broken into a home," he read from the screen. "You may be involved in the death of your roommate, a Mister…" Patel paused as he read the name. The bored expression on his face shifted for just a brief second. He looked surprised, "… John Chen. You went to see his father and told him you were Johnny's psychotherapist. You're under a delusion that Reeds Lake is God and the lake wants you to solve the murder of Mr. Chen."

Patel shook his head.

"That's not totally accurate," I added. My medical records always seemed to be filled with errors. I wouldn't be half surprised if they thought that I worshiped monkeys because of their soft fur.

"All the same, it's a troublesome situation," he added.

Patel tapped his pen on the desk and nodded at me. I'd seen him do this before, when the little cogs in his head were working overtime. I'd known people like Patel for long enough to know how they saw the world. Even back in college, I'd known materialists like Patel. He thought he was just one organic machine trying to fix another organic machine. He saw himself as an expensive car mechanic. There were no ghosts in the machine for him.

"So," he said after much cogitation. "When all

of these events happened, were you taking your medication? Were you also taking the street drugs?"

"Believe it or not," I told him. "I *was* taking my meds. Just like you asked me to. And I never do street drugs."

He seemed puzzled. He didn't seem to understand how I could still be broken after he had fixed me.

Patel asked me about what symptoms I was having but I didn't know what to tell him. He wasn't the only mental health professional to ask me about "symptoms" over the years. I'd heard it many times before and I never knew how to answer. Things like social isolation, hearing things and seeing things were "symptoms." But over the past few years, those things had just become a part of my personality. They'd come, to one degree or another, to define who I was. I didn't like to hear things that other people couldn't hear but as the years had gone by, I had a harder and harder time imagining my life without those voices.

Patel made some notes on the computer and told me that he was changing my medications. I really didn't care. I'd been on so many medications that I was starting to have a hard time telling one from the other. None seemed to make me much better or worse than any others.

Exactly 15 minutes later, Patel stood up and our little consultation was over.

"Good luck with your legal problems, Mr. Plowman. I think, if you keep taking my medications, you will have much relief of your symptoms."

I nodded and left.

When I got back to my room, Walt was there.

He had a big bandage on his head and he was sitting up in bed reading a magazine.

"Walt!" I nearly shouted.

I ran over and hugged him. He may have been old and had wrinkled skin but in that moment he was the most beautiful person in the world.

"Hey, Jack," he said with a smile. Until that moment, I hadn't seen him smile before.

"Are you all right?" I asked him.

"Yeah, I'm okay. They tell me it looks worse than it was. I blacked out but they don't think it's a concussion. It was just the loss of blood and stress that made me faint. They kept me overnight at Spectrum to make sure nothing else would go wrong, but I guess I'm gonna be okay."

"Who, what…" I started. I had so many questions I wanted to ask and they all seemed to be coming out at once.

"It was some big white guy. The cops I talked to said you knew his name. He works here but he missed his last shift. Cops said there's no sign of him at his house. White bastard must have run off now that he know he in trouble."

"Do you remember what happened?"

"Some of it. I was trying to sleep but not having much luck. I heard someone come in, walkin' real slow and quiet like they don't want to

be heard. At first I didn't think nothin' of it.
Nurses got to check on us to make sure we ain't
killed ourselves and all, so I just laid there and then
I heard you start to struggle. I asked you if you
were okay but your voice was just muffled. I got
scared and got up and saw that big ol' ox trying to
suffocate you with a pillow. He glared at me and I
tried to punch the motherfucker before he could hit
me first. Well, I landed my punch but it didn't hurt
him a bit. He stopped with you and grabbed me. It
didn't take him long to really mess me up. One
punch in the gut, I lost my breath and fell to the
floor. Once I was totally helpless, he took my head
and slammed it against the steel footboard of your
bed."

Telling the story was making Walt a little
anxious. I thought about telling him he could stop
but before I could get the words out, he kept going.

"So here I am, head banged up and bleeding.
He goes back to suffocating you with the pillow, but
I think you was awake by then. You were
struggling and struggling but that guy was just too
big. He could have killed us both with his bare
hands in a street fight. We wouldn't have a chance.
I figured fighting was a waste and so I called out for
help as loud as I could. That piece of shit hit me
hard in the head again. After I yelled, panic must
have set in, 'cause he ran off after that."

"You saved my life, Walt." I said sincerely. "I
won't forget that. I owe you my life, man."

"You'd a done the same for me," he said.

I'd like to think I would have acted the same
way, but I doubt it. I was more coward than hero. I

hadn't done anything half as brave and courageous in my life as what Walt had done for me. I decided right then and there that I wanted to be his friend. Walt was the kind of man you wanted in your corner.   Maybe God brought us together for something. Maybe to help each other.

"So, you just getting back from group?" Walt asked me, changing the subject.

"No, I had an appointment with Patel."

"Good ol' Doc Patel. I've been seeing him for years. You'd think the way he talk, I should be happy as a damn singing lark by now."

He tried to joke about it, but I got the impression that Walt still held out hope that his depression could be lifted for good if Patel could just find the right pill. It was an idea that persisted solely on the strength of our desire to believe it.

"You like Patel?" Walt asked.

"Not really," I told him. "He never hears anything I say to him. Just asks a few questions and gives me a prescription. He thinks he's a big deal though."

"Yeah. Always dressed up fancy, like the fancy man that he is."

"Fancy man?" I said, puzzled.

"Oh yeah. You didn't know? Guess I'm not surprised. Patel tries to keep it on the down low, doesn't make a big deal about it or nothing. But one time I was downtown and saw him walk out of one of those gay clubs holding hands with a guy. I met his eyes for a moment and he looked away. More than a few of the gay patients have seen him out in the clubs. He likes to dance apparently. Pretty good, too."

I never would have guessed that Patel was gay. I never, in a million years, would have guessed it. But I suppose you never can tell.

"I never knew that," I told Walt. "Did I tell you that my roommate that was murdered was gay? He liked to go to those clubs too. You think he ever would have run into Patel there?"

"I don't know much about the gay nightlife, Jack. Can't imagine that there are too awful many of those clubs in Grand Rapids though…" he trailed off into a conspiratorial whisper. "You don't think Patel had anything to do with Johnny's murder, do you?"

"I doubt it. But you never know. I bet Johnny was his patient at some point. You know anybody that might be able to tell me if Patel knew my roommate?"

Walt pondered that.

"Well," he said. "I know a guy in my neighborhood, Matt Henry. His neighbor is really into that scene. I could ask Matt to ask some questions. What was your roommate's name?"

"Johnny Chen."

Walt opened the drawer in the nightstand next to my bed. In it was a pen and a small note pad with the hospital's name across the top of it, just like in hotels that I'd stayed in. Walt wrote down Johnny's name on the pad, then circled it.

"I'll call Matt tonight and ask him to ask his friend for you," he said, folding the paper and putting it in his pocket.

"Thanks, Walt. I owe you another one."

33

I barely slept that night. All I could think about was Bruce Daniels sneaking onto the unit and trying to kill me again. I tossed and turned, and on the few occasions that I actually fell asleep, I had dreams of being chased. It was never clear who was after me or where I was. I never knew what was going on, but I knew I was in danger. In my dreams, I ran down country roads and city streets; down riverbanks and through forests full of huge sycamore trees, so tall they seemed to hide me from the watchful gaze of God. That feeling of being alone, separated from God, was worse than the unseen monstrosity chasing me.

Around three o'clock in the morning, I gave up on sleep all together.

Walt was sleeping like a baby on the other side of the curtain. I could hear his gentle exhalations waft around the room like some soothing metronome.

I couldn't stop thinking about Johnny's murder. The fact that Patel might know something about the people that Johnny hung out with in the clubs made me wonder if he was somehow involved. The fact that they were both gay probably didn't mean anything -- unless it did. I looked out my window at the stars shining over the garden and racked my brain for memories of my conversations with Johnny. We hadn't talked much, and when we did, half the time I wasn't paying much attention. I remember that Johnny didn't like to talk about his treatment, and neither did I. That was one thing we had in common.

As I sat in the quiet night and let my mind roam, it occurred to me that we had talked about Community Mental Health once. I was sitting in the living room reading my Bible. This must have been soon after I moved into the apartment because that was when I'd started to get very interested in reading the Bible, cover to cover.

Fr. Chris had discouraged it; he thought that my time could be better spent first reading the gospels. But I wanted to read every word of the Bible, starting with Genesis and ending in Revelation. I was reading the book of Numbers around then. It was page after page of building specs or God's massive grocery list. The book was well named; there were lots and lots of numbers there. I was busy trying to find the hidden birth dates of me or Anna when Johnny walked in.

He was angry. He threw down his backpack as soon as he walked in the door, but instead of stomping off to his room like he usually did, he sat down on one of the white plastic chairs in the living room. I kept on reading and tried to ignore him but I could feel him staring at me.

"What?" I asked him.

He didn't say anything at first, but I could tell that he was glad he had my attention. Johnny was used to getting what he wanted from people. When his boyfriends would come over, he acted like a toddler throwing a tantrum if he didn't feel like they were paying enough attention to him. When he threw a fit, people did what he wanted. I was the farthest thing away from his boyfriend, but I knew that ignoring him would just make things worse for me.

"Do you think I'm schizophrenic?" he asked me.

"What?"

"My new psychiatrist thinks I'm crazy. Do you think I'm crazy?"

"Johnny," I told him. "I'm the wrong guy to be asking that question. They think I'm the loon of the year. Maybe you ought to ask someone else."

I turned away from him and went back to reading my Bible.

"It's just that this new shrink of mine thinks I'm schizo. No one's ever said that about me before. They've said I'm bipolar and depressed and all that but never schizo."

I didn't know what he wanted me to say but in that moment I would have said anything to make him go away. This was one of the few times that we'd shared more than a few passing words and it made me uncomfortable.

"Okay, listen," I said to him. "You've got to take it with a grain of salt. Whatever they say. Don't take it too seriously. Regardless of what they say, they don't know any more about you than I do. Schizophrenia is just a word."

He didn't reply. He just got up and walked to his room.

The way I remembered it, Johnny had never mentioned that the new shrink was Patel. It could have been, but it just as easily might not have been. It didn't prove anything. I'd have to wait on Walt's friend and see if he turned anything up.

Mary caught my gaze after group as I was walking down to the community room to take a little break. She motioned for me to come over as she stood by the nurse's station talking to one of the nurses about rescheduling Dr. Patel's patients for the day. The two had a stack of green charts between them and Mary made notes in them as the nurse rescheduled their appointments. I waited until the last patient was rescheduled.

"Patel out sick?" I asked her when she was done.

"Not exactly. He just had a…," Mary sought for the right words, "a family emergency to attend to. He'll be back soon, don't you worry."

"Well, I hope everything's okay with him," I said. "One of his kids sick or something?"

I was fishing. I just hoped that Mary didn't pick up on it.

"No. Just a family issue." Mary looked at me and away from the charts and changed the subject.

"There's going to be a meeting in a few minutes about your case," she said. "Now don't worry. It's nothing bad. Actually, I think you're going to be relieved. I just wanted to tell you so you wouldn't be shocked. A lot of people are going to be there: Detective Robinson, your brother, myself, and Mr. Chen."

"Mr. Chen?" I didn't know why he would be invited to one of my mental health meetings. What right did he have to know about my treatment?

"What's Mr. Chen doing here?" I asked her, not able to hide the anger in my voice.

"His son was killed, Jack, and then you went to his house while the family was gathering for the funeral and posed as a social worker in order to question him about Johnny. You're lucky that he isn't pursuing legal action against you."

She had a point. Maybe I should just let this one be.

"What are we going to be talking about?"

"Be in the conference room in…," she looked down at her watch, "10 minutes. Okay?"

"Sure. Whatever you say, Mary."

Mary smiled and walked off, probably to give some of the same reassuring kindness to some other patient. Instead of going down to the community room and watching a few minutes of television, I went to the bathroom. I didn't feel like I had to go, but stress always got my bladder going. Although I've always been at a loss to explain it, there was something about stress and my bladder that didn't mix very well. It's like the anxiety creates pee inside me. The more anxious I get, the more my bladder fills up. It's always worse when running off to pee is impossible or difficult. The worst time was with Anna.

We'd been dating for about five months and we were getting pretty serious. I really wanted to make love to her and told her so repeatedly during the make-out sessions we had whenever her roommate left. We'd gotten to the point where she'd let me touch her wherever I wanted to as long as her clothes stayed on. I could touch her breasts as long as her bra stayed on, or I could cup her rear with my hands as long as my hands stayed outside her jeans.

Looking back, her sexual legalism doesn't make much sense to me, but I was in love with her then and didn't question it.

One Saturday night, Anna's roommate, Ramona, an international student from Malaysia, I think, told us out of nowhere that she was going to a movie and then go stay overnight with a friend. We'd have the dorm to ourselves for the whole night. Total privacy.

As soon as Ramona walked out the door, Anna looked at me in a way that no one had ever looked at me before...and no one has since. It's hard to explain. She knew that I loved her and that I'd been waiting for her to be ready, but we never really ever had the opportunity.

Until that night. It was going to finally happen, and for the first time in my life I was going to make love to a woman instead of just having sex with her. I'd wanted this for so long. Anna walked over to me, and started to kiss me when out of nowhere I felt it.

I had to pee.

One moment, I'd felt like my bladder was empty and then, in a half a second, it felt like it was overflowing. I told Anna that I'd be right back and walked to the bathroom that she and Ramona shared. I'm sure that Anna thought I was doing something sexy in there, but all that I was really doing was trying my damndest to point my urine stream onto the side of the bowl so that Anna wouldn't hear the pee splash into the toilet.

When I thought I was done, I washed my hands and started to open the door, but the feeling of urgency came right back. Again and again it happened. Eventually, I just told Anna that *I* wasn't ready. I told her that because I was in love with her, I wanted our first time to be romantic and special, and my bladder had decided that tonight was not the night. Amazingly, she understood.

During the next week, I starting planning the romantic night that I envisioned. I made reservations at a nice hotel a few weeks out and made a CD with "our" songs. It was going to be perfect.

But a few days before our big night, I had my first break. I went inpatient soon after and our relationship started to unravel in lock step with my mind.

34

When I walked into the conference room, everyone was already there. Jake was dressed in a nice suit as usual, a nice charcoal gray one today. Detective Robinson was also in a suit but his was wrinkled and ill fitting. It was a suit obviously not coordinated by Jake's wife, the illustrious and always fashionable Lisa Plowman. Mary was there too. She sat next to a very stern-looking Mr. Chen and next to them were Tiffini and her boss, Ken.

There was one surprise guest too. Someone that I didn't expect to see. Seeing him there all dressed in black, save for that gleaming notch of white just over his Adam's apple, made me feel like everything would be okay.

Fr. Chris smiled at me as I walked in. Then he gave me a thumbs up. It was so corny that I almost laughed. Jake must have told him about this meeting. Fr. Chris knew that I'd need him and here he was.

As I sat down, Mary asked Detective Robinson to close the door.

"Thank you all for coming today," she began. "Jack's situation is surely a complex one and I am grateful that we could all meet here today to talk about it. I know that Attorney Plowman and Detective Robinson have already come to an agreement about how the legal case will be proceeding, but there are new developments in the case of Mr. Chen's son that we should discuss as well. I thought that it was important for me to start by simply expressing my gratitude to be working with such a compassionate and professional group of people."

Everyone nodded.

"I suppose," Mary continued, "that we should start with Attorney Plowman."

Mary looked over at my always handsome brother.

"Thank you, Mary. Let me start by saying that you are the one we should all be thanking. My brother is very fortunate to have such a caring therapist. I am very grateful that you were assigned to Jack's case."

Typical Jake. This was why he was going to be a very successful lawyer.

"Well," Jake continued, looking at me like he knew what I had been thinking. "You will be happy to learn, little brother, that the prosecutor and Detective Robinson here have agreed to drop all the charges with the exception of evading arrest. They have also agreed to release you to my care once your treatment here is completed. Mary has told me that Dr. Patel thinks you can be discharged very soon. The police are requesting, however, that you meet with Tiffini and Ken five days a week, at least for the time being. We all want to make sure that you stay stable. The way the agreement works, as long as you do what is asked of you, take your medication and meet with Tiffini , you will not have to go back to the county jail."

In spite of all the supervision, it was a good deal. I could handle being babysat if it kept me out of jail. Tiffini smiled her million dollar smile at me from across the table just then, and for the first time in a long while, it warmed my heart. Ken sat next to her. He was *her* babysitter. If she had one, I guess I could have one.

"The police also expect you to cooperate with them and to be available for questioning," Jake continued. "I know from my discussions with Detective Robinson that the case of Johnny Chen's death is one that the G.R.P.D. is desperate to solve."

Mr. Chen sat stoically as Jake talked about his son's murder. You would've thought he was watching the evening news on TV.

"Maybe Detective Robinson would be so kind as to give us an update on his investigation."

The focus of the group turned to the older man. He had a few papers in front of him that were filled with his illegible handwriting. He'd made numerous sections and enclosed them with circles. Curling arrows connected the circled areas to show how each balloon connected to the other. As I watched him and waited for him to start, I noticed for the first time that in spite of his wrinkled clothes, the detective had an almost perfectly shaved face.

"We're following up some leads," he began, looking down at the papers that only he could understand, "and one of those leads is this man Daniels."

Bruce Daniels, the man that had now tried to kill me twice.

"We got a warrant, searched his home, but he seems to have packed up his belongings rather quickly. He also hasn't been in for work at the hospital since the night of the alleged attack against

Mr. Plowman. We've reviewed his work history and it appears that he and Jack Plowman had not met professionally prior to the alleged attack."

I thought that for an alleged attack, it sure has hell hurt a hell of a lot.

"These facts have led him to be classified in my mind as a person of interest in this investigation."

"Detective," Mr. Chen spoke up for the first time, "did Bruce Daniels kill my son?"

He asked the question in a calm and even tone that betrayed now the smallest hint of emotion.

"We don't know yet, Mr. Chen," Robinson replied. "We think we have enough evidence to suggest that he is involved somehow. Fr. Parsons identified Daniels as the man that attacked him at his church while he was meeting with Mr. Plowman, and it appears that he was involved with the second attack against Mr. Plowman here."

"Daniels tried to kill me and Walt, my roommate," I said. "Walt saw him."

"The night staff on the unit also saw him run off and were able to identify him," Robinson added, looking at me.

That seemed to make it gospel for him, that some of the non-crazy people saw him.

"We've started to contact some of Daniels' family and friends in the area to see if he has holed up with them. It may take a while, Mr. Chen, but we will find this man."

The way Robinson said it, I believed it. I just hoped they found Daniels before he could finish me off. I'd been lucky to be with friends the two times that he attacked me before. Who knew if I'd be as lucky the next time around?

"From my run-in with him," Fr. Chris added, "I can attest to the fact that he's a very dangerous man. God knows what he would have done to me if my parishioners hadn't been there to help me."

"We can handle him, Father. Our officers are trained to deal with rougher customers than him," Robinson said.

"Can you tell me about any other leads that you are looking into?" Mr. Chen asked the detective.

"We have a few other leads, but none of them are really advanced enough that I can talk about them now. I'll stay in touch with you as our investigation progresses, Mr. Chen. I'll make sure you are kept informed."

Mr. Chen didn't show much emotion but his lack of a follow-up question seemed to mean he was satisfied with what he'd heard.

I still didn't know what to think about Chen. He clearly had had some very serious problems getting along with Johnny, but he was the man's only son and now he was dead. Maybe his reserve was just a façade hiding his inner torment. But then again, maybe the show of concern about finding the murderer was the façade and he was just glad that Johnny wasn't around anymore to shame his family.

"To say that this has been a difficult situation for everyone involved is an understatement," Mary said to the group. She made sure to look each of us in the eye as she spoke.

"I have no way of understanding the pain that you and your wife must be going through, Mr. Chen. Losing a child is one of the most difficult traumas that anyone can experience. But I can tell you that the attack that happened on our unit has committed the staff here to bring justice to the person involved. We've taken up a donation, and would, with your permission, Mr. Chen, like to offer a reward of one thousand dollars for information leading to the apprehension of Bruce Daniels."

"My thanks to you and your staff," he said.

"I know that I speak for all of the hospital staff," she continued, "when I say that we pray this man is found quickly so that we can all start the difficult work of grieving what we have each lost."

The room was silent. A moment of holy reverence in that windowless conference room.

"Mary," my brother said, breaking the silence, "when do you think Jack will be able to be discharged?"

"That's up to Dr. Patel, but he'll need a few more days of monitoring to make sure the medication has returned him to baseline functioning. Still, we should be able to get him discharged by early next week."

You don't really understand the beauty of the word "discharge" unless you've spent any time in the hospital. Hearing it in that meeting was almost like Easter morning for me. Jesus raised from the grave and taking me to glory.

I must have been smiling without even being aware of it. Because when Jake looked at me he started to smirk.

"Is there anything anyone else would like to add?" Jake asked.

"I'd like to say one thing," Chen said and turned his head to look directly at me. "Jack, I want you to know that I bear you no ill will for the deception that you used to gain entry to my home. I've come to believe that your mental illness compromised your abilities to make wise decisions. I forgive you for the additional pain that you caused my family in our hour of grief."

I knew that it would be polite to just thank him for forgiving me, but I didn't feel like I'd done anything to need forgiveness for. I was answering a call from God to bring justice to his son's murderer. If that made him uncomfortable, he should take it up with his maker, not me. But I was the mental patient, and he wasn't.

"Thank you," I said, biting my lip to resist the urge to say more.

"I think that went very well," Mary said after we got back to her office and sat down for our individual session. Mary was as matronly as ever, sitting in her chair and looking at me in the same way she probably looked at her own children. She was one of the few shrinks that I'd worked with that seemed to genuinely care about what happened to me. She wasn't a phony.

"I'm just glad to get out of here," I told her.

"I thought you said this place was good for you. Safe."

"It has been," I told her truthfully. "But a couple of days is enough of it. I know what happened now. I have insight, as you people like to say. Finding Johnny's body and then getting beat up at the church and all the rest was just more than I could handle. Stress makes my symptoms worse. A lot worse. I know that, but I forgot about it for a while. I'm better now and ready to get back to business."

"Business?"

"The business of finding Johnny's murderer."

Mary looked at me like I'd just broken her window with my baseball. She was not happy with my plans. But what had she expected me to do, just go back to Jake's house and sit on the couch for the rest of my life? For one thing, Lisa Plowman would never allow that. She had a pristine white couch that she always lead me away from when I visited. She never said so, but I knew that she didn't want me to even sit on it, for fear that my crazy would defile it forever. To her, I was like a dirty dog with a weak bladder. I was certainly no dog, but...well, maybe she was half right.

Regardless of what Lisa or Mary thought, God had given me a job to do and I intended to complete it.

"Don't you think the police would be better equipped to handle that, Jack?"

"No, I don't."

"Why is that?"

"Because he was my roommate and God has put it upon me to find his killer. I don't make it a habit of questioning God, Mary."

"I'd thought your delusions had decreased, Jack."

I was incensed.

"Mary," I began, trying hard to hide my seething anger, "I cannot believe you are implying that my faith in God is a delusion. I am deeply offended."

And I was. I was so offended that I turned my back on her and faced the wall.

"Jack," she said sternly, "that's not what I'm saying at all. I do not regard belief in God as a delusion. You know that. What I consider a delusion is all that stuff about Reeds Lake. That goes way beyond belief in God. What you saw at the bottom of that lake was a part of your delusion."

"So, it's that simple, huh?"

"What's that simple?"

"My religious experiences. You just want to write them all off as crazy, don't you? How can you say that it's okay for me to believe in God but then label my relationship with God as psychotic? That doesn't make any sense, Mary. I think you're the one that doesn't want to hear the voice of God. He might offend the comfortable life that you've made for yourself. And what good is a God that never speaks? That might be the passive middle-class God that you worship, but that's not my God. My God whispers in my ear on dark nights. He tells me to get up and fight for righteousness, for justice. He tells me to love my neighbor as I love myself. He doesn't say to love my neighbor as I love myself, unless it makes me uncomfortable. That's not my God, Mary. And that's not the God of the

Bible either."

"I hear what you're saying, Jack. You feel like I'm invalidating your faith by questioning the visions that you had about the lake. The way you know God is through visions like the one you had out in East G.R. and you can't imagine faith without them. Plus, you think that I'm a tad bourgeois."

"Exactly."

"You're right," she continued. "I can be like that. Especially the part about being bourgeois. I am that."

"Not that there's anything wrong with that," I said. "But I'm different. I see a different voice and I hear a different vision. I don't think that's a bad thing. I don't think that's mental illness. I think that it's my special gift from God."

"Hmm," she said. "And what you just said is what we call a reframe."

"A reframe?"

"It's a way to understand a situation in a more positive way, in a way that allows possibility and growth. It's like taking an old photo out of its cheap plastic frame and putting it in a new frame that suits the picture better."

"But you still think my vision in the lake is crazy, right?"

"I think," she said, "that I cannot possibly know the mind of God. I cannot know how God chooses to work in people's lives. But I do know a little bit about mental illness. It can be sly and sneak up on you. It's a trickster, Jack, kind of like the devil. What I'm talking about is to be aware of this trickster and not fall into his traps. When you fall into his traps, you end up sick and in here."

"Kind of like Jesus being tempted by the devil after he was baptized?"

"I suppose so. I think that you've got to be careful not to let this lead you into a situation that might hurt you. You said yourself that too much stress was what led you here. I think that if you want to stay well, you've got to minimize your stress. Trying to solve a murder is stressful. You learned that the hard way."

"Okay," I told her. "I see what you're saying. You're afraid that if I go out and continue to investigate Johnny's murder, I'll go nuts again and end up back here?"

"Right. That's what I'm saying."

"But what I'm saying is that I've got to do it. I'm called by God to do it. But that doesn't mean I have to do it alone... maybe I can get other people to help me."

"That's better," she said. "I'd rather you stay out of this all together, but if you must do it, I hope that you'll be very careful and manage your stress. Do you know any stress management techniques?"

"Yeah, a few," I said. "But I suppose that it wouldn't hurt if you taught me a few more."

"I'd be happy to."

35

When my session with Mary ended, I walked back to my room feeling optimistic for the future. I wanted to share the good news of my upcoming discharge with Walt but I also hated to have to leave him here. The man had saved my life and I felt deeply in his debt. I wanted to help him somehow and repay that debt. I vowed that someday I would do just that.

When I got to the door of our room, it was halfway ajar and I heard muffled voices coming from Walt's side of the room. I peeked my head in the door, not wanting to disturb Walt if he was talking to his therapist or Dr. Patel. He wasn't talking to either of them.

He was talking to Fr. Chris.

As far as I'd known, the two didn't know each other, but Fr. Chris seemed to know a lot of people from every imaginable walk of life. Maybe it was just the job, but he seemed to have some kind of connection to everyone in Grand Rapids. Without fail, he ran into someone he knew every time we went somewhere together.

With only half my head in the room, I could see that Walt was sitting on his bed and Fr. Chris had pulled up one of the wooden chairs to sit close to him. I took a quick look around the hallway. No one was coming.

"So, you have to just open your mind, Walt."

"I've tried, Father. I really have."

"I'm sure you have. I'm sure you've tried.

256

You know, I think God's music is always playing, Walt. Sometimes you can hear it in the crackle of lightning that wakes you up in the middle of the night and other times you can hear it in a crowded elevator. Little kids, they always seem to hear it. But I think many of us, as we get older and more serious and rational, we just get so used to hearing it that we no longer notice. It becomes like the background hum of the refrigerator; you learn to filter it out most of the time. But it's always there, Walt. You just have to relearn how to hear it."

"I think I've grown deaf," Walt said dejectedly and started to knead his hands together.

"Why don't you come to church sometime? There's a lot of interesting things to be heard there."

"I appreciate it, Father. But it just wouldn't do any good."

"Easter's coming," Fr. Chris told him. "And the way I understand the story is that Jesus isn't the only one who gets raised from the dead."

Fr. Chris was priesting for all he was worth. God bless him for it too.

My conscience was getting the best of me, so I knocked on the door. Fr. Chris turned and smiled when he saw me.

"Jack! Good news, huh? I'll bet you're happy as a clam."

I couldn't hold back a smile. "Yeah, I'm pretty happy about getting out of here. But I'm going to miss my friend Walt here. Did he tell you that he saved my life?"

Fr. Chris raised his eyes at Walt in an expression of surprise.

"No, I don't think he mentioned that. I've been sitting here with a bona fide hero and I had no idea."

Walt stopped the churning motion he was making with his hands and folded them demurely in his lap. He clearly wasn't used to being called a hero and his face showed it. He was the same sad old man that I'd met when I was admitted. Saving me and getting beat up for it hadn't altered the course of his despair one bit.

"You'd done the same for me, Jack. It was nothing."

"Nothing, my ass!" Fr. Chris exclaimed. "You *are* a hero, Walt."

"If you say so, Father."

I opened my mouth to start to argue with him but then thought better of it. This wasn't something I was going to be able to reason him into. Walt had on emotional blinders. He couldn't see the hero that he was now. I suppose that was part of the reason he was here in the first place.

Fr. Chris knew better than to argue with him too. He changed the subject.

"So what are you going to do when you get out, Jack?"

"I'm going back to what I was doing, Father. Finding out who killed Johnny."

Lines formed on his brow. The same lines that must have formed on his forehead when I talked to him on the pay phone a few days ago. This time, he took a different tack.

"I'd like to try and talk you out of it, but I know that won't do any good. I guess the only thing that I can do is offer my help."

"Great," I told him.

"Speaking of helping," Walt broke in, "I called my buddy Matt and he said that he'd ask around if anyone ever saw Patel with Johnny."

"By Patel, you mean Dr. Patel, Jack's psychiatrist?" Fr. Chris asked.

"Yep. The same one," I said to him.

"So you think Patel is involved? That's a pretty serious accusation," Fr. Chris said in a whisper. His face told me that even saying things like that was a very bad idea.

"I'm not saying anything, Father. I'm just following up on a lead."

I leaned over to the nightstand and took out a sheet of paper.

"Can you call me at my brother's house when you hear, Walt?" I wrote down Jake's number. "I'd like to hear what you learn as soon as you know anything."

"No problem, man."

"Plus, I want to stay in touch with you, Walt. I owe you a lot and I intend to pay you back if I can."

"Like I said, it was nothing."

"When are you being discharged?" Fr. Chris asked Walt.

"My therapist tells me that I'll be here a few more days yet. They want to make sure that the beating hasn't made me want to hurt myself again. I'll be out soon, though."

He said it like he didn't seem to care one way or the other. Walt lived his life like it was some river that carried you away down its twisty trail and there was nothing you could do about it. Someone needed to teach him how to swim against the tide instead of just float.

That night I had the dream again. I hadn't had it for so long that I was just about starting to think it was gone forever. But as soon as I closed my eyes, there I was again back in the theater to watch that same old film.

I was up there on the screen but I was also the only one in the theater. When the bad part came, I always screamed at the Jack in the movie. I told him not to do it, that it was a mistake that he'd regret for the rest of his life. But regardless of what I said, the action played out like it always did. I couldn't stop what the other me did up on the big screen anymore than I could stop what the doctors did to me in the state hospital.

The movie always opened on a busy college quad. Then it cut to me back in my dorm at Michigan. It was winter and a brisk wind blew in little gusts outside my window, piling up mounds of snow on the sill. My roommate was still gone on winter break and I was sprawled out on my bed with my world religion textbook. I'd highlighted phrases, many of them multiple times and in different colors so the page that lay open looked less like a page from a college textbook and more like an amateurish watercolor. I always turned the heat up when my roommate wasn't there because I liked it warmer than he did so the room was very warm. I felt comfortable and relaxed, peaceful even.

Then came the knock on the door. I got up. I had on a white tee shirt and a pair of plaid boxers. The boxers were a Christmas gift from my mother. She always gave me socks and underwear for Christmas. She'd done it every year as far back as I could remember. Before I answered the door, the me on the screen glanced down and noticed that the tee shirt was stained orange with grease. I'd been eating from the bag of Cheetos that lay on the floor by my bed and absent-mindedly wiping my hands on my shirt. By the looks of things, I'd done it a lot.

But the me up on the screen didn't seem to care about how he looked. He just bounded up and opened the door.

When the door opened, Anna was standing there. Her face was wet from freshly cried tears. A few unmelted flakes of snow were still lodged in her long brown hair, and I remember that I wanted to pick them out, but I resisted. I'd had enough restraint to not do that at least.

Anna was wearing her big glasses and not the contacts that she usually wore when she came over. Snow had melted on the outside of the lenses and it almost looked like those droplets were also tears.

"Hey," I said, letting her in.

She just stood in the doorway and looked at me, expecting me to say something. The me in the theater knew that what she expected was an apology but the me up on the screen didn't have a clue.

"What?" I asked her.

"Is that all you have to say for yourself?"

Saying the words took real effort. She started breathing heavy like she'd run up the four flights of stairs to my room instead of taking the elevator like she always did.

"What?"

Anna looked at me like she didn't know me. I suppose that by this point it was true.

"Is that all you have to say for yourself, Jack Plowman?" she accused me. "What happened to you? My parents were expecting us. You knew. Don't you care about me anymore?"

The question was too much for her and she burst out in tears, her face contorting like someone was torturing her. I didn't know what to say or what to do.

I put my arm around her and led her into my room. I didn't want my neighbors to see Anna like this.

"What's the matter?" I asked her as I shut the door behind us.

She sobbed and sobbed and when I tried to hug her she pushed me away. Not knowing what else to do, I sat down on the bed and waited for the crying to stop.

The heat of my room quickly melted the snow that was stuck in her hair. I watched it slowly change into water before my eyes. I was fascinated by it. The change of state had religious significance to the Jack up on the screen. As Anna stood in front of my bed sobbing, I walked over to a notebook that

I had just started to keep and wrote down my observation.

It jarred Anna out of her despair and her crying stopped. She looked at me, puzzled.

"What are you doing?" she asked me.

"Seeing the snow melt in your hair made me think of something and I need to write it down now before I forget it."

"Made you think of what?"

"It's all about transformation, Anna. Water seems to be the essential essence. Maybe it's a metaphor for all of sinful humanity. When you came into my room, you had snow in your hair but the heat of my room melted it and it reverted back to water. We can be transformed just like that snow. God transforms us. I'm starting to see that now. Jesus walked on water to point to this exact fact. He wanted to show us that we can be just like that water, we can be changed by the heat of His love."

Anna looked confused.

"Stay with me. Water is H2O, right? Jesus is the Alpha and the Omega. Alpha is the letter A and the Omega is our letter Z. So it all starts and ends with Jesus. We can all be in Jesus. If that's true, then the two H's and the O are in Jesus as well. Water is in Jesus, and Jesus is in water. Jesus is the force that transforms the snow when it comes in contact with the light of his love. See?"

That Jack was getting excited. He was talking louder and faster and pacing around the small room.

"The light of Jesus transforms us, Anna.

Oh, my God. I'm just starting to see that now. We ARE the water. We can be transformed, that's why Jesus was baptized! It all goes back to water. How could I not have seen this before?"

The Jack in the movie started to scribble furiously into the notebook. Anna blankly stared at me as I did and waited. I wanted to tell him to stop but I'd seen the movie before and I knew that it wouldn't do any good. I was powerless to change what happened next.

"Jack, I think you need to go the hospital," Anna said, the tears now gone.

"What are you talking about?"

"You've been acting a little obsessively for the past few weeks," she explained, all the previous emotion gone from her voice. "I mean, I've really liked going to all those churches with you. I learned a lot and we met some really smart people, especially Fr. Brooks. It's been great. But you can't seem to let it go come Monday morning. You've got other classes besides world religion, Jack."

"This is important, Anna."

"I know it is," she said. "But so is world history. So is chemistry."

"Anna!" I yelled out, making her jump. "God is calling me. All of that other stuff doesn't matter anymore. This is what matters. Don't you understand that?"

"Look at you, Jack," she yelled back at me. "You sound like you're going crazy. You aren't making any sense anymore. All this stuff about Jesus is…"

That's when it happened. I've relived the moment many times, in the dream world and in the waking. I've relived it when I'm alone and thinking about my life. I've relived it to countless therapists. For a long time, I told myself that my reaction was automatic, that I didn't have time to even think about it. But in my heart, I know that's not true. I knew what I was doing. I was just so angry at her that nothing else mattered to me.

Up on the screen, Jack pulls his hand back and whips it forward violently. He strikes Anna hard on the face with his open palm. A ghostly red imprint forms immediately and Anna's glasses hit the wall in slow motion and shatter.

36

"So you'll follow up with Tiffini and Ken tomorrow at 9:00 AM and see Dr. Patel at the C.M.H. office next Wednesday at 1:45 PM."

Mary was filling out my discharge forms in her office. Jake was sitting next to me. He was going to drop me off at his house and then go to work. I was supposed to just stay inside and not get into trouble until I met with my case manager, make that case managers. Being connected to a murder meant that now I had two, Tiffini and her boss Ken too.

"Does that sound like what we agreed to?" Mary asked me.

"Yep."

"Good," Mary smiled at me. "Now you take care of yourself and try to stay healthy. If you want to work with me to continue psychotherapy, you can talk to Tiffini about it. I have an office downtown and I've got a contract with C.M.H."

"Thanks, Mary," Jake said to her. "You've been such a blessing to Jack and to our whole family."

"It's been my pleasure to be of service."

Those two could have gone on telling each other how great the other was for hours but I didn't want to have to sit there and listen to it. I wanted to get back and finish the business that I had to finish.

"Okay, I'm ready to go," I said, and the two of them laughed.

I'd already packed my bags and said my goodbye to Walt. I planned to call him in a few days to learn what he found out about Patel and if he had any connection to Johnny. When we exchanged addresses it turned out that Walt didn't live that far away from my apartment on Prospect. I also promised to buy some beer and hamburgers and bring them over to his place as soon as he got out. I had a little hibachi grill that I'd picked up for about five bucks but I'd never gotten around to using it. Now I had my chance.

Mary opened the big metal door for us with her key and we walked down the hall to the front entrance, the same place that I'd been roughed up a few days before. The hallway was pretty empty; it was just the three of us walking, and none of us said anything.

When we got to the front door, Mary opened it and said to me, "Keep in touch, Jack." I nodded and walked out.

Jake had parked his old Honda near the entrance. It was an older silver Accord, the same car that he had when he was in law school. The same car that he'd driven to pick me up that time in Ohio when I went off the deep end and ended up in the county jail.

"I'm surprised you haven't gotten a new car since you graduated," I said to him as the sun blared its heat down on me. It felt good to be outside. It felt good to feel the sun on my face again.

"Lisa's got the new car. She drives around town a lot, so she needs the more comfortable car. This thing just sits in the garage downtown all day."

"She still trying to get that real estate thing going?" I asked him.

He started up the Accord and pulled out of the parking lot. As we rode down the driveway, I saw the hospital recede in the rearview mirror. God speed, Walt, I thought to myself.

"Yeah, it's not easy to get started. There's a lot of competition in East Grand Rapids and that's where Lisa wants to work. She's been putting in a lot of hours trying to establish herself. Most of it's on the weekends, open hours and stuff. She'll be home with you during the week. Is that going to be okay?"

It was a reasonable question. I'd never gotten along with my brother's wife. She came from money, her father was a well-respected plastic surgeon in Lansing, and she seemed to have a hard time relating to people who weren't upper middle class like she was. She *tried* not to be mean, but some of the things she said made me resent her pampered lifestyle.

But I didn't want to talk about Lisa as we drove down the road. Jake already knew how I felt about her. I didn't need to say it again.

"We'll get along okay as long as we don't spend much time together," I told him, hoping that his new house was big enough to give us some distance.

Jake nodded at me but kept his eyes on the road. "We're going to set you up in the bedroom we use for storage. I put up an inflatable bed for you last night. It's a little crowded in there with boxes and Lisa's winter clothes, but it should work out all right for you. I know for a fact that you've stayed in much worse places than this."

That was the truth.

"Do you have a computer that I can use?" I asked him.

"I've got one in my office that I use for work, but that's the only one in the house. Why do you need a computer?"

"I just want to check email, that's all."

Jake shot a quick glance at me.

"I don't want you getting into any more trouble than you're already in, Jack. It wasn't easy to get the prosecutor to release you to my care, you know. I had to really call in a favor that I had hoped to keep for more impor...I mean, more important work things. If you get yourself in trouble, I'm not going to be able to pull your ass out of the fire again. Do you get me?"

Jake wasn't usually angry like this.

"Okay," I said like a chastised child. "But you've told me that you wouldn't be able to help me before and you always seem to come through somehow."

"Yeah, that's been true so far, Jack. But one of these days, you're going to get yourself into a kind of trouble that an attorney can't bail you out of. I can't raise people from the dead, you know. If you don't keep your nose clean, you might just be heading that way."

"Okay, Dad. I understand."

"Don't get smart with me, young man!" he yelled in mock fury, pounding his fist on the steering wheel just like our old man used to do.

"Oh, that's right," I said. "I almost forgot. You're the wise older brother. Born a whole three minutes before me."

He was laughing now.

"And don't you forget it. The early bird gets the worm, son. A stitch in time saves nine…"

"And the first one out of the womb gets a ribbon!" I added, laughing so much tears were forming in my eyes.

For a minute there, it was like we were kids again.

Jake turned the Honda off Franklin and onto a side street called Cambridge Boulevard. In most of the cities that I've visited in my psychotically fueled travels, they'll call any street a boulevard or an avenue, just so they can get more mileage out of a good name like Cambridge. If a city already has a Cambridge Street, a new developer could call his new road Cambridge Avenue and still benefit from the Oxbridge pomposity of the name. Most of the time, what comes after the name of the street doesn't matter. Not in this case.

Cambridge Boulevard was indeed a boulevard. The east and west lanes were separated by a grassy island spruced up every few feet or so with a flowering bush or some other organic eye candy. The houses on either side of the boulevard were old and big and sat off the road far enough to allow for large green lawns. The lawns were home to grand trees that formed a canopy over the road, letting in just enough light to perfectly illuminate the homes.

It occurred to me as we drove down the wide road that I was back in East Grand Rapids again for the first time since my visit to the Chen house. Not that I planned to pay a return visit or anything, but a part of me wondered how far the walk would be if I had a change of heart.

As we rolled down the road, I noticed that the houses, along with the boulevard, kept getting smaller and smaller as we went. It was as if seventy-five years ago, the richest one hundred people in Grand Rapids had decided to build homes here, only to catch the attention of a group of slightly less rich people who followed suit further down the road. It went on like that until the just barely upper middle class staked a claim on their little piece of Cambridge Blvd.

Jake's house was old like the others, but had probably been built by an upper middle class family at the tail end of the building boom. It was a brick ranch that sprawled over a large lot. The architect seemed to have been inspired by Frank Lloyd Wright. The brick was dark, as brown as you could get without bleeding over into black, and the lines were straight and low. I didn't see a way into the place.

"Here we are," Jake said, parking the car on the curb. "Let's go in and see if we can get you settled."

"How do you get into the place?" I asked him.

He chuckled. "The door is behind that porch. Don't laugh. Not having an obvious door to knock at comes in handy when the Jehovah's Witnesses come around."

"They may not have all the details right," I said as we walked up the cement path, "but they love the Lord too."

"Sorry," he said unconvincingly. "The last thing I want to get into with you is a religious debate. They expect me back at work soon. I don't have three hours to chew the holy fat with you, bro."

"Wait a minute. What's that supposed to mean?" I asked him.

Jake bounded up the last steps and opened the door with his key.

"Like I said. I don't have time to get into it now."

The door opened to a small living room. There was an art print of a European landscape on one wall and an old-looking wood fireplace sitting stoically on the other. Lisa, long and lean and dressed in a gray business suit, was sitting reading a magazine on a gaudy plaid couch that was so bright it left an afterimage on my eye when I looked away from it.

"Hello, Jack," Lisa said, looking up from her magazine. I was touched. Against every fiber of her being, she'd forced a granite smile onto her face.

"Hi, Lisa. Thanks for having me," I said as I set my backpack down on their bland carpet.

I was surprised at how small the living room actually was. The place had looked like it was pretty big from the outside. A little wave of terror ran through me when I thought about being stuck in a small house with Lisa Plowman.

"Let me show you to your bedroom," Jake said. I just nodded to Lisa, acknowledging her and followed my brother down the long narrow hallway. There were a few pictures of Lisa's family lining the wall. I saw her tanned father and mother standing on the deck of a boat and a group picture taken at some fancy restaurant. At the end of the hallway, Jake turned into the last room on the right.

"Here it is," he said to me.

It looked just like Jake had described it in the car. Cardboard boxes, stacked three or four high, filled most of the room. The inflatable bed was tucked into the far corner near a window that looked out onto the pool in the back yard. Jake had made me a path through the boxes from the door to the bed.

"You can use the bathroom just down the hall. Our room is right across the hallway, so no trying to sneak your girlfriend in at night," he said, nudging me.

"No problem with that, Pops. I haven't had a real girlfriend in a long time."

"Speaking of which," he said, taking my bag from me and setting it on the blow-up bed, "you'll never guess who's been calling me lately and asking about you."

"You're right, I can't even begin to imagine."

"Anna."

A part of me was surprised but another part of me had expected it. That girl could never let anything go. Back when we were dating, I remember one time when we went and saw some old Ingmar Bergman movie at one of the artsy cinemas in Ann Arbor. It was *Wild Strawberries*, I think. After the movie, as we were walking home (hand in hand as we always did when we were together), I said to her that I wondered how long Bergman had been dead. Anna was sure he was still alive. No, I told her. I was quite sure that he was dead. I'd read about his death, years ago, I told her.

She was adamant that he was still walking the earth.

"Either way," I said. "It was a moving film, wasn't it?"

It was my way of changing the subject to a topic more likely to make her want to make out with me back in her dorm room.

"Yeah, it was good," she said, the gears still turning in her head. "But I'm almost positive that Bergman is still alive. What time is it? Maybe, if we hurry, we can hop into the library."

Researching whether some Swedish director was alive or dead was the last thing I wanted to do with my pretty girlfriend on a romantic moonlit night. Anna was no technophobe but she never trusted the Internet to get pressing questions like this answered. It was the library or nothing for her. Don't get me wrong, libraries are fine places during the day time. But I've always thought that the night was made for other things.

"We can check it out tomorrow," I said. "Why don't we go back to your dorm and just hang out?" By hanging out, I really meant making out.

"But I really want to know if he's alive or dead. You started this, Jack."

She was right.

"How about I just admit that you're right. Then we can go back to the dorm now. I'm sure you're right anyway."

"No," she said. She was having none of it. "I don't want to win by forfeit. Now I'm really curious. You might be right. He could be long dead."

"And if he's dead, there's no hurry to verify it now. He won't be any less dead in the morning," I said, putting my arm around her.

"Let's just peek into the library," she said. "We've got lots of time to hang out. It's become a little mystery for me now. I've got to find out how it ends."

"It ends with death," I said. "Always death. Whether it's now or in the future is just a little detail."

It didn't do any good. We changed course and walked all the way across campus to the main library. It was open and we spent about an hour getting Anna her answer. Predictably, she was tired by the time we got back to her dorm, and all the action that I got that night was a quick goodnight kiss on the check.

As I got to know her better, I saw that she could get obsessive with little things like that. She was a very detail-oriented person. She was the kind of person that would search all night to find a missing piece to a jigsaw puzzle so she could finish it. The little loose ends of life drove her nuts and I was the biggest loose end of her life.

I'd never even really broken up with her. After I went into the hospital and had to drop out of school, I just stopped returning her calls and moved back to Grand Rapids. Eventually, I talked to her a few times on the phone, but we never had a formal goodbye. She would just call Jake to check up on me from time to time.

"What'd she say?" I asked him.

"Not much. She just wanted to know how you were doing. She's an elementary school teacher somewhere down in Kalamazoo now. Did you know that?"

"No, can't say as I did."

"She left her number for you, if you want to call her."

It'd been years since I'd spoken to Anna, although I often sat up in bed thinking about her, especially on cool rainy nights in the summer. Her memory always came to me on those nights where it had been oppressively hot during the day but then cooled down after a hard evening rain. I don't know why, but the musky scent of rain in the summer air always reminded me of her. That scent would always wake me up, even out of a sound sleep. I'd sit up in whatever bed I was sleeping in, in whatever place I was in, and think about the life that Anna and I could have had if I hadn't gone bat shit crazy. As the rain came down, I'd sit in the dark thinking about what it would have been like to wake up to Anna's face every morning. I'd think about what our children would have looked like. I thought about the joy we could have shared together.

The life that I didn't have now.

Instead of that life, I'd lost my mind. Worse than that, I'd lost who I was. As much as I wanted to, I knew I couldn't go back to that life. The Jack that Anna had fallen in love with was gone. He was dead. He'd died a slow death on a psych ward in Ann Arbor, Michigan, years ago.

But I never told Anna that. I just walked out of her life without a word.   I never told her to her face that it was over, that I was over. Maybe she needed that to be able to move on with her life. Maybe I owed it to her to talk to her and let her go.

Maybe then I could move on, too. Maybe if I made a formal break with her, then those haunting memories I had of her would go away. Standing there talking to my brother in that little storage closet of a bedroom, I felt a warm breeze against my skin. It could have been the furnace starting up, but I thought it was more likely that it was the Holy Spirit.

"Where's her number?" I asked.

"I've got it written down by the phone. You know, she's probably at school now anyway."

"Yeah, maybe I'll call her tonight."

37

After Jake left to go back to work, I sat down on the couch and started to read one of the magazines on the coffee table. Lisa came in, turned on the TV and just sat there, blankly staring at the screen. I knew she felt like she had to babysit me. She felt like I was some mischievous toddler that would stick his finger in a light socket and kill himself if left unattended for even for a second. There she sat in her fancy real estate clothes, wasting valuable networking time. The scent of her resentment filled the room like sulfur. I gave up on the magazine and watched television in silence with Lisa for a while. We sat there, each of us barely moving, eyes fixated on the screen.

After about an hour, I'd had enough.

"Okay, I'm going out," I told her.

"I'm not sure that's such a good idea, Jack," she said.

"What do you mean?"

She knew what she wanted to say, and I could almost see the cogs in her head trying to translate her meaning into simple words, words even a man like me would understand.

"You've been through a lot," she eventually said. "Wouldn't you like to just sit here on the couch and relax a little? Put all your cares aside?"

"No, I really don't. I want to go out and do the work that I've been given to do."

"But, Jack, the doctor said that…"

"Lisa," I said to her, openly showing my anger for the first time, "did Jake tell you someone had to stay here with me?"

Silence.

"No," she said after a moment's consideration. "No, he didn't."

"Good. Then there's no reason for you to be here. I'm going out to settle some things that need settling. I'm doing it whether you like it or not. You can either call my brother from here or from work. You might as well do it from work. If you're lucky, you might get something productive done today after you tell Jake what a pain in the ass I am."

I've learned a few things about people from my endless hours sitting with shrinks. One of those things is that when you tell someone what they want to hear, they don't argue with you. Lisa didn't argue with me that day. She just nodded and went to the door. I followed her out in silent procession.

"I'm locking the door and no one will be home until six tonight. You're on your own until then. You got a problem with that?"

"None whatsoever."

With that, Lisa walked out the door and into her black Lexus, buckled herself in and without even a look in my direction. In a moment, she was down the driveway and off to work. I waited until her car was just a black dot at the far end of the road before I set off. I turned right down Cambridge Blvd. and started walking. I didn't know exactly where I was going but I did know that I was back on the job, doing the work God had given me to do. It made me smile.

The day was cool but dry. I walked down

the sidewalk, past fancier and fancier homes, until I got to Franklin Street. I took a right there and started walking downtown. It didn't take long for the neighborhood to get rough and the houses to get dumpier. I felt more at home here, like I was back in my element.

I decided to go to the Grand Rapids Public Library and do a little research on Missy Chen. Johnny's sister was running for mayor and so I expected to see quite a bit of ink on her in the *Grand Rapids Press*. She was young, attractive and ambitious, not the kind of woman that you typically think of as a killer. Yet her ambition might be a motive to kill. History was filled with stories about the terrible things people did for ambition's sake. Johnny certainly couldn't have done anything to help her get elected. Having a mentally ill gay brother might help you get elected in California but not in conservative Grand Rapids. If word got out about Johnny's lifestyle and drug use, it'd be bad news for her campaign. But would she be willing to kill to stop that from happening?

I didn't think so. But I'd learned enough about sin in church, and about human nature in the nut house, not to rule out the possibility completely.

When I got to the library, I found it very busy as usual. The library was within walking distance to the mission and a lot of the homeless guys hung out there. The mission pushed them out the door during the day, and the library was a place where they could go and no one would hassle them about loitering. Most of the guys just sat at a table and looked at magazines but some surfed the

Internet on the library's computers. I didn't know why they would even be interested in the Internet until one day I looked across the reading room and saw a guy scrolling through a pornography website. I was shocked by the incongruous sight of a naked woman on the screen below the reference books. That guy was as open about it as he could be, too. No shame.

I made my way back to the newspapers and started browsing. After coming up empty for an hour, I got bored and moved on to *Grand Rapids Magazine*. It took a few hours but eventually I found what I was looking for. My hunch had been right. There was a lot of ink being spilled about the upcoming mayoral election. The current mayor, a Christian Reformed pastor turned Amway distributor turned politician, had chosen to retire and not run for another term. His decision took the local Republican Party by surprise. All the party big shots had expected him to run again and so no one had laid the groundwork for a campaign. There was a political vacuum, and we all know that nature abhors a vacuum.

Within a month of his announcement, every opportunistic Republican in town had thrown their hat in the ring. The field was ridiculously big at first, but narrowed slowly as some of the lighter weight candidates came to their senses. According to what I read, the Chen campaign was still strong. Missy Chen was a real contender. She even had a storefront campaign headquarters downtown.

I decided to pay her a visit.

It was late afternoon by the time I got to

Chen HQ. I'd never been to a campaign headquarters before but by the way they were portrayed on television, I expected a big sign-filled room with a gaggle of college kids answering phones and licking envelopes. I expected the energy and the passion that come with youth.

The Chen headquarters was nothing like that. I decided to walk in and ask directions to the bus station just to get a feel for the place. When I walked in, there were only two men inside; both were over fifty and just sitting around a big desk listening to some blowhard talk radio station. Missy Chen was nowhere in sight so I went over to the little café across the street and ordered a coffee. I found a seat with a view and sat down.

I sat there for two hours nursing that cup of joe. I waited in the dwindling sunlight hoping to see Missy Chen walk up but she never showed. The thought crossed my mind that if she was involved with Bruce Daniels and Johnny's murder, and she saw me sitting outside her office, I'd be in big trouble. She could just call Bruce and before I knew it, his big fat hands would be dragging me into a car. I decided to call it a day.

I walked back to Jake's as the light slowly left the sky to make way for the moon and the stars. It was a nice clear night.

When I reached Cambridge Boulevard, my watch said it was just after six-thirty. Jake and Lisa would both be home and if I was lucky I would enjoy a home-cooked meal before I retired to the inflatable bed.

The light in the living room was on as I

walked up the walkway. I went to open the door
but then realized that I didn't have a key, so I
knocked instead. Lisa, still in her work clothes,
answered the door.

"Jake is working late," she said to me
without a word of welcome. "I already ate dinner.
You can help yourself to whatever you find in the
kitchen."

What a loving sister-in-law. I scrounged
around in the refrigerator but there wasn't a lot
there. Jake and Lisa Plowman were young strivers
and young strivers usually ate all their meals at their
desks. No point in going grocery shopping when
you don't have time to cook. Eventually, I made
myself a peanut butter and jelly sandwich and ate it
with a big helping of potato chips. It wasn't the
home-cooked meal that I'd hoped for but it tasted
better than the hospital food I'd been eating.

When I was done, I refilled a big bowl with
chips and went into the living room. Lisa was
watching some crime drama on television. The
handsome detective on the screen held Lisa in rapt
attention as she nibbled on a small plate of baby
carrots and dip.

I watched the show with her for a bit and
then during one of the commercial breaks, I broke
the silence.

"Lisa, could I use your computer to check
my email?"

She looked at me as if I had asked her what
twelve times thirty-six was and she was struggling
to work the math in her head.

"The computer is in the office down the

hall," she said to me, "but I've got a block on inappropriate content to protect my nieces."

"What do you think I was going to…" I started but then I didn't let myself finish the rest of it. I was a guest in her house. It was either stay here for a while or go back to the hospital or the jail or some other place I didn't want to be.

"Could I please use it?"

"Okay, but remember, be appropriate."

I got up and calmly walked down the hall. It took all the effort that I had not to lose my shit with her, to tell her what I really thought about her. But I held it together. I half-wished Patel was there to see it.

The office was a small bedroom that had been converted into an office. The computer, an old desktop model, sat on top of a flimsy desk Jake probably put together by hand. The chair was old and cheap too, but comfortable. I recognized the chair from Jake's law school apartment. Nothing was on the walls except a black and white copy of Jake's law degree. This room was clear of even the slightest influence of Lisa Plowman. I liked it very much.

As the computer booted up, I tried to remember Johnny's hotmail password. His email address, <u>FabulousChen@hotmail.com</u>, was not something that I was going to forget anytime soon. Its flamboyance fit Johnny to a tee. His password was another story. When I'd first read it on his laptop, the one that the cops had taken from me and was now probably in some evidence locker somewhere, the password hadn't been unique enough to stick with me. I double-clicked on the web browser and called up the Hotmail site. It was up on my screen almost as soon as I had hit Enter. Jake had some really fast Internet service.

Was the password big something?

Just then, I started to feel that I was being watched. It hit me like that blow to the head Daniels had given me the first time I had the pleasure of making his acquaintance. I turned around, hoping to catch Lisa watching me, but there was no one else in the room. Just to make sure, I rolled the old chair over to the doorway so that I could peek around the corner. No one was there either.

I could hear the dialogue of Lisa's crime show down the hall and assumed that Lisa was still watching. The show would be nearing the climax. She probably wouldn't get up now even if the house was on fire. I rolled the chair back to the screen and sat there staring at it. I waited for the password to come to me but it wouldn't.

I tried to imagine sitting there in the Three Kings coffee shop typing in the words that gave me access to Johnny's online life. He'd put all his passwords in a word processing document that I'd found. I remembered he had used a derivation of this password for some other site too. Maybe it was You Tube. He had used...

Bigdaddy. That was his password.

I hurriedly typed it into the little box and hit Enter.

The page didn't load immediately and for a minute I was sure that I had the password wrong. I was sure my crazy brain had failed me once again. Another Jack Plowman failure. But after a few seconds the page loaded, and Johnny's email was open.

He had three new emails. Two of them were just spam. Both Viagra advertisements disguised to look like emails from friends. The third one wasn't spam. It was a real email from a real person and it scared the hell out of me.

Staring at that blue inbox screen, all I could see was the name of the familiar sender and the glaring subject header. The subject was "WARNING" in big bold capitals.

I'd always thought those people who always complained about people typing in all caps didn't have enough real problems to deal with. But sitting there, I understood how all those large letters could get to you, except instead of feeling irritation, I felt fear. Pearls of sweat formed on my forehead and upper lip. I could feel my heart beat like the bass drum in some techno song. A flood of anxiety washed over me, my head swimming in that old familiar murky water. I felt sick and faint and had the sudden urge to lie on the floor and piss myself.

All alone and with no one watching, I let myself lie down on the floor, but I held my bladder, at least for now. Lying on the carpet made me feel better, so I just let myself lay there and tried to will myself calm. I closed my eyes, thought about Jesus and tried to blank out that name on the screen. I tried to forget about the mess I'd gotten myself into. I laid there and thought about Anna and the times we spent walking together around campus. I thought of God's love for the weak.

After a few minutes, I felt better and got up. What I really wanted was a cool glass of water but I knew I had to read that email before I did anything else. If I didn't read it now, I might never have enough nerve.

I clicked it:

> From: Bruce Daniels
> <bruce.daniels.23@yahoo.com >
> To: FabulousChen@hotmail.com
> Subject: WARNING

I know where you are jack. You are staying with your brother on Cambridge drive in east grand rapids. His address is 1134 cambridge. You get this straight, you mother fucker. You don't step one god damn foot outside that door. No more snooping around. Got it? Otherwise I don't just kill you, but I also kill your brother and his hot piece of ass wife. Not one foot out the door, or everyone dies. I'm watching.

38

I couldn't believe what I was reading. I stood there shell shocked for so long that the computer had gone to sleep by the time I'd regained my composure. I had to wiggle the mouse around to wake it up, mouse wiggling being the smelling salt of computers.

I thought about what to do. I told myself that I should probably print off the message and give it to Jake when he got home. It wasn't just me in this now, it was all three of us. I had a responsibility to try and protect them. As much as I didn't like my sister-in-law, I didn't want anyone to get hurt and I knew that Bruce Daniels was capable of violence and probably murder too. If he'd been watching me like he said he was and he'd seen me make my little trip this afternoon, things were about to get bad.

Really bad.

I sent the email to Jake's ancient printer but when the paper jammed, I decided that this wasn't the time to play tech support and ran off to the living room without the paper copy

"We've got serious problems," I said to Lisa.

"What?" she asked, looking up from the television. She was watching another crime drama but this one was different. This investigator, while still handsome, had blond hair instead of brown.

"Jack, are you okay? You look as pale as a ghost."

I opened my mouth to start telling her all

about Bruce Daniels and how he very well might be on his way over to kill us both right now when I saw a car out on the street slow down and turn into the driveway. It inched up the drive cautiously, unsure of itself. Lisa saw me stare out at it.

"Jack?"

The car came to a halt and the engine died. The headlights that announced its presence were gone too. The night outside returned to total darkness. I waited for the sound of a door opening but it didn't come. It should have come, but it didn't. The only sound that I could hear was the weeping of a woman recounting her rape on television. I grabbed the remote and turned the TV off. Lisa looked at me, puzzled.

"Jack, I was watching that," she protested.

"Shhh," I said and switched off the lamp beside her as well. It was the only light on in the room, so when I switched it off, the room was blanketed with the same darkness that was outside.

"What are you doing?" she asked, but the anger was gone from her voice. In its place was fear. Pure, cold fear. The fear that you have when you know you're going to get hurt.

"Be quiet," I told her sotto voce. I hunched down next to her between the couch and the coffee table and tried to stay perfectly still. Lisa did the same. I watched out the window. With the light off, I could make out the bushes outside the window and the long slope of the lawn down to the street. I didn't see any movement. All was still.

But the house had more than one entrance. If he'd seen the light in the living room, he may have decided to try the back door, or a back window. I turned my head around in an attempt to find a window to the back yard to look out, and that's when the front door knob wiggled.

Someone was at the front door and they weren't knocking.

I turned my head around to the moving door knob and motioned for Lisa to stay down. The look she gave me was one that I knew I'd seen before. It was the same look that I'd seen on my face in the mirror of Mr. Chen's bathroom. She started to speak but then didn't.

I crept up slowly to the door and positioned myself behind it so the person who opened it wouldn't be able to see me. As I was flattening myself against the wall, the tumblers in the lock fell into place with a click and the door slowly opened.

"What's going on?" a familiar voice said.

I didn't move, frozen with fear. The intruder turned on a light.

"Oh, my God," Lisa gasped.

Using both my hands, I pushed the door back towards him, hitting the intruder with a thud. I heard him gasp and, sensing my chance, bolted out from behind the door to face him.

It was Jake. I'd knocked the wind out of him. He stood hunched over in the doorway trying to get it back.

"Oh, man, I'm so sorry," I said.

"What the hell is wrong with you?" Lisa screamed at me. "What are you trying to do? You're fucking crazy! I will not have this goddamned head case in my house, Jake! What the fuck is wrong with you, Jack?"

I had no response. Lisa, for all her faults, was right this time.

Jake struggled to regain his composure and finally stood up. He was actually smiling.

"Not exactly the way I expect to be greeted after a hard day," he said, bracing himself on the doorjamb, "but you certainly got my attention."

He chuckled a little and so did I, more in the hope of lightening the mood than actually thinking something was very funny. But it didn't work. Lisa was still enraged.

"I told you this was a bad idea, Jake," she seethed. "Your brother belongs in an institution, not in our home! He is not fit for society. He's almost killed you within a few hours of you bringing him into our home! This is not going to work for me. Either he goes or I go. Mother would be glad to have me back, you know. She never thought that you had the drive to be successful anyway. I'm always telling you that you need to make more money, Jake. We can't live like this. Maybe Mother was right. Maybe I should have married Max Anderson. He's already vice president of his father's company. You should see the house they have. I'm starting to feel like…"

Jake interrupted her.

"Just relax, Lisa. No one got hurt. I just got the wind knocked out of me, that's all."

My brother closed the door I'd just hit him with. As his twin, I knew how Jake operated. His preference was to just forget this had ever happened, to just move on. He didn't like to argue, which, come to think of it, was a strange trait in a lawyer.

"I'm fine. I understand how you feel, Lisa, but my brother is my brother and I can't just push him out onto the street. Besides, I'm sure Jack has a reasonable explanation for this. Don't you, Jack?"

"Well, kind of," I said.

"My God," Lisa yelled. "The man is a fucking mental defective, Jake!"

"Lisa, give him a chance. Take it easy."

Jake went and sat next to Lisa on the couch. He put his arm around her and she begrudgingly accepted it. Touching her husband seemed to open her up emotionally. She started to silently cry into his suit jacket. It made me feel even worse.

"What's happening, brother?" Jake asked me from across the room. I still stood stunned beside the door. I was disoriented.

you're crazy

I wasn't sure that I could trust myself. I couldn't seem to think clearly. Overcome with doubt and unsure that I'd even read what I thought I had, I sat down on the tile of the foyer.

"I thought," I began. "I thought you might be Bruce Daniels. I…I just…there was this email that I think he sent but I'm not really sure…"

"Jack, just relax and tell me what's going on."

"Well, it's like this." I took a couple of deep breaths and tried to let the tension blow away. "I got into Johnny Chen's email. I found his password on his computer before they put me in jail. I've been reading his email, you know, looking for clues. The killer knows that I'm reading it and when I got home tonight, I checked it again and there was a threatening email from Bruce Daniels. He said that if I left your house, he'd come and kill us all and I went out today and I thought that he might've seen me and was trying to get us. Honest, Lisa. I was just trying to protect you. I know we don't get along, but I really thought that we were in danger…"

Jake nodded and looked down at Lisa, her head on his shoulder. "Okay," he said. "That makes sense. Right, honey?"

Lisa nodded, but ever so slightly.

"I need to see this email, Jack," my brother said, standing up. "Log back on right now. We need to call the police if this is true."

Jake said if it was true. If. I know that being a mental patient brings this kind of automatic skepticism from strangers, but hearing it from my brother really hurt.

"It's true," I told him, as if my word meant anything to him. "He knows your address. He knows that Lisa is hot. This guy is the crazy one, Jake. Not me."

"Jack," my brother began. "I didn't mean…"

"He said I was hot?" Lisa broke in. "Were those his exact words or did he say cute or attractive?"

There she was. The self-involved Lisa Plowman that I knew so well.

"Let's go read that email," Jake said, walking back to his little office. I started to follow but then stopped when I heard the noise outside the front window. Neither Jake nor Lisa had heard it, or if they had heard it, they treated it like one of the many background noises that we all eventually learn to ignore. You know the sounds. The low hissing that the fan on computers makes. That sizzling noise that fluorescent lights make. Sounds that are all around us all the time, but that no one hears anymore.

But I heard this one.

I froze in place as Jake continued to walk down the hallway. Lisa looked at me like some confused dog but then the noise came again, louder. Lisa heard it this time and turned to look out the big picture window. The fear that had disappeared from her face was back. I was close enough to see the goose pimples rise on her arm. They made her arms look like they were covered with chicken skin.

he's gonna fuck you up

"Get Jake," she said, barely moving her lips.

I started towards Jake but then thunderous banging erupted from the front door. The door frame and the drywall around the door shook from the force. It was the force of powerful fists. The same big meaty fists that had already worked me over twice before.

"Open up," the man bellowed. There was no doubt about it. It really was Bruce Daniels outside the door this time, and only a thin slice of wood separated him from the people he wanted to kill.

I expected Lisa to lose it, to burst into tears and turn into a blubbering mess. I expected her to become another problem that we'd have to deal with. But that's not the way it went down that night. Hearing the threatening voice must have flipped some self- preservation switch in her head, because as Bruce continued to yell at us from outside, Lisa turned to me calmly and said, "Get something to barricade the door, Jack."

There was another thud at the door, this time much stronger. Bruce must have thrown his whole body weight this time because even an end table across the room shook. An empty vase tottered back and forth, threatening to fall.

The only thing that I saw that would be of any use as a barricade were the oak chairs in the kitchen. I ran on shaky legs and grabbed one. It was heavy, but I managed to get it wedged under the doorknob before the next blow came. I could almost feel his hatred come through the vibrations in the wood.

"Open the goddamn door!"

"Jake!" Lisa yelled. "Get in here now! He's here! He's here!"

Another blow hit the door and the frame bulged inward perversely. Bruce laughed.

I looked over at Lisa and saw that she was punching the three numbers you never want to have to dial into her cell phone. She got up off the couch and looked me straight in the eye, the drama of a few minutes ago totally forgotten.

"Get something to protect yourself with," she barked at me, her face washed in terror. "He's coming."

the devil's at the door. i'm at the door.

knock knock.

She was right and so were the voices.

Just as Lisa was grabbed the poker from the fireplace, the front door exploded inward. Lisa dropped the phone in shock and it fell to the floor in front of the fireplace. The door's explosion was so violent that it was almost like Daniels had dynamite in his hands. Wood shards filled the air in such number that I reflexively covered my eyes. When the wood shards had all fallen, Bruce was standing where the door used to be, panting and full of sweat. His hands were dripping in his own blood and for some strange reason the sight made me think of Jesus on the cross.

"Oh, man," he said between deep breaths. "You should have opened up, Jack. I told you to open up, brother."

He looked over at Lisa, the poker defiantly out in front of her.

"Oh, yeah. You and me gonna have some fun, Ms. Plowman. You gonna see what a real man is all about."

If I'd been more of a man, I would have attacked him right then as a matter of principle. But I didn't. I just stood frozen in fear, more full of piss than courage.

Bruce stepped over the shattered door frame and pointed his finger at me. "I'm gonna make you watch what I do to her, and then you're gonna die, Jack Plowman. You'll never mess up another deal again, fuck face."

He lumbered toward us, a growl on his face. Lisa started to swing the brass poker in his direction.

prepare to meet Satan, jack.

That's when I heard Jake's voice behind us.

"You have just committed home invasion, Mr. Daniels," he said without a hint of fear in his voice. "That is a very serious crime."

Daniels turned to him and laughed. Jake was standing in the kitchen, his body in complete shadow.

"Oh, I'm very sorry," Daniels hissed. "But I don't give a good goddamn about you and your laws. The only law I recognize is survival of the fittest, and you don't look very fit to me."

Daniels must have thought that he was pretty funny because he laughed deeply then. He laughed so hard that he had to steady himself on the recliner. As for me, I didn't get where my brother was going with this.

"Might I suggest," Jake continued, "that you surrender right now and make this easy for yourself."

Daniels laughed derisively but not as hard as he had at his own joke.

"I'm gonna fuck you up real good, law boy. You won't be able to think straight when I'm done with you."

Daniels started towards Jake, and Jake, as brave as I was cowardly, went to meet him. As he stepped from the shadows, I could see why it had taken so long for him to get here. He wanted to come prepared.

"Mr. Daniels," my brother calmly intoned, "if you take one more step toward me, so help me

God I will blow your motherfucking head off."

Daniels looked up as Jake raised the gleaming pistol and took aim. It stopped him dead in his tracks.

"You don't look much like a marksman to me," Daniels said. "I bet you ain't never even shot that thing. I bet you couldn't even hit me if I was standing still."

"Maybe," Jake said to him, firm as steel, "but to find out you have to take one hell of a chance, Mr. Daniels."

Daniels seemed to consider it. He looked over at Lisa and I, huddled together in the far corner trying to be invisible, and then back at Jake. "I'm in a position," he said, "where I've got to take chances in order to stay alive. You ain't gonna use that gun. You ain't got the guts to kill a man. You're weak, soft."

"I'm a lawyer," Jake said. "Haven't you heard what scumbags we are? I could kill a filthy pig like you in a heartbeat and then sit down immediately and enjoy a nice dinner."

Daniels shrugged and then, out of nowhere, made a jumping lunge at my brother. I saw the muzzle flash and then a moment later heard the deafening crack of the shot blasting off the walls. Daniels and Jake fell into a heap on the kitchen floor, and the gun went sliding across the tile. I got up to help my brother but Lisa was ahead of me. She ran into the kitchen, jumped over the men fighting on the floor, and grabbed for the gun.

By the time I got to Daniels and Jake, Jake had already taken quite a pounding. Daniels was on top of him blasting punch after punch into my brother's head. In spite of this, Jake was still trying to fight back. As Daniels delivered blow after devastating blow, I came from behind him and put my arm around his neck in a choke hold. Feeling the pressure on his neck, Daniels thrashed his head back and forth and stood up. I held on and was lifted off my feet as he stood up. Daniels staggered, then turned around and ran backwards as fast as he could into the living room wall. Needles of pain pierced my back and I let go, dropping to the floor. My moment of heroism over.

Fortunately, by the time I fell, Jake had gotten up. He stood in the kitchen doorway with rigid determination in his eyes. Daniels hit him square in the gut, so fast that Jake didn't even have time to block. Jake doubled over in pain and Daniels raised both his fists together to strike my defenseless brother's neck.

"Get away from my husband," Lisa yelled, "or so help me I will shoot you!"

Daniels looked at her and then positioned Jake like a shield.

"You people don't know what you've gotten yourselves into," he said. "This is more than just a dead queer. This is serious shit. I suggest that you quit while you're ahead and put the gun down before you kill your husband."

Daniels darted a glance backwards towards me to make sure I didn't pose a threat and then started to ease back towards where the front door used to be.

"You mark my words. Even if they catch

me, you're still not safe. This shit goes beyond me. If I'm out of the game, someone else will come for you. Get out of town now while you can."

Lisa followed Daniels to the door. She kept the gun pointed at him as he backed away.

"Let my husband go," she said.

"Forget Johnny Chen. Forget all this," Daniels said as he took my staggering brother's head in his powerful hands.

"Forget everything," he said as he bashed Jake's head into what was left of the jagged door frame.

"Jake!" Lisa cried as Jake's head made contact with a loud hollow thunk.

As Daniels sprinted down the lawn, Lisa and I ran to Jake. He was barely conscious. Tears rolled down Lisa's face as she sobbed and held him in her arms. Jake mumbled something unintelligible and Lisa lowered her ear to hear.

"He wants you," she said to me and I knelt down to face him.

"Are you okay, man?" I asked.

"It's...it's some kind of blackmail," he wheezed. "The cops know that much. Johnny got a lot of money blackmailing someone. Detectives don't have any more leads though."

"Okay. Thanks, Jake. You're going to be all right, bro. Just hang on. Help will be here soon."

Jake nodded.

"Lisa," he said. "Go stay with your friend Jacki in Detroit. Get away from here."

"I won't leave you," she sobbed and grasped

Jake's hand.

He shook his head. "Too dangerous to stay here. They'll find you. Jack, you need to get away too. Find somewhere safe. Find…"

But he wasn't able to finish what he wanted to say. I looked down and saw Jake's eyes roll back into his head as he grew slack in Lisa's arms.

39

The police talked to Lisa and I at the hospital for a long time. We were interviewed separately by two different officers to make sure our stories matched up. When it was clear that they did, the cops let us go.

Jake was admitted to the intensive care unit. Lisa said that the doctor had told her that he was stable but that he'd suffered a serious head trauma. It would be impossible to know the extent of the damage for at least a day. He told her to go home for the night and get some sleep.

Lisa suggested that we drive down to Kalamazoo together and get a hotel room for the night. In the morning, we could drive to Detroit and stay with her friend. We'd both be safe there.

I thanked her but declined. I had things to do in Grand Rapids. I promised Lisa that I'd find a safe place for the night and started to walk away. She begged me to reconsider, but I told her that I couldn't, especially after what had happened tonight. This was personal now. They were messing with my family and there would be hell to pay.

I walked Lisa out to her car in the Michigan Street ramp and she kissed me on the cheek as if she really loved me like family. I watched her drive off down the big hill towards the highway and then I set off the other way, cradling the stuffed duffle bag that held all my possessions. The hill was steep and the night air was as cold as Bruce Daniels' heart. When I got to the top of the hill, I stopped at the all-night Burger King to treat myself to a chocolate shake. Lord knows I deserved at least that.

The place was deserted this time of night so I sat all alone in the dining room. Once in a while a group of teenagers would walk in and order something, but they always took their food to go. I sat there thinking for a bit and then made the call. I apologized like crazy for waking him up, but he didn't seem to mind. He wanted to help, he said.

It was very late when he finally showed up. As usual, he had on his collar, even though it must have been almost five in the morning by then.

"Hey, Jack," he said, taking a seat next to me in the plastic booth. "I'm glad you're okay. Why don't we just go back to the rectory and get some sleep?"

"I'm really tired," I told him. "But I also really need to talk about what happened."

jake looked like a smashed up watermelon, didn't he

"There's no hurry, Jack. We can talk a little in the car on the way if you want. In the morning, we can have coffee and you can tell me all about it, okay?"

I was dead from exhaustion. I'd almost fallen asleep in the Burger King a few times while I'd been waiting. But for some reason, once we were in Fr. Chris's car and I started telling him all about Jake's beating and Jake's insinuation that there was more to Johnny's death than I knew about, I just couldn't stop the flow of words. Halfway into my story I noticed that Fr. Chris had driven past the church and down Division Street.

"So what's your next move?"

"Same as it has been from the beginning. I've got to find out who killed Johnny and now why. It's my call from God, but now it's more than that."

Fr. Chris didn't push me to talk anymore that night. When we got to the rectory, he showed me to the same room I'd slept in a few days ago. I thanked him, took a long hot shower, changed into clean clothes and then got into bed. I tried to sleep but the rest my body needed just wouldn't come. All the events of the day ran through my head like I was watching a movie on fast forward. My world had been turned upside down. As I lay there looking at the cracks in the old plaster of the ceiling, I realized that if I continued down this path I was probably going to die.

I waited for the fear to come and take me like it always did, but that night the monster never came. Instead, I laid there as calm as if I was sleeping next to Anna. For the first time in my life, I was truly ready to die. If bringing justice was what God wanted me to do, I'd do it. If that meant that I was going to end up dead, so be it. I'd found something worth dying for and in that I'd also found a holy peace.

I wondered how Jake would react to my death. I wondered how our parents would react when they heard the news that their black sheep son was dead. I pictured my funeral. Fr. Chris would have people sing all my favorite hymns, especially that one about Eden and sunlight and morning. That hymn was so beautiful and so joyful. It was

my all-time favorite. All my friends would be
there. I hoped they would know that I was in
heaven and happy.

I lay there and fantasized about my funeral
for at least an hour before it occurred to me that if I
really was going to die, I had one more thing I had
to do. I turned on the bedside light, found my
wallet and dialed the phone number.

It was late so the phone rang four times
before it picked up.

"Hello?" said a groggy voice that I hadn't
heard in years. A wave of unexpected memories
crashed upon me and I nearly lost my breath.

"Anna?"

"Yes," she said, trying to clear her head.
"Who is this?"

"It's Jack. Jack Plowman."

She was silent for a moment, confused about
whether what she was hearing was real or a dream.

"It's really me, Anna. I'm sorry to call so
late. It's just that the time is growing short now and
I needed to talk to you."

I could hear the rustling of covers and then
the click of a light switch.

"Is it really you, Jack?"

"Yes. It's really me. I'm sorry that I
haven't called you. I shouldn't have left you
hanging like that. That was wrong of me."

"Well, I understand," she said. "It got really
bad, really quickly, and then when you went in the
hospital, I just didn't know what to say or…"

"No," I interrupted her. "You don't have
anything to apologize for. I was the one that pushed

you away, which was stupid because it wasn't you that I was angry at. I was angry at God for doing this to me. I was angry that my life was over and that my dreams were dead even though I wasn't."

"But, Jack," she said, "your dreams didn't have to die. Your life wasn't over. *We* didn't have to die."

"It never would have been the same, Anna. You know that's the truth. The man you loved died in that hospital. The man they discharged still had my name, but that was all that was left of me."

"No," she whispered into the phone. "That's not true. You're calling me tonight, aren't you?"

"I am, but the reason that I'm calling is to let you go, Anna. I'm calling to finally say goodbye to you so that you can move on with your life. I should have been man enough to do this years ago, but I just couldn't bear to let you go until tonight. Probably because the thought of you, and our memories, have kept me alive on some of my worst nights. There's been a lot of terrible nights since I last talked to you, Anna. You can't imagine what it's like to live like this. To never know when you're going to crack. But thinking of you when I was like that always made me feel better, grounded. You've always been with me, even if you didn't realize it, Anna."

"Jack…"

"No, let me finish. I couldn't let you go until now because I wasn't ready. But I'm ready tonight. This is probably the end for me, so I want to let you know that I release you, Anna. I release my claim on your heart. I release you from feeling guilty about me, from wondering what if. All that. You are set free."

Anna was silent. The only sound coming from the other end of the receiver was faint static.

"I still," she said, pausing to collect her thoughts, "I still want to be your friend, Jack. I want us to be friends. Why can't we just do that? There's no reason that we can't talk on the phone and have dinner once in a while."

It was a nice thought, to have Anna back in my life.

"Maybe," I told her, "maybe at one time that would have been possible, but not now, Anna. It's the end for me…"

"What are you talking about? Are you sick or something?"

"No, nothing like that. Listen, Anna. I regret that my mental illness has hurt you. Please move on with your life. I have to go now."

"No," she pleaded. "None of this sounds right. Are you having an episode or something? Are you sick?"

"No," I told her. "I have to go now. Goodbye. I'll always love you."

I placed the receiver back in the cradle, waited for a full minute and then picked it back up. I listened to the hum of the dial tone for awhile, thinking. But then I sat the receiver down on the nightstand once again and went to sleep.

The next morning, Fr. Chris found me

staring out at the road from the church's front steps. I'd been there since sunrise, thinking about what came next and what God was going to demand of me. Last night's calm acceptance had been replaced with creeping fear and doubt. It was one thing to think about dying and quite another to actually do it.

"I thought that I'd find you here," Fr. Chris said as he bounded up the steps and sat next to me. "I've got coffee inside if you want it."

"No. I'm fine. Thanks."

"I called the hospital right after I woke up this morning to check on Jake. I played the clergy card and the nurse said they plan to release Jake the day after tomorrow. It looks like he's going to be okay, but they have a neuropsychologist coming in to do some tests just to make sure. The GRPD has been guarding his room as a precaution, Jack. So you don't have to worry about him. He's in good hands."

I nodded, glad that at least Jake wouldn't be hurt any more than he already was. As I sat out on the steps of the church and watched the world come alive that morning, everything that had happened the night before started to settle in.

"Father Chris, why did God allow this to happen to my brother?"

It's the sort of question that priests get asked all the time in the movies, but Fr. Chris didn't seem ready for it. He sat there pondering an answer for quite some time.

"That's the big question, isn't it? In seminary, they called it the theodicy problem, or as a famous rabbi once asked, 'Why do bad things happen to good people?' I must have read at least 15 different answers to that problem from 15 different theologians, but in the end they all seemed like nothing more than philosophical rationalizing. I guess I don't have a good answer, Jack."

That wasn't what I wanted to hear. I needed to understand what was going on in my life, now more than ever. Fr. Chris's answer left me feeling alone and for the first time that I could remember, disappointed in his guidance.

"That's not to say," he continued, "that we are left with nothing to help us. Remember, Jack. We are very small. The world does a good job of telling us how brilliant humans are, about how much of the world we've already figured out and how it's only a matter of time before we'll be able to explain everything. But you know, as great as our minds are, as wonderful as all the discoveries we've made about our world, we can never even approach the understanding that God has. God's ways are mysterious to us because God is so much larger than we are. You know, Jack, I've known a few people that have dealt with terrible evil in their lives and I've learned from them that the only way to deal with all the pain in the world is to trust. We may not understand it, but we must trust that God can make something good come out of even the worst tragedy. Good Friday has to happen before Easter Sunday."

I sat there and looked out over the growing phalanx of cars that had come to a standstill at the bottom of the steps. Morning rush hour in Grand

Rapids. People were going to work, just like they always did. And here I was: in a mess that I never intended to be in, just trying to play yet another crappy hand, and working like hell to resist that familiar impulse to fold.

"Thanks," I told Fr. Chris, getting up. "That helps. I've got an appointment to get to now. Please pray for me."

"I will," he said, "just like I always do. What time are you going to be back? I usually have dinner at about six."

After what happened the last time he let me stay with him, I was shocked that he was going to offer it again.

"No," I told him, grabbing my trusty bag on the step below, "I'm going to see if my friend Walt can put me up. If not, then I guess I'll try someone else or sleep outside. I don't want you getting hurt like Jake."

"Jack, I know that you…"

"I thank God for you, Father, but you know as well as me that you're better off without me here. I'll keep in touch."

He accepted my decision without making a show of trying to talk me out of it. We were past that now.

"Okay. You know you can call me."

I shook his hand and then headed off down Division alone. The Community Mental Health building was only a few blocks away from St. Mark's and a quick glance at my watch assured me that I had plenty of time before my nine o'clock appointment with Tiffini and her boss, Ken. I thought about what my next move should be. Bruce Daniels had made a brazen attack after I had made my trip to talk to Missy Chen. That could mean that Missy was an important link in Johnny's murder. Talking to her would be my first priority after my meeting.

Although I resented being babysat by Tiffini, I knew that her supervision and my brother's lobbying were the only things keeping me out of the nut house. It really was a small price to pay for my freedom. Besides, there was no reason that this trip would have to be a total waste of time. Johnny had been a mental health client just like I was. I might be able to weasel some information about him out of Tiffini or one of the many people that hang out in the C.M.H. lobby during the day.

My hopes of running into someone who knew Johnny were dashed as soon as I walked in the door. The lobby was empty. There wasn't a soul to be seen besides the old black woman behind the receptionist's desk. I told her my name, that I had an appointment with Tiffini, and then sat down to read one of the many magazines they had sitting out. That was one of the nice things about Community Mental Health. They always had loads of magazines.

I didn't get very long to enjoy the brand new *People* before Tiffini was at the door calling me back. I guess I'd have to find out who Tom Huddleston was sleeping with later.

"Hey, Jack," she said to me. She was looking fantastic as usual in a short red dress and pearls. "Come on back. We're going to meet in

Ken's office."

I followed her back through a hallway until Tiffini stopped at an office that bore a brass nameplate that said, "Kenneth J. Albany, Ed.D." and motioned for me to go in.

When I stepped into the office, it was like I'd stepped through the wardrobe into the land of Narnia. Ken's office was a completely different world than the rest of the C.M.H. building. Albany's office was more like the offices that the partners at Jake's law firm had than any community mental health office that I'd seen. Instead of the old metal desks from the 1970s that most of the social workers toiled behind, Ken had an oak behemoth that was delicately carved. He had a shiny oak cabinet to match his desk on the right wall and two elaborately upholstered side chairs for guests like me. I sat down in one and Tiffini took the other.

"So, Jack," Ken said to me from behind his desk, "I heard that you had a pretty busy night last night. Someone tried to break into your brother's house to assault you and ended up hurting your brother. How is he?"

"He's okay," I said. Albany looked ridiculous behind that desk. He looked like a little kid playing president.

"I've got a lot to do today, so if you don't mind, can we keep this short?"

"You've got a lot to do today?" Albany asked. "If I remember the agreement that we made at the hospital, you were to keep out of trouble until the police are able to finish their investigation of your roommate's death. You don't plan on playing detective again, do you? I would think that after what happened to your brother, you'd stop all that nonsense. Leave the detecting to the detectives, Jack. It's for your own good."

I wanted to argue with him, but I knew that was pointless.

"I understand your point, Dr. Albany," I said. "But this Bruce Daniels guy and whoever he works for are trying to kill me. I don't see how I can just sit back and be a target."

"We're not asking you to let someone victimize you, Jack. We're just asking that you take a good long look at your limitations. You are not a trained investigator. You are not a police officer. You shouldn't be messing around trying to capture criminals like you were in some movie. On top of all that, you have a very serious brain disease called schizophrenia. It impacts your ability to process information in a rational way."

He was so wrong. First off, I wasn't a schizophrenic. No doctor had ever given me that label. Never. Second, he *was* asking me to be a victim. Albany wanted me to sit quietly while I was hunted down and killed by Daniels. There was no way I was going to let that happen.

But I knew my place. Albany was the man with the power here. If he thought that I was not following the treatment agreement, he'd have me back in the hospital in a minute. As much as I hated to lie, I knew that the greater good demanded it. I saw no other way to achieve the mission that God had given me, but to lie to Albany. And so, that's just what I did.

"I'm not planning on any more mischief," I lied. "When I said that I had a busy day planned, what I meant was that I was planning on getting together with my friend Dan. He used to work in the security business and said that he'd help me set up a security system in Fr. Chris' rectory so that we'd be safer there."

Albany nodded and looked at Tiffini. She nodded back.

"When you say the rectory, you mean the rectory at St. Mark's downtown? Are you planning on staying with your priest friend while your brother is in the hospital?"

"That was my plan," I lied again, "assuming that staying with him is acceptable to you, Doctor."

Albany leaned back in his chair. "I think that would be acceptable. I'll let Detective Robinson know that you'll be there. I don't suppose we could hope for a much better guardian for you than a clergy person, huh?"

Albany laughed. Tiffini laughed. And then even I joined the stupid chuckle choir.

"Did you take your medication this morning?" Tiffini asked.

"Oh, yes. I've learned my lesson about that, too. I need my medication to keep me stable. I understand that now."

"Good," Albany said. "I'm glad to hear that. Is there anything you want to add, Tiffini?"

"No, Ken. I'm satisfied that Jack is stable. Should we check in tomorrow, same time?"

"That sounds good to me," Albany said, making some notation on his computer. "Let's make it a standing appointment for now, shall we?"

"I've got a training next Thursday," Tiffini said. "Is it okay if I miss that one, Ken?"

"Sure. I can do it that day." He typed another notation in the computer and then turned to me.

"Okay, Jack. I'll let the police know where you'll be staying. I'm sure that they'll keep their eyes on the place. You'll be fine."

"Thank you, Dr. Albany," I said, getting up.

"You are most welcome, Jack. Don't you worry, son. This will be over soon and you'll be able to get back to your normal life. Won't that be nice?"

"Absolutely," I lied again. I was becoming almost Clintonesque in my ability to lie and it was surprisingly easy once you got the hang of it.

Dr. Albany stuck out his hand and I shook it like I was his dog.

"See you tomorrow," he said.

40

I knocked on the rotting wood as hard as I could, stinging my knuckles on the chipped paint. His house looked like all the other run-down houses on the street. Many of the dusty lawns had been fenced in by cheap chain link so that the owners' dogs could run free. My knocking set them all off like some weird canine alarm system.

He came to the door after about a minute. I heard him disengaging the door's dead bolts before he opened it. I must have woken him up. He was groggy and I saw sleepers in his hound dog eyes.

"Jack?" he squinted at me.

"Sorry to come over unannounced, Walt, but I need your help again and I think I'm running out of time."

Walt let me in and shut the door behind me.

"How did you find my house?"

"Easy. You gave me your phone number. I just went to the library and cross referenced it in the City Directory."

"By why not just call?"

"Listen, Walt," I said. "Here's the deal. Bruce Daniels attacked my brother Jake last night. He hurt him real bad. He is serious about killing me. He's watching me. He knows my every move. I have to finish this, and fast."

Walt led me from the little entryway into his tiny kitchen. The wallpaper was some floral motif with lots of pink and green. It looked like it'd been put up in the 1940s. Even though Walt had been asleep until a few minutes ago, the room still smelled faintly of lard.

"I know I have no right to ask you to help me again. You've already done so much for me, but I need just a little bit more. "

He stared blankly at me, trying to take it all in. He looked like he wasn't sure if this was all just some sort of weird dream. He rubbed his wrinkled hand over his head and then looked me straight in the eyes.

"Jack, you know you're my friend. I'd help you any way I can, but I ain't no criminal if that's what you talking about. I don't want no trouble with the law."

"Neither do I. The Bible says to respect the laws of men. I try to do that. But God has called me to finish this and I cannot let anything get in my way. I have a higher purpose."

"Okay," Walt said. "Why don't you tell me what you have in mind and then I'll decide if I can help you or not."

He led me into his living room and we each took a seat in one of his two green plaid recliners. The room was drab and filled with old furniture, but neat. Walt obviously took pride in his home, modest as it was. Seeing his home and imagining the island of stability that it granted him made me regret asking him to be involved. But I had to. I laid it all out on the line then. I told him everything that had happened to me since the hospital. I told him all about the attack, about how Daniels had as much as said that the death of Johnny was bigger than I'd imagined, and about how Community Mental Health was keeping me on a short leash. He sat there and listened, nodding at the appropriate times. Then I told him what I had planned. I explained it in as much detail as I had worked out, which wasn't much. It was risky, but I thought we could pull it off. I told him that if we succeeded, we might have the evidence we'd need to finish this thing once and for all. Finally, I told him that this wasn't really my plan, it was God's.

"As I was walking around after my appointment at C.M.H., it hit me like I was Paul on the road to Damascus. The plan came fully hatched into my brain, Walt. It wasn't me. It was the Holy Spirit! I just know it!"

Walt nodded but sat there impassively.

"That's it?" I asked. "God speaks to me through the Holy Spirit and all you can do is nod? This is genuine divine intervention, my friend! This is the path that God wants us to take!"

Walt looked away from me and glanced out the window. A man in a long white tee shirt was across the street in his yard, playing with two large pit bulls. The grass was dead and the dogs were kicking up a huge cloud of dust.

"So?" I asked him.

"The plan is cool, man," he said slowly. "I mean, I think it could work. It's just I ain't so sure about God givin' you the idea. Why God gonna tell you to do something dangerous like this?"

"The Lord works," I explained to him, "in mysterious ways."

"So you say," he said, getting up and staring out the window at the man and his dogs.

"You want some coffee or something?" he

asked without looking at me. "I could use some. You woke me out of a sound sleep and I'm still dog tired."

"I'm fine," I said.

Walt went into the kitchen and I heard him go about making the coffee.

"Oh, Jack," he called out from the other room as the coffee brewed. "I talked to my friend down the road. As far as he knows, Patel never knew Johnny. Patel's a high class guy, big shot. He wouldn't even talk to a guy like Johnny when he was at the club. I guess he got enough of that at work."

It didn't really surprise me. Patel, for all his shortcomings, didn't seem like the kind of guy to be involved with murder.

I sat there and waited for Walt to come back. He'd been gone long enough to brew five pots of coffee. He was doing more stewing than brewing in there. As much as I hated to admit it, Walt was the real linchpin. The entire plan would fall to pieces if he balked.

When Walt came back he held a steaming cup of coffee in an old chipped mug. He'd been gone twenty minutes, but I acted like he had stepped away for only a moment.

"It's like this, Jack," he began, sipping the coffee. "I like you, but we ain't known each other for long. We just getting to know each other but now you asking me to put myself in danger for you. This time on purpose. I don't know, man. I'm not sure I could keep it together. I'm holding on here, trying not to think about killin' myself, but I tell you, it ain't easy. I feel like I'm starting to get more stable, like I'm gettin' better. My case manager sees it too. The last attempt I made, the one that got me put in the hospital with you, was half-hearted. I actually called and told someone that I took the pills. That ain't like me, man. I usually want death for real. No bullshit. This time was different. I was makin' progress. But that shit back at St. Mary's..." he trailed off. "You don't know how hard it is, man. You just can't."

He paused and pointed to two small pictures on the wall.

"Those two are my kids, Jack. Dante and Yvette. They all the family I got, man. Wife left me years ago. Didn't let me see 'em much when they was growing up and, honestly, that was probably for the best. I was messed up with the drugs and all. Dante, he's a lost cause. Been in prison since he was twenty for manslaughter. He ain't never getting out. But Yvette, she's doin' pretty good. Going to college downtown at C.C. She gonna get a college degree."

I started to say something but then thought better of it.

"At first, Yvette didn't want to even talk to me when I reached out a few years back, but then she warmed up. I'm the only daddy she ever gonna have. She ain't got no choice but to love me. That girl's special, Jack. In spite of all I put her through, she have me over for dinner once a week. Even calls me Daddy."

Walt looked out to where the man and his dogs had been.

"I can't lose her, Jack. I just can't. She all I got now."

Walt continued to look out the window, at nothing at all.

"I know it sounds dangerous, but you've bested him before, Walt. Fr. Chris and I both tangled with him before and he beat the daylights out of us. But you were able to actually hurt him."

Walt chuckled. "All the street fightin' I did when I was a kid, I guess. Still got the instinct."

"You do have the instinct, Walt. You're the only man for the job. And it's not just me saying it. God thinks so too."

"You and all that God talk," he said. "You know that talkin' like God is whispering in your ear likely get you put in Pine Rest again."

"Maybe," I told him. "and you know it wouldn't be the first time I went right back in after getting out."

We both laughed at that and some of the tension in the room went away.

"You've never really heard God speak?" I asked Walt.

"Nope. Maybe I need some hearing aids, man."

"No, your hearing's good enough. You just have to learn to read God's music."

"Maybe," he said. "You know, Jack. I ain't never met another person like you."

"That goes for me too," I said to him and he smiled at me from his chair. "So, are you in, my friend?"

He didn't answer, he never actually said a

single word, but then again he didn't really have to. The look on his face told me everything I needed to know.

      I sat at the table sipping the expensive coffee and waited. I didn't know when she would show up, but I knew that it was just a matter of time before she did. Waiting like this, in plain sight in a heavily trafficked area, was dangerous. I knew that and yet I sat there anyway, I sat there *because* it was so dangerous. From what I knew of her, she was a busy, hard driving woman but I was pretty sure that she'd show up sooner or later.

      The weather, which until recently had been making the turn to spring, seemed to have decided to make a U-turn that day. It was cold and the temperature made the metal of the chair seem cold. I wondered if it would be better to die in the cold. Something about that seemed right to me for some reason. Jesus probably felt pretty cold up on Golgotha. Death was always cold.

      She showed up even sooner than I could have hoped for. I didn't even get a chance to finish my coffee before she came into sight in her black skirt and high heels. She was carrying a large, black leather messenger bag, the kind that everyone used now in place of suitcases.

      I got up and ran to catch up with her. I knew that once she got inside, I'd never be able to talk to her. Leaving my coffee cup half full, I leaped over the fancy metal fence that divided the café seating area from the public sidewalk and walked quickly towards her.

It didn't surprise me that she was a fast walker and that I had to struggle to catch up with her. This woman knew what she wanted and wasn't one to waste time. It wouldn't have surprised me a bit to find out that she worked 16 hours a day.

I was huffing and puffing by the time I reached her.

"Ms. Chen," I said, trying to hide how winded I was, "could I talk to you for a minute?"

Missy Chen stopped in her tracks and turned around. She was as beautiful today as she was when I first saw her at her father's house. She looked at me quizzically as people passed us on the sidewalk. I knew she recognized me but couldn't place from where.

"I'm Jack Plowman," I told her. "I was your brother's roommate."

At the mention of her brother, the color faded from her face. She stood on the sidewalk, shocked to be confronted with the memory of her dead brother unexpectedly. She didn't know what to do.

"All I want to do is to talk," I told her. "That's all. We don't even have to go back to your campaign office if you don't want to. We can just go for a walk. Actually, I'd prefer that. Lately, I find that it's in my best interest to keep moving."

She thought about what I was saying for a second and as she did, she seemed to relax.

"Okay, we'll talk," she said. "But just for a few minutes. I've got a lot of work to do. The debate is coming up and I have a lot of prepping to do."

"That's fine," I said, walking up to stand beside her. "Just a short walk then."

She continued on the way she'd been going and I walked with her. She seemed to be walking slower now that I'd joined her.

"So it must be exciting to be running for mayor," I said.

She shot me a harsh glance. "Let's not make small talk, shall we? You didn't come here to hear me talk about what it's like to run for mayor, did you?"

"You've got me there," I said.

"So let's just cut to the chase," she said as her campaign headquarters came into view. When we came to her door, Missy passed by it, making one furtive look back. I had the strong feeling that she wished she were there doing something more productive than taking a leisurely walk in downtown Grand Rapids with a mental patient.

"You must have come to talk to me about Johnny," she said. "If you're here to try and get me to pay you for staying quiet about my brother's…idiosyncrasies, then you're barking up the wrong tree. I've never hid anything. The press realizes that this is a private family matter and has no bearing on my ability to be this city's mayor."

For the first time, she sounded like a politician. She'd thought about this before.

"It's nothing like that," I told her. "I'm not after your money. I'm after the person that killed Johnny because he is now trying to kill me as well."

She didn't seem impressed but said, "Go

on."

I told her about Bruce Daniels and his attempts to hurt me and the people that were closest to me. I told her that I wanted to bring justice to the people that killed Johnny. I left out the part about God calling me to do it. That might turn her off. A prophet never being appreciated in their own home town and all that.

"So that's why you went to my father's house? You were playing detective?"

"I don't like how that sounds, but I suppose that's what I was doing."

We walked on until we came to the DeVos Place Convention Center. The Convention Center's curved steel form reminded me of a single angel's wing. It was like the city's protector.

"So now you want to question me?" she asked. "What do you think I could possibly know to help the investigation that I haven't already told the real investigators?"

"Well, you could tell me who *you* think did it."

We passed the protective wing of the DeVos Center and Missy took a left turn on Michigan Ave.

"I'll tell you what I told Detective Robinson. I have no idea who killed my brother. If you lived with him, you know what kind of life he led. He was into drugs and sex. He thought of no one but himself. He dishonored my family and spent his time with any number of scoundrels that would just as soon kill him as not. He lived like an animal and died like one too."

"What about your father? Do you think he

was involved? From what I've learned, Johnny seems to have had something on Mr. Chen and he was using it as leverage to get things from him."

Although her voice seethed with anger, Missy didn't look at me when she answered.

"How dare you imply that my father would kill his own son! If we weren't in public right now, I'd slap you for even suggesting it! My father has his problems but he, unlike Johnny, knows the difference between right and wrong. He would never have harmed Johnny, even if he deserved it."

"You said your father has his own problems. Are you talking about his gambling addiction?"

That stopped her in her tracks and she stared at me, unable to hide the shock from her face. It was a logical guess. I'd seen the horse racing papers in his office and thought it seemed odd.

"Oh, yes. I know about his problem," I said. "If he's anything like my junkie friends, I bet he went to treatment more than once to try and beat it too. Probably failed every time. As much money as your father makes, I bet he did a lot of damage."

She didn't even try to deny it. "It's not something we talk about, you understand," she explained. "My mother forbids me to even mention sports or horses when my father is around, for fear of feeding his addiction. I admit that he has hurt our family a great deal with his gambling. I've even had to intervene to stop him from losing the house. He has so little money left now..." she trailed off.

That the truth was finally out seemed to change her mood dramatically. Missy began to sound less like a polished politician and more like a confessor recounting her sins to a priest.

"If he was so broke, where was the money coming from that he was paying Johnny?" I asked.

"What are you talking about?"

"The payouts. I have proof that your father was paying Johnny to keep his mouth shut about something. Where did he get that money from?"

The look on her face told me that this was news to her.

"You're saying that my father was giving Johnny money?"

"Yes, and probably a lot of it, from what I've read in his emails. There was something that your father wanted kept secret and he was willing to pay Johnny to keep it that way."

We'd crossed over the Grand River and were approaching the Gerald R. Ford Museum where the former president was buried in a crypt cut with a view of the river. Seeing that building always reminded me that death awaits all of us, even presidents.

"Maybe you're a better detective than I gave you credit for, Mr. Plowman. I don't believe that the police told me anything about this. Maybe Detective Robinson chose not to share this with me because it cast a poor light on my dad, but my gut says they don't even know."

"So, where'd the money come from?" I asked again.

"I don't know," she said. She sounded sincere and I was inclined to believe her. "I've seen all his financial records. He hasn't had any savings to speak of in at least three years."

"Has he been gambling? Maybe he had some big wins and has kept it secret from you and your mom."

"He's quit many times before, but he always goes back to it. It wouldn't surprise me at all that he was back at it. But there's no way that he could have squirreled away any real money. My dad has always been a gambler and he's always been a really bad one. For a man that places as many bets as he has in his life, he hardly ever wins."

"But he did have money, and he was turning it over Johnny. So where else could it have come from?"

Missy walked onto the grounds of the Ford Museum as she pondered my question. A group of school children were filing in in as orderly a fashion as could be expected. There were a few people paying their respects at the grave site as well.

"Dad's been an accountant for years," Missy said. "He's very well respected at his firm and has worked on some very big accounts. I'm sure that he'd be a full partner by now if it weren't for the gambling. Maybe he's been playing games with the books on one of his accounts."

"Maybe," I said. "But wouldn't the company figure that out pretty quickly? I mean, a smart guy might have been able to pull that sort of stuff off before the Enron debacle but not after, right?"

"You've got a point there," she said as we got close enough to the group of kids for me to hear their young teacher admonish them for not staying in line. That teacher, I thought, must have forgotten the joy of being a child and going on a field trip.

"But if you're sure about Dad making payments to Johnny, then he must have gotten it somewhere."

"I'm as sure about those payouts as I am that your brother is rotting in the ground right now, Ms. Chen."

If I'd spent more time developing people skills and less time in mental institutions, maybe I wouldn't have reminded her about her dead brother then. I would have just kept talking, getting more and more useful information. But that wasn't what I did. No, Jack Plowman, in his great wisdom, decided that this was a great moment to remind Ms. Chen that her brother's earthly body was now rotting in the cold ground. When I mentioned Johnny, Missy grew silent.

The cacophonous sounds of the school children grew louder. They must have been fifth or sixth graders by the looks of them. The girls in the group were taller than the boys.

As Missy and I became enveloped in the group of students, teachers and reluctant parent chaperones, I decided to try and salvage what was left of my relationship with Missy.

"I'm sorry about Johnny's passing," I told her as we were forced to slow down. "But I came to talk to you today because God has called me to bring justice to whoever is responsible for his murder. I need your help to do that, Ms. Chen. Please."

Missy stopped completely and looked at me

the way she might look if one of the kids standing around us had said something amusing.

"I want to find out who is responsible for what happened to Johnny too, Mr. Plowman," she said. "But I think the people that are best suited for doing that are the police. You have a good day."

With that, she turned around and started back the way she came.

I thought about trying to follow her, to keep asking questions, to stay with her, but then I decided it wouldn't do any good. I'd had her for a minute. She'd been talking, but then I blew it. Dr. Patel would call my little social faux pas a negative symptom of my mental illness. Maybe he was right. But then again, maybe I just had a tendency to put my damn foot in my mouth.

The kids went on filing their way into the museum. For a moment, I considered following suit and taking a lazy walk around the exhibits myself. But then I thought of my brother laying in that hospital bed, and of his not-so-terrible-after-all wife, staying with a friend. This wasn't the time to take a break.

I started to make my way through the long line of children, listening in on their conversations as I passed, when all of a sudden I started to feel like I was being watched. At first I thought it was just the kids, their eyes unconsciously drawn to me, the only stranger over five feet tall among them. But that wasn't it. Someone besides those kids was watching me. I could feel the eyes locked on me. I glanced backward, but there was nothing except a sea of children. I did a complete 360 degree rotation and saw someone that looked familiar over at the section of the Berlin wall on display outside the museum. It was a man. And not just any man, a big man with big hands.

It was Bruce Daniels.

I tried to blink it away, thinking that my paranoia had finally gotten the best of me, but when I looked again he was still there. Except this time he was staring right at me.

I walked into the lobby of the Ford Museum in the middle of the swarm. I tried to look like a teacher, or at least a parent who'd had gotten stuck chaperoning a trip to a boring museum. As we moved forward in the line, I saw Daniels moved towards us.

Maybe it was because of the countless number of kids in the vast lobby, or maybe it was because no one could even fathom someone trying to sneak into this place, but no one questioned me or asked to see any ID as I walked in. Once I cleared the lobby, I looked back and saw that Bruce had followed my lead and joined the long line of people snaking into the building. He was about twenty feet back and when he caught me looking at him, he waved.

I stuck close to the kids as they moved through the building. As soon as the classes started to break apart from one another and disperse around the museum and I felt it was safe, I broke away and hid behind a big concrete column on the second floor that offered me a protected view of the lobby below. I stood there and tried to make out Bruce in the sea of people. All the kids looked the same but the few adults stood out. I made three passes over the crowd before I found Bruce. He was standing in the middle of the lobby looking around like he'd lost his own child.

I stayed out of his line of sight and kept my eye on him, my face pressed against the cold concrete of the pillar. Daniels didn't seem to see me, but moved to walk up the stairs. My old friend, the cold sweats, descended on me right on cue. Daniels had given no indication that he even knew I was up here, but I was still terrified. As busy as it was here today, if he did it right (and I was sure he knew how to do it right), he could stab me and then just walk away like nothing had ever happened as I became a bleeding mess on the floor.

he means business this time, jack

It was true. No denying it this time. When the voices were right, they were right.

When Daniels reached the top of the stairs, he peered around. I stood ramrod stiff behind the column. If he laid eyes on me, I'd run like hell. If security came and tackled me, so be it.

But he didn't see me. He walked right over to where the exhibit began and started to glance through the sea of kids. He must have known that I couldn't have gotten very far ahead of him. The way the exhibit was laid out, he could see at least fifty feet in front of him but the entire area was like a highway at rush hour, bumper to bumper. He just stood there, much to the chagrin of the people forced to walk around him. The thought occurred to me that if this had been New York City and not Grand Rapids with all its upright Calvinist courtesy, someone would have at least yelled at him by now.

I decided that this was my chance to make a run for it. I might not get another. I was smaller than he was and I was a good twenty feet closer to the stairs. I was reasonably sure that he wouldn't be able to catch me before I hit the front door. I took three long breaths and sprinted away, blasting out from behind the column like I was running across a prison yard filled with sharpshooters. I ran straight down the stairs with all I had.

But he saw me instantly.

41

I've never run faster in my entire life, but halfway down the concrete steps I glanced over my shoulder to see Daniels, right on my tail, pushing kids out of the way and gaining on me fast. As I neared the front doors, I noticed an old security guard near the entrance that hadn't been there when I came in. He was really old, at least seventy, and thin. If he tried to stop me, I'd have to push him out of the way, but a man that old could get hurt bad if he fell down. God only knew what would happen to him if Bruce decided to shove him.

As I neared him the guard surprised me and just moved out of the way. He stepped a good 10 feet from the door and might as well have said, "Have a nice day" to me as I passed him.

Out the door and onto the plaza I ran, sprinting toward the pedestrian bridge that spanned the Grand River a few yards away. The Amway Grand Hotel cast a dark shadow over the little bridge as the concrete sped under my feet. There wasn't another soul on the bridge. I was about a quarter of the way across when Bruce crested the hill and joined me on the bridge. I had a good fifty feet on him but he continued to gain ground on me.

When I reached the end of the bridge, the stitch in my side that had been growing intensified. I sprinted along the river toward the big hotel that loomed over the city. Daniels kept gaining on me and he didn't seem winded at all.

I hit Pearl Street and my breath grew labored. My lungs couldn't get enough air. I knew

that I couldn't run this fast much longer. I passed
by the Amway Hotel where a couple of neatly
dressed bellhops were helping a car full of guests
unpack, and ran towards Campau Avenue. One of
the bellhops stared at me questionably as I ran by.

Fr. Chris' car was parked illegally across the
street from where they were building the new J.W.
Marriott Hotel. The Camry had a fresh new layer of
dust from the earth they were moving around, but it
looked beautiful to me when I saw it. I found the
key fob in my pocket and pressed the button to open
its doors as I sprinted towards it.

Bruce was right behind me and saw me get
into the car. I locked the doors and turned the key
in the ignition.

But it didn't start.

this is it jack, you're dead

Terror flooded over me and I started to feel
faint. Little white lights flashed across my vision as
Bruce sprinted towards me, helpless in the car. It
didn't make sense. The car wasn't that old. What
could possibly be wrong?

My hand trembled around the key as I
turned it again. I told myself that I had to pull it
together. I asked God to help me. I closed my eyes
and thought of Anna.

My hand steadied just enough to give the
ignition one more turn. This time the engine roared
to life. I was so shocked that I just sat there grateful
for a second that I wasn't going to get murdered
sitting alone in my friend's car.

When I came to my senses, I slammed the
shifter into drive and accelerated towards Bruce

Daniels, who was still advancing on me from across the street. As the car bore down on him, I saw that he was more winded than I'd thought. Dark circles of sweat covered both his armpits.

I sped past him but the stopped traffic at the corner of Campau and Pearl forced me to slam on my brakes. Daniels ran to catch up with me but he too was stopped by a wave of streaming oncoming cars.

Daniels stood panting across the street from me, killing me with his eyes.

We sat there like two cowboys in a standoff in a Western movie—me in the car and him standing winded. Both of us forced into inaction by a sudden surge in afternoon traffic.

It was funny, almost.

As the traffic cleared, I turned left onto Pearl with a confident smile before Bruce could reach me. From the rearview mirror, I saw him standing there considering his options. There were only two ways that this could go from here and I was ready for both. A strange feeling of confidence, so rare for me, swelled up and filled me like holy light. God was with me.

Instead of attacking my car, Daniels turned away from me as I made the turn. Just before he passed out of my view, I saw him run up to the valet and toss a man out of his car.

Fr. Chris's cell phone was sitting on the passenger seat. I picked it up when I hit a red light where Pearl Street met the 131 highway. I thought about running it, getting away from Bruce for sure, but then decided against it. That was not the Lord's will. This had to end sometime, and God had given me a plan. I had to follow it.

As I waited at the light, I dialed Walt's number on the phone. He answered on the first ring.

"Hello...Jack?"

"It's happening, Walt."

He let it sink in. "I didn't think it would be this soon."

"The Lord works in mysterious ways," I said through the crackle of the phone.

"You always say that, man."

"I'm going to be there in about ten minutes. You better leave now."

"Okay, see you in ten," he said and hung up.

Just before the light turned green, I heard a screech of tires behind me. I looked back and saw a white Oldsmobile skid onto Pearl Street. It was coming towards me at an alarming rate of speed. The car was big and powerful and surely had a bigger engine than my Camry.

I turned onto the on-ramp and merged onto US 131 heading south. Gunning the Camry's engine as I entered the S-curve , the car whined in resistance. It was no speed machine, that was for sure, but it didn't really have to be. It just had to get me a few miles up the road. I hit sixty by the time I was in the middle of the S, the centrifugal force pushing me against the door frame, and then seventy and eighty as I finally straightened out. I looked back and saw the Olds was gaining on me.

I hit ninety about the time I passed the Hall Street exit. I tried to keep pushing the little Toyota further, but it just wouldn't go any faster. I had the accelerator floored, but the speedometer was stuck at ninety-three.

Daniels could go faster than that. Much faster.

By the time I got to 28th Street, Daniels was right on my tail. The two of us zigged and zagged through the midday traffic like it wasn't even there. Other cars that saw us moved out of the way.

When I saw the 44th Street exit, I got into the right lane and exited the highway. Daniels followed. The light on the off ramp was green, and I made the turn at sixty miles per hour.

The car skidded wildly. For a brief panicked moment, I thought that I was going to flip it, but then I regained control and straightened the car out. All my experience slipping and sliding around the road during all those Michigan winters had finally paid off.

Back in control, I floored the gas pedal and roared down the hill. The light at the next corner was red and cars blocked the intersection, so I slowed down as I reached the dead cars.

That's when he hit me. I felt the jolt push my body forward as Daniels rammed me from behind with his big Olds. If I'd been going any slower, he would have given me whiplash.

Waiting for the light to change was no longer an option.

I veered off left into opposing traffic and floored it. The cars laid on their horns and turned off the road to avoid me as I maneuvered around them and through the intersection. Daniels stayed on my tail as I swerved around the tangle of traffic.

He was within two inches of my bumper when I turned into the cemetery.

I slowed way down as I entered the cemetery grounds and Daniels did likewise. He backed off a little too. He finally had me exactly where he wanted me.

It was time for him to finish the job.

I drove deeper and deeper into the cemetery, towards the mausoleums. Daniels stayed back and matched my speed as if we were part of a funeral procession. The cemetery was Catholic, and the graves were interspersed with statues of various saints. As I passed a statute of Mary, I made the sign of the cross.

"Mary, mother of God," I said. "Please protect me."

I slowed to a stop in front of the two-story brick building that housed the mausoleum. Daniels did the same.

The pale brick architecture of the mausoleum couldn't have been uglier. It was like the architect had decided that the dead were in no position to complain about the aesthetics of their final resting place and so had spent as little time on the building as possible.

As I opened the door of the Camry, I could hear my heart beating in my ears over the traffic from the highway that raged just beyond me. Stepping out of the car, I couldn't seem to find a stable piece of ground to plant my foot. The ground was like Jello.

Daniels had already exited his car and

was already waiting for me. He stood twenty feet from me next to his big Olds, a Cheshire grin on his face.

"What's going on, Jack?" he asked. "You knew it was me. The smart thing to do would be to run to the cops. But I suppose that I can't expect a head case like you to do something that makes sense."

He laughed a little at how crazy I was.

"Instead," he continued, "you decide to drive to a cemetery. That's an interesting choice, my friend. Very interesting indeed. But I suppose this is a fitting place for you to die. Makes things easier. They can just dump you in the nearest hole and be done with it."

He started to walk towards me. His gait, slow and casual. He knew I had nowhere to run.

As he advanced on me, I took a quick look around. There was no one in the cemetery this time of day. No groundskeepers mowing the lawn. No mourners. It was just like I'd planned.

"Not so fast," I said, realizing too late that I sounded like some cliché in a bad movie. My voice crackled.

"It's not that simple, Daniels. You're not going to be killing anyone today. Today God is bringing you to justice. You're going to jail."

He stopped in his tracks about ten feet from me. I thought I saw a glimmer of fear rise in him for a second.

"Yeah," he said. "I don't see any cops around here, so unless God decides to throw a lightning bolt down from heaven, it looks like you're on your own here."

In the movies, that would have been the moment where Walt walked out and came to my aid. But that wasn't what happened. What happened next was...nothing.

I just stood there looking at that evil hulk of a man that meant to kill me as the sweat gathered on my forehead and my arms started to tremble.

he didn't come. You're gonna die.

It occurred to me then what a stupid plan this was, and how stupid I had been once again. Walt was probably stuck in traffic somewhere, or else he'd gotten second thoughts at the last minute. My talking about God with him had probably convinced him that I was crazy again, so he left a message on Tiffini's voice mail and then went back to whatever it was he'd been doing.

But then, there he was, coming around the other side of the mausoleum. A frail old black man, with graying hair and wrinkles around his eyes. My guardian angel.

Daniels saw him and stiffened up in a defensive stance.

"You think that this old nigger is going to protect you, Jack? I'll kill you both with my bare hands and leave you rotting on the ground. How'd you boys like that?"

Walt walked over and stood beside me. His mere presence calmed me. It was as if by simply standing next to him, I shared his strength.

"I don't appreciate you calling me no names," Walt said to him defiantly. "You ought be more respectful to a man. But people like you all the same. Got no respect for nobody. You live your life like a school yard bully. People like you think might make right. Well, if that's what you think," he said, sticking his hand into the waistband of his pants and pulling out the pistol, "then I guess that this makes me right, don't it?"

In that moment, Daniels was no longer a bully. He looked like a slow kid who just can't seem to grasp what the teacher is saying. He was flabbergasted that my friend, a fellow mental patient, was standing there pointing a gun at him.

"Now," I said. "We're going to take you to the police. But first, I want to know who it is that you're working for. Who killed Johnny? And why? And what is this all about?"

The questions just flew out of me. I wanted to know why my life had been turned upside down and I wanted to be finally done with it all.

"Okay," Daniels said, backing up a few steps. As he backed up, Walt raised the gun and kept a bead on him.

"If you want to know, I'll tell you. I'm the one that killed Johnny but I don't have a beef with the man. I'm just hired muscle. I'm not really the man that you're looking for. I was just doing a job."

Daniels remained calm as he spoke. He'd regained his cocky demeanor and it worried me. I was about to say something to Walt when Daniels started to walk backwards again.

"That's far enough," Walt yelled at him. "Don't take another step unless you want a bullet in your head!"

Daniels stopped and raised his hands. He looked right down the barrel of the gun at Walt.

"Just relax, man. Like I told you. I'm not the man you're looking for. If you want to find out who's really responsible for this shit, you need to lower that gun and calm the fuck down."

Walt looked at me for guidance on what to do next.

"Okay," I said to Daniels. "Who are you working for?"

"I'd be happy to tell you, but first you need to put that gun down on the ground and promise me that once I tell you, you'll let me drive out of this place and forget that you ever saw me. Is that a deal?"

When God had given me this plan, I hadn't expected this. It was supposed to go something like this: Walt comes out with the gun and Daniels melts into a little puddle right before our eyes. He gives up who he's working for and then begs for our forgiveness. I say something like, "Only the Lord can forgive you, Daniels. I suggest you ask him." Something like that. Then we take him in to the cops and are given medals by the mayor for our heroics.

I'd never imagined that Daniels would want to deal.

"So you want us to let you go?" I asked incredulously.

"That's the only way I'm gonna tell you anything."

I looked over at Walt but the look on his face told me he didn't know what we should do next either. This whole mess had been my idea and he wanted me to be the one to decide our next move. Daniels stood before us, hands still raised in submission, but the look on his face was not one of powerlessness. Daniels knew that we were not tough guys. We had no business doing any of this. I was no professional investigator. Even so, I had to make a decision in that moment whether the risk of Daniels getting away was worth the information he was offering.

"Put the gun down on the pavement," I said to Walt.

He nodded and did as I asked.

"Okay," Daniels said. "Now I'm going to slowly walk back to my car, then I'm going to get in and start her up. Once I'm safely inside, I'll open the window and tell you who's really behind this."

Daniels started to slowly walk backwards toward the car that he'd stolen a few minutes before. He kept his eyes on Walt and I, watching us closely to see if we made a move toward the gun.

It occurred to me then that I was again thinking like an idiot. What was to keep Daniels from just getting in the car and taking off? Were either one of us a good enough shot to blow out one of his tires? I looked over at Walt and his face said that he was as unsure about this as I was.

"Wait a minute," I said to him. "This isn't going to work. We need to…"

That was when he made his move. As I tried to renegotiate, Daniels turned and sprinted to the Olds. I was stunned into inaction but Walt was faster than I was. He bent down and picked the gun up off the blacktop and pointed it at Daniels.

"Stop," he yelled, but Daniels had already reached the car.

Before we knew it, he had opened up the door on the big Olds and ducked behind it, invisible except for his feet. I just stood there stunned, not able to believe the plan that had seemed so foolproof in my head had gone so awry. Self-loathing started to flood me but then Daniels stood up so that we could see him again.

He was holding a pistol of his own.

Before Walt could react, Daniels took aim and fired. I instinctively fell to the ground. The gun's report echoed off the mausoleum walls as I hit the blacktop face first. Red pain screamed in my head.

you got shot in the head.

I thought about what it would be like to die here, in a cemetery of all places. I thought about what heaven would be like, what my funeral would be like. I saw Anna coming to my funeral alone.

But then another shot rang out louder than the first. The smooth black of the pavement was all I could see. I felt all over my head looking for a gunshot wound but I couldn't find one. Maybe I hadn't been shot after all. I didn't *feel* like I had been shot, but I also had never been shot before so I had no idea what being shot felt like.

I turned over on the ground. Walt was crouched down near the trunk of Fr. Chris' car. I could see Daniels' feet still behind his door.

The next thing I knew, Daniels stood up from his crouch and fired at Walt. The bullet zipped through the air and made a metallic zing as it pinged off the door of the Camry. A second later, Walt returned his fire, missing wildly.

I knew that I had to get to cover quickly. I sprang up and made a dash for the back of the Camry before either of the men could fire again.

Walt didn't even look at me until I put my hand on his shoulder. He was softly crying.

"I don't wanna do this, Jack," he said to no one as the tears glistened down his creased brown face. "This ain't right, man."

"I'm sorry," was all I could say. Walt was right. I'd made a huge mess of things...again.

"Hey, you two," Daniels yelled to us from behind the door of the Olds. "I see the nigger ain't much of a shot. You guys don't have a chance against me. Throw out the gun now before the cops show up and I might just let you both live."

Things had gotten so out of control. I'd put my friend's and my own life in jeopardy on a foolish scheme. I wanted to be a hero. That was my biggest mistake. As I sat crouched behind Fr. Chris's bullet-ridden car, my greatest wish was for things just not to get any worse.

But that's exactly what happened.

At that point, I just wanted to cut our losses, to get out of this thing alive. I didn't give a damn about Johnny or his killer. I didn't give a damn about justice. And although it pains me to admit it, I didn't even give a damn about the will of God either. I just wanted to go home.

"Walt," I said to him, "I've never even held a gun before but if you want me to give it a try, I'll…"

"I never thought I'd have to do this again," he whispered.

I didn't understand. "What are you talking about? Do what again?"

But Walt didn't answer my question, at least he didn't answer it with words. What he did do astounded me. It still astounds me to think of it now. Walt closed his eyes and took three deep breaths and then he stood up and looked at the big Olds.

Nothing happened for a moment. Daniels remained shielded behind the door, unaware that Walt was standing up, making himself an easy target. When Daniels stood up to check on us, Walt fired. The shot was another wild one but Daniels reflexively sunk down and sought cover. When he did, Walt started walking towards him. I couldn't believe my eyes. He took five steps and then blasted off another shot in the vicinity of the Olds. I jumped as the shot rang out like thunder through the air although it didn't hit a single thing as far as I could tell. When he was about three feet from Daniels, he fired again. This time the shot was so low I saw it skip off the blacktop.

I sat peeking out from the car, transfixed. It seemed real but at the same time, misty and dreamlike. It was like I could have been hallucinating it all.

Daniels was so busy trying to cover himself that he didn't notice Walt as he took his final steps and stood before him. From where I was, all I could see was the big rectangle of the car door, Daniels' feet beneath it, and Walt pointing the gun towards the ground.

"I ain't no nigger," he said and then the muzzle of the gun flashed.

42

To this day, I thank God for the engineer that designed the big doors on that Oldsmobile. That engineer saved me from having to see the bullet enter Daniels' body and to see the red wine stain grow on his chest afterward. I never had to see the actual violent act. It was almost like God had chosen to censor it for me, like he was using a version of that black bar they used to use to cover up nudity on TV.

A moment after he shot Daniels, Walt took the gun and held it to his own head. He was crying and looking down at the man he'd just shot.

"Walt!" I yelled. "Don't do it!"

In the aftermath of what had happened and with all the things what must have been running through his head, I doubt that Walt even heard me. He was all alone in the universe at that moment. If he *did* hear me, he chose to ignore what I said.

I got up off the ground and started to walk towards him.

"Walt, take it easy. You just did what had to be done. God will forgive you, Walt. He's a forgiving God. Nothing you can do can separate you from God's love!"

The barrel of the gun was pressed hard against his brown skin, his finger tight against the trigger. He couldn't seem to take his eyes off of Daniels, who had slumped down on the blacktop in a sprawling mess. I could see the lower half of his torso, but there wasn't any blood.

"Walt, put the gun down," I said as I slowly

approached him. "Please, just put the gun down. Let's talk about what happened. There's no need for anyone else to get hurt today. It's been bad enough already."

As I got closer to the car, I couldn't help but imagine what Daniels must look like. I imagined his chest being torn open like a grenade had gone off inside him. I imagined his rib cage exposed, blown open, his heart a hanging piece of raw meat inside. I tried to push the images out of my mind by thinking of Anna but when I did that, it was her face on the mutilated corpse.

"Walt, please," I said when I reached him. I kept my eyes focused on Walt and not on what laid below on the ground. Walt was wet with sweat and crying the same silent tears that he seemed to have been crying forever.

Guilt flooded over me then and I started to cry, too. I cried for Walt and for what I had done to him. Walt was a good man but he was no more emotionally stable than I was. I cried for all the things that God had chosen to deny the two of us. Clear heads and strong hearts. I really was as crazy as the shrinks said I was. Maybe more crazy, because I hadn't even respected the limits they placed on me for my own good.

I wanted to reach out and hug Walt at that moment. I wanted him to feel how sorry I was about what I'd done to him.

All of a sudden, I saw Walt's face tense up like he was in great pain.

"Walt?"

His finger shuddered once and then he

pulled the trigger.

death death death death death death.

There was a click as the hammer fell in the empty chamber.

The gun was empty. He must have shot Daniels with the sixth and final bullet. I looked over at Walt and he seemed honestly surprised by what had happened. A part of me wanted to laugh. God had let us get so close to total death but then pulled us back at that last moment.

It was only then that I took my first look down at Daniels. The shot had hit him square in the chest. A red circle like a rose had formed where he'd been hit. His eyes were open but I wasn't sure if he was dead or not.

"Coward," he hissed at my friend. Walt just stood there mute, his eyes now closed.

I crouched down next to Daniels and inspected his wound. The flower on his chest was growing into a massive bloom.

"You're losing a lot of blood," I told him. "We need to get you to the hospital."

"No," he said. "No point. Let me die. Can't feel my legs."

"There's still time to redeem yourself," I said. "Tell me who you've been working for. Make at least a little bit of what you've done wrong, right before you die."

Daniels smiled at me. His lips were covered in blood.

"Go to hell."

I didn't know what to do. I was as lost as I'd ever been.

"Lord," I called out to heaven, "what should I do?"

And the fire of the Holy Spirit was set upon me.

I jumped up and ran back to Fr. Chris' car. In the back seat, he had a number of books. One of them was a Book of Common Prayer with a beat up red cover. I grabbed it and ran back to Bruce.

Walt still stood there mute, but I ignored him. I sat down next to Bruce and started to feverishly page through the book. Bruce seemed half awake, but seemed interested in what I was doing. After some effort, I found what I was looking for. It was the section in the book called "Ministration at the Time of Death."

"Almighty God," I began, "look on this your servant, lying in great weakness, and comfort him with the promise of life everlasting, given in the resurrection of your Son Jesus Christ our Lord. Amen."

Bruce and Walt were both silent.

"God, the Father," I said. There was a reply to be said by the dying in the book. I turned the book so that Bruce could see it. He looked at the page and I pointed to the response.

"Have mercy," he said, " on…I…I don't feel right saying it. I'm not religious."

I skipped ahead and found another prayer that seemed appropriate. Before saying it, I reached my right hand out and touched Bruce's head. I made the sign of the cross in the sweat of his forehead and then I read:

"Deliver your servant, Bruce Daniels, O

Sovereign Lord Christ, from all evil, and set him free from every bond; that he may rest with all your saints in the eternal habitations; where with the Father and the Holy Spirit you live and reign, one God, for ever and ever. Amen."

Bruce closed his eyes and was silent.

He was dead.. until he opened his eyes again and looked at me, resurrected.

"Jack," he whispered with great effort. I put my ear close to his mouth so that I could hear what he wanted to say.

Bruce Daniels then spoke his last words and I was the one to hear them. When he was done, he closed his eyes for the last time. I felt his final breath on my cheek and then he was gone.

I gave the moment the respect of silence and when I thought it was the right time, I read again from the book:

"Depart, O soul, out of this world;
In the Name of God the Father Almighty who created you;
In the Name of Jesus Christ who redeemed you;
In the Name of the Holy Spirit who sanctifies you.
May your rest be this day in peace,
and your dwelling place in the Paradise of God."

43

Walt couldn't speak, but I managed to get him into Fr. Chris' car and belted him in. He stared mutely out the front window of the bullet-ridden Camry.

We drove away from that killing field, going back the way we came. No one seemed to have heard the gun shots, or if they had they didn't seem to have bothered to call the police. Walt and I drove out to the highway and back downtown. When we got to the church, I parked the car outside St. Mark's, locked the doors and left Walt alone. I made a beeline to the rectory and knocked on the door as hard as I had knocked on Walt's door.

Fr. Chris was there by the second knock. He must have known from the look on my face that something had gone terribly wrong.

"Lord Jesus, what's happened, Jack?"

"There's too much to explain. Walt and I need your help. Especially Walt."

We went out to the car, and Fr. Chris looked down at Walt, totally motionless except for the blinking of his eyes.

"Are you all right, Walt?" Fr. Chris asked but got no answer. Walt didn't even acknowledge us. He sat mute and stared out the front window at the brick wall of the church like it was Dali's Crucifixion.

Fr. Chris and I ended up picking Walt up like a roll of carpet, rigid and heavy. Eventually we got him inside the rectory and into one of Fr. Chris' old recliners.

"I don't suppose you want to tell me what happened to make him this way, do you, Jack?"

"Not now, Father. I need to use your computer."

"What?" He looked at me like I was crazy. Which of course I was. Always had been, always would be.

"I'll explain later, I promise," I said to him. "Can I use your computer or not?"

Frowning, he took me back to his study, showed me his computer, and then went back to attend to Walt. I spent about half an hour trying to verify what Bruce had told me was true. Although everything he'd said made sense to me, I had to make sure it was the truth before I acted on it.

Everything that I could verify online, I did. It all checked out. Every last word.

When I came back out to the living room, Fr. Chris was trying to get Walt to sip water out of a glass. It wasn't working so well. Walt had little streams of water running down his shirt. I sat down on the couch as Fr. Chris gave up and sat next to me.

"Is now the time to tell me what happened?" he asked.

"No. Not now," I told him and took a sip of water. It was cool and refreshing. Living water.

"What are we going to do with Walt?" Fr. Chris said, letting the panic slip into his voice. He was usually the calm one, the sane one with the level head, but not this time.

"I'm not a psychiatrist, Jack. We have to get him to the hospital so that he can get appropriate medical care. I want you to know that I cannot in good conscience keep him here and withhold treatment from him if that's what you have in mind. I will not do it!"

I could tell that Fr. Chris was put off by my coolness. It was not something that he'd seen in me before. Hell, I hadn't even seen it in myself in a very, very long time.

I remember when I was in college, I had this professor who always talked about flow. Flow was the term, he told us, that a Russian psychologist coined to describe the feeling of being so enraptured by an activity, so clear in your goal, so focused and confident in the outcome, that you lose your sense of self–consciousness. You lose your sense of self and become the action. I'd understood the concept, but I can't say as I had ever felt like that, until that day in the rectory. My vision was clear. The Holy Spirit was a vast river and I was floating on the top, free and easy.

"Don't worry. I'm not asking you to do anything like that," I told him. "You know how much I hate the psychiatric unit. What they do to you there, the power plays, the deadening drugs, and all that, but in this case there's no avoiding it. He's got to go. You just have to be the one to take him."

"Come again?"

"You have to be the one to take him, Father. That's why I've brought him to you."

He looked at me quizzically. "And why can't you take him?"

I smiled. "I've got something to do and I

need to do it now, before I lose this feeling, before I lose my nerve."

"I wish," he said, exasperated, "that I knew what the hell you were talking about."

"Have faith, Father. I'll explain it all. But first I need to borrow a few things."

The place was just the way I'd left it. The broken cement of the driveway, the faded glory of the façade, the wobbly wooden staircase up to the cheap apartment. It was all the same. I walked up the staircase to my old apartment and tried the door but it was locked. Some cop must have used some common sense and locked it behind him. I tried my key. It still worked. I opened the door, expecting to see the inside turned upside down.

But just like the outside, the inside looked exactly the same as it had when I'd left. Still disheveled but not any more than usual.

I wondered if the police had even bothered to search the place after they found Johnny. More than likely, they just called the morgue to pick up the body and then filed the report. One more dead nut case. Nothing to get too worked up about.

I made a pass through the place, checking all the rooms to make sure they were empty. Lord knew that there were enough desperate people in the neighborhood, and any one of them would've been happy to crash here if they knew the place was empty. Locked doors meant nothing to desperate people. Nothing looked out of the ordinary with the exception that Johnny's bed was gone. Other than that, the place looked no different than it had a few weeks ago, when I still had a roommate and I was just another mental patient.

I clicked on one of the old lamps and a faint yellow glow filled the room. It was starting to get dark outside and the extra light helped me see better. I took a glance out the one window I had. I don't know why I even did it, but I did. I guess I was worried that someone might sneak up on me before I was ready. I unpacked my gear and then took a look in the refrigerator. There were still two cans of Coke rolling around in the vegetable cooler. I took one out and drank it down as I sat in one of the white plastic chairs where I used to watch TV.

The Coke was cold and sweet. I was amazed that I could enjoy it while knowing what was coming next. I was going to be facing possible death again, two times in one day. Even thinking about doing something like this a few months ago would have been enough to put me in the psych ward. But not anymore. Here I was, Jack Plowman, sitting in my old plastic chair, enjoying a soft drink, and ready for whatever came through the door. God was good. I felt protected sitting there, like nothing could go wrong. I felt like even if things did go awry, I would find a way through. Whatever happened, God was still God, and that was the most important thing.

I felt like the Old Testament prophets must have felt after they had received guidance from God. Even now when I have a hard time getting to sleep, I'll think about sitting there and drinking that Coke, watching the moon rise over the trees outside that window. I like to remember how I felt then.

When I was done with my Coke, I went to the phone and picked it up. As luck would have it, it hadn't been disconnected yet. I made two short phone calls and then sat back and waited.

About ten minutes later, a pair of very bright headlights came up the driveway. I could see them from the big picture window. A car door slammed and then I heard rapid footsteps on the stairs.

"Shit," came the voice from outside. The footsteps were slower then. The wobbly stairs had claimed yet another victim.

Three hard knocks rattled at the door.

I opened it up and stood face to face with the man Daniels had told me about with his last breath. He was wearing a wool overcoat, black leather gloves and was holding a pistol out in front of him.

"Jack Plowman," he said to me, pushing his way into the apartment, "you are the dumbest man that I have ever met."

Ken Albany stood there in the tiny kitchen that was my foyer and smirked.

"You crazies are so fucking stupid that it surprises even me sometimes. I've seen some epically stupid decisions in my years working with you people but this takes the cake. Did you really think that I was going to cut you into the game, Jack? Why would I do that when I can just come over here and kill you instead?"

He laughed a derisive laugh that I'd heard before, but never from a mental health professional like Ken.

"I mean, come on, Jack! I expected a little

better from you. Didn't you go to college?"

"I went to the University of Michigan," I told him.

"Ah," he sneered, "they must have extended affirmative action to mental patients when I wasn't paying attention."

"I bet your bosses at Community Mental Health would be for that, Ken."

"Oh, they'd say they were for it, but you should hear what we say about you people behind your backs. You'd be surprised how many of us secretly despise you people."

Albany motioned me further inside and closed the door. For all my hatred of Tiffini, I knew that she wouldn't be included in the group Ken said secretly hated us. She was naïve and sheltered but she wanted to make the world a better place, if only in her own naïve and sheltered way.

"In case you didn't understand me the first time, I'm going to kill you, Jack. Right here in your apartment, but first I want to know how you figured out what was going on."

"You want to know if there's anyone else who knows about the blackmail?" I asked him.

Albany nodded his head. "Now you're getting it, you fuck up. I want to know who told you about our little arrangement. I sure as hell know that you didn't figure this out by yourself. If you were that smart, you would have sent the cops on my ass."

"You esteem your own intelligence too much, Ken. It wasn't really all that complicated. Once I got a different view of things, it all fell into place. Your neurotic need to be successful and measure up to your dad. You have a tendency to have exploitive relationships, Ken. If it hadn't been me to bring you down, it certainly would have been somebody else that you crossed down the line. You're a really flashy guy. But behind that flash, you feel like a worm. I should have seen that sooner. You call yourself a doctor, but what you really are is a doctoral *student*. And you don't even go to a real college, just some online joke of a school that no one respects."

I knew that my accusations were hitting home by the stunned look on Albany's face.

"Even your promotion to supervisor of case management wasn't based on merit. It was your dad again. He made a big donation to the clinic and a few months later people suddenly realized what a great employee you were."

"That's bullshit!" he yelled. "He was just trying to control me, to show off. I would have gotten that promotion without him. He just couldn't let me succeed on my own. He had to express his dominance."

"Well, Ken, you've got to admit that he is pretty dominant. Davidson Furniture is the oldest and most respected furniture company in a town known for its furniture companies. They did over a hundred and fifty million dollars in sales last year if you believe the Internet. They're big and powerful but are still owned by the Davidson family. No one on the outside knows exactly how much money they make. Having no shareholders means that they can keep it that way. No earnings reports or SEC filings to let the cat out of the bag. It's kind of like an old mom and pop restaurant, except this time mom and pop are multi-millionaires."

Albany's face was twisted in rage.

"Your father becoming president of the company was a shock to everyone. He was the first non-Davidson to lead the company in its 124 years of existence. It was a desperate measure by Sam Davidson. Apparently, all of his children were just like you, Ken. Disappointments."

"Fuck you," he said, stabbing the gun in my face.

"So your dad takes over the company, and because he's *not* like you, he does an amazing job. Double digit growth for five years straight. Record profits, according to the business press. He forms a whole new business division that almost single-handedly creates and then corners a market for office cubicles. The model corporate leader. A man like that starts thinking that he can do no wrong, that he can't make a mistake…"

"That *his* shit doesn't stink," Albany added.

"Right. People like that get built up so much by the media, by other business leaders, by hangers-on, after a while they start thinking they're God. Doesn't take long before they start *acting* like God too. Making their own rules when the rules that the government set are inconvenient."

"You mean tax laws?"

"That's right. Your father couldn't understand why Davidson Furniture should have to pay those cumbersome federal taxes, taxes that threatened Davidson's explosive growth. Plus, it didn't seem fair to your father. The opposite was what was fair. He thought Davidson deserved a special tax *break* for all the good-paying jobs they were creating. And if the government didn't get that, then it was time for a higher power to intervene, namely your idolatrous father, with his full-blown God complex."

"I've never thought about it like that before, Jack, but you're right. My father thinks that he's God."

"And God doesn't pay any taxes, does he? So your dad decided to call up a guy he'd heard had a way with numbers. A man who'd learned to lie with a spreadsheet, more out of necessity than anything else. A man with a secret addiction."

"Edward Chen," Albany said with disdain.

"That's right. Johnny's CPA father. Mr. Chen had become an expert in cooking the books over the years to hide his growing gambling addiction. He stole money out of the family budget and then from his employers' budgets to cover his losses. He was a real wiz. He pulled the wool over everyone's eyes for a long time. He even fooled your father."

"You're half right. Dad's not that stupid. He figured out something was funny within a couple of years."

"But by then what was he to do? Your father had hand-picked Chen to reduce the company's tax liability and just like everything else he did, this too worked perfectly. Davidson continued to grow at twice the rate of its nearest competitor and everyone kept thinking that your father was one of the most brilliant business minds in the country."

Albany shook his head.

"But his continued success came with a big cost. He'd made a deal with the devil, your father had. He'd yoked himself with an unstable man with a raging addiction. A man that, although he tried to stop, couldn't pull himself away from gambling. A man that stole more and more of Davidson's money to feed his habit. A man that your father had to prop up again and again for fear that if he let him fall and Chen spilled his guts, the resulting tax evasion prosecutions and penalties could very well send the whole company into bankruptcy."

"Dad grew to hate Chen with such a passion," Albany thought out loud, "some nights when he'd been drinking, I honestly thought that he might just go out and kill him himself."

"I'll bet you did," I said. "And if you'd loved your father, you might have even volunteered to help him do it. But you didn't love your father even back then, did you, Ken? No, you didn't love him because he's always dominated you. He's always made you feel small and powerless."

"I'll bet you didn't know that he fucked my wife a year after we were married, did you, Jack? That bastard couldn't let me have anything of my own, he even had to take Shari from me."

"And that's why when Mr. Chen's son, fresh from his first manic episode, ended up on your caseload at Community Mental Health, you knew that your day had finally come."

Albany smiled. "Yeah, I was finally going

to show him."

"How long did it take?" I asked him. "How long did it take before you convinced Johnny that together, the two of you could get very rich and humiliate both of your fathers at the same time? I'll bet that it didn't take much to get Johnny on board. He hated his father as much as you did yours."

A lusty laugh erupted from Albany.

"So you two go in together. The plan is set. Armed with your knowledge of the accounting tricks, Johnny blackmails money out of his father just like Mr. Chen had been stealing money from your father and Davidson Furniture. I'll bet it felt like sweet justice to the both of you. Johnny thinking that he deserved the money because of the way he'd been shunned and abandoned by his family and you feeling justified in finally getting the upper hand on your old man."

Albany stood there and held the gun inches from my nose but I was as relaxed as I'd ever been in my life.

"But things started to go bad when Johnny started to get lost in his own addiction. All the clubbing and crack made it difficult to keep the con going. Not to mention the fact that Johnny started to talk about your scheme when he was high. You tried to help him but eventually decided that Johnny was a lost cause. The only thing you could do to avoid exposure was to get rid of Johnny, for good."

"But you," I said to Ken as his quivering hand held the gun to my face, "you, Mr. Albany, are a world class pussy."

"What?" Albany yelled.

"You're a coward. You like to act tough, but you aren't up to doing the real dirty work. You don't have the stomach for it, I guess. So you befriend Bruce Daniels, a big goon I bet you met when he roughed up one of your clients at the hospital. You knew that Bruce was the man you needed. He isn't above violence, so you paid him to take Johnny out and end your liability."

"And a good job he did. My only complaint is that he never finished off Johnny's worthless roommate."

Albany's arm shook as he held the barrel of the gun at the tip of my nose and put his index finger on the trigger.

"Daniels wasn't able to finish the job, but I will," Albany sneered. "You're damaged goods, Jack Plowman. Maybe someday we'll have tests so that we can abort people like you before you're even born, but until then…"

Albany gripped the trigger and started flexing his index finger.

"Don't kid yourself, Ken," I said without a single break in my voice. "You don't have the guts to kill anyone. If you did, you wouldn't have hired Daniels in the first place. Face it. Your father's been right about you all along. In the moment of truth, you're a coward *and* a failure. It's funny. All your attempts to prove yourself, the stolen money and the fake doctorate, just prove what kind of man you are. You've devoted your entire life to earning the respect of an evil man. You've wasted the life God gave you, Ken."

Albany wanted nothing more than to kill me

right then. I could see it in his eyes. I could feel his hate for me like a cold breath on my face. Albany wanted to pull the trigger, but his finger just wouldn't move.

"Don't be so surprised," I told him. "It had to end this way. In the end, love always wins."

As if I'd said a magic word, Albany dropped the gun on the floor and covered his eyes with his hands. I didn't make a move for the gun. There was no need to. I heard the floor creak in the tiny bathroom and my priest walked over to the now sobbing Albany and put his arm around him.

"Why don't we sit down for a minute?" Fr. Chris said to him. "Let's sit down a moment before we call the police."

44

Det. Robinson separated Fr. Chris and I when we got to the police station. Robinson was his regular rumpled self, clearly aggravated to be called out this late at night. He sat me in the tiny interrogation room, and I told him my story.

Fr. Chris, I told him, had been over at the apartment counseling me like he does every week. I felt like going back to my apartment would be healing, so I'd met him there. When Fr. Chris had gotten up to use the bathroom, Albany stormed in and threatened me. I told him that Albany had confessed that he and Johnny had been blackmailing Mr. Chen and that he had hired Daniels to do the dirty work. I told him that if he checked Albany's bank accounts, he'd find more money than any social worker should have, even ones with phony doctorates.

The wrinkled detective listened to my story and then left me alone while he spoke to Fr. Chris. I sat in that tiny room with its reflective windows for about another twenty minutes before a uniformed cop came and told me I was free to go. I met Fr. Chris in the lobby and we walked out together.

Once we were about a block away from the station, Fr. Chris turned to me with downcast eyes. "You know, Jack, I'm a priest. I'm not supposed to be lying, especially to the police."

He was right. I'd told him what his story was going to be when I called him from the apartment before I'd called Albany. I'd asked Fr.

Chris to lie for me knowing that his words would be unquestioned. No one expected a priest to lie.

"I know that, Father, you're right. But the true story is complicated and the police might think that Walt and I did something immoral, illegal, if we told them the whole truth."

We walked down the mall together as the night grew colder. All the stores were closed, save for a few of the restaurants and bars. It was a silent, peaceful night. When he got to where they were building the new art museum, Fr. Chris stopped in his tracks.

"I've given you the benefit of the doubt through all this. Don't you think that I deserve the truth?"

He did, so I told him. I told him the whole gospel truth. I told him all about what had happened with Daniels at the cemetery and how Walt had saved me by sacrificing himself and his sanity. Walt had paid a very high price already. I told Fr. Chris that I didn't think it was fair for the police to charge him with murder on top of all that. Fr. Chris listened as we walked and reluctantly agreed to keep my secret, at least for now. He wanted me to meet with him to do some sort of penance though. I agreed.

We parted ways at the church, and I went back to the apartment that I had shared with Johnny.

The next day the story was on the front page of the newspaper. My phone rang like it never had before but I didn't answer. A few of the local television stations even made a visit to the apartment. They knocked at the door, and when I didn't answer they set up and did live shots in front of my house. It was so surreal to see a live picture of the outside of my apartment, while I was inside watching it on television.

The story was big news for three days and during that time I only left my apartment twice. For a while it felt like I was going to be trapped forever, but then some drunk driver plowed into a house in Granville, almost killing twin five-year-old boys. The journalists had a new hot story and moved on from me. No one gave a damn about Jack Plowman anymore.

Tiffini came by on day four. She brought me a bag of groceries, assuming that I wouldn't want to go out and face the media. She was right, of course, just a tad late. I took the groceries anyway.

Jake was released from the hospital exactly a week after the media barrage ended. Lisa came and picked me up the weekend following his discharge and we had a nice quiet dinner at their place. The doctors told Jake that his prognosis was very good but that he would need extensive physical therapy and would have to be off of work for at least a month. My brother took the news better than I expected. Lisa had never been so kind to me.

When I attended my scheduled appointment with Dr. Patel a week later, both he and Tiffini were happy when I reported that I'd been taking my medication religiously.

As I said, Lisa and I had a new and much better relationship. Gone was the fighting and anger. That had been replaced by a fresh familial love. It started to feel like she was the stuck-up sister I'd always wanted but never had.

One day, I asked Lisa if I might borrow one of their cars to run a few errands. Lisa insisted that I take her Lexus.

At first I was a little reluctant to take it. The Lexus was so new and so expensive. The last thing that I wanted was to get in an accident and wreck it, along with our new friendship. But when she assured me that nothing I could do to the car would change the way she felt about me, I believed her. Before I left the garage, I looked around and found a shovel and put it in the trunk.

In spite of what she said, I was really careful driving that car. I never went even a single mile over the speed limit on the way to the library and I double-checked to make sure that I locked it before I went inside.

The East Grand Rapids Library was just as dead that day as it had been when I'd been there a few months before. I looked up his address in the phone book and then used the library computer to show me how to get there.

The trip out to Dorr took me about 25 minutes. It would have been quicker if I hadn't been driving so cautiously, but I took it easy and listened to my sister-in-law's satellite radio. There was no doubt about it. That car was nicer than my apartment.

The farmhouse was out in the middle of nowhere. It was a very faded green and sat next to two dilapidated barns. Everything was really run down. You never would have guessed that someone had been living there until a few weeks ago.

I pulled up the dirt drive and tried to park so that I couldn't be seen from the road. There wasn't a neighbor anywhere nearby, but you could never tell when someone might drive by and start asking questions. I took the shovel from the back of the car and pulled on the big red door of the larger of the two barns. The door's rusty track resisted me with everything it had, but I eventually got it open.

The barn was full of very old hay and almost nothing else except a few half- empty bags of feed and some old tools. It was clear that no one had used the place in a long time, but the dry, musty hay smell still hung in the air like the memory of better days.

I stood in the doorway of the barn and methodically counted off 15 paces, then stopped and knelt down. Old hay covered the dirt. It was just like he said it would be.

I started to dig a hole in the floor with the shovel. It was supposed to be three feet down. I dug and dug but didn't hit anything. After a while, I gave up, filled the hole back up and sat down to rest in a pile of ancient hay. I tried to remember back to what he'd told me. I worried that I might have misheard him. This was the very last thing that Daniels had said to me before he died, even after he told me about Albany and how he was involved. I remember thanking him for telling me about Albany, but then he said that he wanted to tell me one more thing. His voice was very dry at that point and he wasn't breathing well. It had been very hard to understand him.

I decided to try to count off the steps from the wall opposite the door. I walked over and again counted off the steps. I marked the spot and then double-checked it.

Then I started digging again.

I hit the case about 10 minutes later. I felt the shovel hit the edge and knelt down and used my hands to finish digging it out. It was an old suitcase made out of thin brown leather with faded brass latches. I opened it up right there on the floor, my heart beating like it had been back in Mr. Chen's house.

The case was filled with stacks of twenty dollar bills. It was Daniels' fee for killing Johnny.

My hands were shaking so much that I had a hard time counting it. Assuming that I counted correctly, there was exactly $19,160 in the case.

A couple weeks later, I called Anna and she agreed to meet me for coffee. We sat together at the Three Kings, sipping lattes that I bought from the same guy that had kicked me out before. He didn't seem to recognize me. Thank God for that. I didn't want to explain that story to Anna.

I got right to the point. I told Anna that I knew I didn't even deserve to be sitting with her, the way I'd treated her. I apologized to her for what

I had done to her in college, especially hitting her when I first got sick. I told her that I'd lost control of myself during that first battle with mental illness but even at my sickest, I'd never wanted to hurt her.

The illness took over, messed up my judgment, and I took it out on her. I told her that I finally understood how she felt about all the things that had happened in the past between us. I'd done some terrible things to her and I knew that I couldn't put all the blame for it on my mental illness either.

I asked her to forgive me, and I told her how sorry I was. Even though my mental illness had changed me in profound ways, I knew that there was still a lot of the old Jack left. I told her that I would be honored to be her friend, and if that was all I ever was, I would thank God for it every day.

I meant it.

Anna smiled that bright toothy smile that I hadn't seen since college. We talked for a long time, catching up and trying to recapture some of the closeness that we'd felt in college. I told her some about my road years when I was sick and drunk and never sleeping in the same place twice. She told me about teaching elementary school, and missing me and moving on. Anna and I talked so much that time got away from us. It was already five minutes past ten when I glanced down at my watch. We were late.

In a panic, I told Anna we had to go, now, and frantically grabbed her hand and led her through the throngs of people to the door of the coffee shop. I freed her hand when we reached the door, but Anna retook it and held it all the way to the church. Her grip was tight on my hand, like she was afraid that I was a balloon that would float away into the clouds if she let go for even a single second.

We walked into St. Mark's as they were singing the first hymn. Late but not too late. We sat down in the last pew in the back and I waved a quick hello to some of the people that I recognized from the mission. Walt was sitting among them. He was still struggling, but each day seemed better than the last.

I opened up the blue hymnal and turned to hymn number eight. I caught up with the rest of the congregation in time to sing the last verse of the hymn:

> Mine is the sunlight, mine is the morning;
> Born of the one light, Eden saw play!
> Praise with elation, praise every morning;
> God's recreation, of the new day!

And to that, all I can say is Amen.

Charles D. Thomas

Headcase

Charles D. Thomas

ABOUT THE AUTHOR

Charles D. Thomas is a writer and psychotherapist from Portage, Michigan. He has worked in the Michigan community mental health system for over twenty years. This is his first novel.

You can read more of his writing at:
www.charlesdthomas.com

71877783R00212

Made in the USA
Middletown, DE
30 April 2018